THE BILLIONAIRE'S NANNY

ELIZABETH MADDREY

PROLOGUE

Scott

I shifted on the couch, getting more comfortable. The TV droned in the background, more for noise than because I cared about the baseball game. Living in Old Town Alexandria, I was a Washington Nationals fan, but it was more about having a chance to go see a game in person than anything else. Opening day only mattered if I could get tickets and hang with the guys. But our team was away, so I was home after work with the TV.

I scrolled social media on my phone, glancing up periodically when I heard the commentators or crowd going crazy, not really registering what I was looking at on either device. The crack of a bat had me looking up. I forgot about my phone as I watched the ball soar across the field and into the stands. The cameras zoomed in on the guy who caught the home run.

"Nice." Were we actually going to open the season with a win? That'd be a welcome change.

I glanced back at my phone and frowned. I must have tapped

a link. I scanned the headline. Hmm. I continued reading, excitement building in my chest.

When I finished reading, I browsed over to the forum responsible for the article and started digging into the threads there. It might actually work. I drummed my fingers on my knee then shot a quick text off to the guys.

Y'ALL SEE WHAT'S GOING ON WITH THE VIDGAMES STOCK?

Some of them were more into the various forums than me, so it was entirely possible they'd been watching since the whole situation started last week.

Austin was the first to text back. YEAH, MAN. IT'S CRAZY. I'VE BEEN WORKING ON A WAY TO MAKE THIS SOMETHING FUN FOR MY SENIORS.

I laughed. Of course Austin, the high school math teacher, was already thinking in lesson plans. Then again, he always had. When I thought of the word "vocation," I thought of Austin.

Cody, Noah, and Wesley asked for the link. Tristan just sent a thumbs-up emoji.

I copied a few links into the group chat. Should I put my suggestion out now, or give them time to read? Would any of them have the same thought?

With a shrug, I started typing. I THINK WE SHOULD GET IN ON IT.

ARE YOU NUTS? I'M ALL FOR THE STOCK MARKET, BUT NOT LIKE THIS.

I smiled reading Austin's fast reply. It was the math teacher in him. I knew he taught some of his upper-level classes about investing and dollar cost averaging and all those long-term strategies.

Normally, I'd agree with him.

My dad had started me off with some long-term investments right out of college. Managed right—and he definitely helped with that—they should provide a decent nest egg for retirement by the time I was sixty or so. But this...this could be such a great opportunity. And I had some extra money I'd just come into from my grandmother's estate. I'd been considering using it for a down payment on a house, if I could find something I could afford. The rent on my one-bedroom plus—the "plus" was a space too small to be a bedroom, and it had no closet, but it made a nice office—was close to what some people who lived farther out in the suburbs paid as a mortgage. But I was right here in Old Town and I loved it. I didn't want to move south.

Which was why I still had Grandma's money.

WHAT WOULD IT TAKE TO CONVINCE YOU?

I was mostly asking Austin, but maybe the others would chime in, too. With Austin it was better to have a firm plan. I knew that. I should have thought of that *before* I texted. Of our group, I was the most likely to take a risk. Sometimes it worked out, sometimes it didn't. But I was a firm believer in the idea of nothing ventured, nothing gained. And I could see a lot of potential gain here. If we got on the train before it ran out.

And if we all agreed to go for it.

Even with the money from Grandma, I didn't have enough to invest to make a big splash.

Although.

I got up and crossed to the kitchen to grab the spiral notebook and a pen from beside the fridge. It was my "I'm too lazy to add it to my grocery list app right now but I don't want to forget" notebook. Most of the time, I ended up forgetting to transfer the paper list to my app and thus went a week or two without anyway, which meant I was working on getting better about just adding it to the app. But I kept the notebook there just in case.

I carried it back to the couch and set my phone on the coffee table. Maybe Grandma's money *was* enough. I'd do a little figuring and see what I could come up with.

And if the guys knew I was going for it regardless of their

participation? I was pretty sure that would push them all—even Austin—into joining me.

I rubbed my hands together and reached for my phone. It was time to look up information and run some numbers.

FRIDAY NIGHT, it was my turn to host our weekly poker game, so I'd swung by to pick up pizzas and snacks on the way home from work. I slid the food onto the little island that served as a place to eat in addition to the demarcation between the kitchen and the living area, then headed into my bedroom to change shoes.

Robinson Enterprises didn't have a strict dress code. Not even in the government services arm. I'd been a tiny bit worried about that when Chris and Stephanie were officially put in charge of the division after the big boss, Joe Robinson, ran his contest last spring, but there hadn't been any big changes in the year plus a little since they'd taken over. It had been interesting to watch the contest. Most of the division had expected a clean sweep by Christopher and then been stunned when he and Stephanie fell in love. Now, a little over a year later, they were married and, if the rumor mill was right, she was expecting.

I'm not sure I was quite as surprised as everyone else. Stephanie was a good-looking woman. Maybe a little sharp around the edges, but I liked a woman who knew what she wanted and how to go after it.

I switched out my shoes for the Birkenstocks I tended to wear around the apartment. The guys would rag on me, but I didn't like to be sock-footed, and I wasn't going to tromp around in shoes that I'd worn all over creation during the day. The jeans and T-shirt were good enough.

One-by-one, the guys all knocked then came right in. They

did, at least, remember to kick off their shoes by the door before descending on the pizza like a pack of starved piranha.

"We're still playing poker, right?" Austin held a folded slice of pizza over his plate and looked around the living room.

"Yeah. I got home a little late. Hadn't had time to set up the table yet. You wanna put that food down and come help?" I jerked my head toward the little hall that led to my office area.

Austin shrugged, set his plate down on the coffee table, and followed me. "You get over that crazy stock idea yet?"

"Not yet. I think I'm going to do it, actually. I've got that money from my grandma. Maybe that's just as good a use as anything."

Austin grunted and took the other side of the folding round table we used for our games. "Oh yeah, sure. Throwing it away on the stock market makes so much more sense than buying a house."

I frowned as we moved the table from its storage location into the living area. One of the other guys had shifted the coffee table out of the way to we could set up the poker table in the cleared space.

"There's no guarantee real estate will go up. Or even hold its value. You know prices around here are inflated right now." I locked the legs in place and helped Austin flip the table. "So I could buy a house with the money and still end up losing it."

"Long term, though. This way? You could lose it all in a matter of weeks." Austin shook his head and stalked over to the coffee table to reclaim his pizza.

"What are you talking about?" Cody held a bottle of root beer and frowned after Austin. "Do you have to make him mad before poker? You know he's going to count cards now."

"He always counts the cards." I shook my head. Austin was a math whiz and should probably be doing top secret research for the National Security Agency rather than teaching in a high school, but he loved what he did. "It's why he almost always wins."

"No. I win a lot because the rest of you are terrible at poker. Maybe we should play rummy instead. Or, I don't know, spoons." Austin took a big bite of his slice.

I laughed. "Maybe we should."

"So what did you say to tick him off this time?" Cody took a drink from his bottle before setting it on the card table. "Come on, I'll help you get the chairs."

I followed him back down the hall to collect the folding chairs I also kept stashed against the wall in the office area. "Hang tight, okay? I want to talk to all of you at the same time."

When everyone was finished eating and had pulled their chairs up to the card table, I took a deep breath and started to shuffle.

I was bridging the fourth shuffle when Tristan shot me a pointed look. "You gonna deal or just shuffle all night?"

"Ha. Ha." I rolled my eyes but started to pass out the cards. "Did any of you read the links I sent on Wednesday?"

"Skimmed them. Why? You're not serious about doing it, are you?" Noah collected his cards and peered at them. "Day trading is risky, man."

"It's not like I'm quitting my job so I can day trade full time. This is a one-time opportunity. It feels too good to miss."

"Too good to be true, you mean." Wes rearranged the cards in his hand.

I growled and considered my own cards. Maybe I should keep my plans to myself then. No. I really wanted to do this with my friends. We were kind of like the six musketeers—had been since college. "But what if it isn't?"

Austin sighed and laid his cards down on the table. He looked at me and held my gaze. "You ran numbers?"

I nodded.

"What's the best-case scenario?" Wes collapsed his cards into a pile and tipped them toward his shirt. "I'm serious. Are we talking break-even? Make the same amount back?"

I shook my head. "Best case? More. Way more. One guy has already turned ten K into a little over three mil."

I could feel the pressure of their eyes on me.

"Dollars? You're saying he made three million dollars?" Wes blew out a breath. "Wow."

"It scales. The more you can invest, the bigger the potential return."

"Three million is a half-mil each. We could scrape together ten K." Austin had a glint in his eyes. "That's a decent sized nest egg."

"It is. But what if we invested closer to three hundred K?" My stomach clenched. I didn't mind going all in with the money from Grandma, and I had a little in my savings that I wouldn't mind pulling out to play with. If we lost it, then I wouldn't have a vacation fund or a new car for a while, but that was fine by me. "I can get us to two."

Austin leapt up, his chair clattering to the floor. "Are you insane?"

"No. Hear me out." I held up my hands and scooted my chair back. "Let me get my notepad."

I shouldn't have been surprised by Austin's response. Or the silence from the other four. They were probably in shock. And okay, sure, I was basically asking them to each come up with twenty grand. I grabbed my notepad from my bedroom and took it back to the living room, then tossed it to Austin. "If we can make it work the same way, we'd be looking at a little over two billion. Each."

Austin was scanning my notepad, his lips moving as he went over my figures and theories.

Cody's eyebrows drew together. "Why would we split it evenly if we're not investing evenly."

"Why wouldn't we?" I sat back down and reached for a handful of chips from the bowl in the middle of the table. "The way I see it, none of this works without all of us. At least not as well as it could. And more than two billion bucks? Why would I care if I put more in than you guys?"

"But..." Noah scowled. "I don't like that. You'd be losing more than the rest of us."

"There's that sunny optimism." I forced a smile and refused to look at Austin to see what he was doing. I knew if he was in, everyone else would be. If he wasn't? Maybe a couple of the guys would give it a whirl, but it wasn't going to be anywhere near as impressive. "It's like I was telling Austin in the beginning. If I put it in a house, I'm going to lose it eventually. You all know prices right now are at least double what they should be."

"Sure. But the area's booming. It's not like Washington, DC, is ever going to close down." Wes shrugged. "For all we know, housing prices are going to keep going up."

I started to speak, but stopped when Austin put the notepad down.

I looked at him, eyebrows raised. "Well?"

Austin pressed his lips together and tapped the notepad. "This could actually work."

I grinned and did a mental victory dance. "So?"

"Twenty grand?" Austin's hand stilled.

It was a lot. And of the six of us, it was going to be hardest for him to come up with. Public school teachers weren't known for having heaps of money lying around.

"All right." Austin gave a decisive nod. "I'm in."

1

SCOTT

Six months later

I groaned as I settled onto the sofa and put my feet up. It had been a long day at work, and I was ready for some mindless television. Something without a lot of drama. Definitely not something I had to pay careful attention to if I was going to understand it. I started flipping channels, then paused for a few seconds when something caught my eye.

My phone rang and I glanced at it on the coffee table, smiling slightly when I saw my mom's face.

"Hey, Mom."

"Hi, honey. I'm glad I caught you."

I frowned. She sounded like she'd been crying and that was decidedly not something Mom did with any frequency. "What's wrong? Is it Dad?"

Mom gave a watery laugh. "No. You're father's right here."

"Hi, Scott!" Dad shouted from the background.

I breathed a little more easily, hearing him sound normal. "What is it then?"

"Do you remember your aunt Carol? My sister? I think you met her a couple of times, right?"

I frowned. Mom's side of the family was a mess, and we'd never done a lot with them. Carol was Mom's half sister, if I remembered correctly. I also had another aunt and an uncle who were, technically, step-siblings to my mom. Making them pretty much nothing to me, which is exactly what they said to Mom any time she tried to get the family together.

"Vaguely?"

"She had a daughter a few years older than you. Shelby Ann. I doubt you remember her, though. She was always too cool to hang with the little kids." Mom sighed.

I was still confused. "This is a fascinating trip down memory lane, Mom. What does it have to do with why you're crying?"

I heard Dad start to laugh and then muffle it and Mom's whispered, "Oh, hush." She probably thought she'd covered the microphone, but she hadn't.

"Mom?"

"Shelby Ann has a three-year-old little boy, Beckett. Carol sent some photos over this afternoon, he's the cutest little thing. Seems like he's smart as a whip, too."

How nice for her? I still didn't understand what this could possibly have to do with me. "Okay?"

Mom cleared her throat. "Shelby Ann's remains were found this morning. I guess she'd left Beckett with her friend while she went hiking alone. She was into communing with nature, that kind of thing. I guess she was missing for a week and a half, but now they know."

"I'm sorry, Mom. That sounds awful." It was starting to get a little clearer. "Does Carol need money for the boy? Is that it?"

"Well. Kind of."

I pinched the bridge of my nose and tried to sort through Mom's tones. She wasn't usually cagey like this. "What does that mean?"

"No, honey, I've got it."

"Give me the phone." Dad's voice brooked no argument, and I hunched my shoulders. He didn't pull out his Army voice very often, but when he did, we all still snapped to. "Scott?"

"Yeah. Hi, Dad."

"What your mother is tiptoeing around is that she'd bragged to Carol about your newfound wealth. Carol, of course, gushed about it to Shelby Ann and probably anyone within a six-mile radius, because that's just who Carol is, and Shelby Ann decided you made a perfect guardian for her son and named you as such in her will."

"Wait. What?" I hit mute on the TV remote and sat up a little straighter. "You did not just say that a cousin I never really met made me the guardian of her child in the event something happened to her."

"That's exactly what I said." Dad's calm demeanor did nothing to quiet the screaming in my head.

"No. I refuse. I can do that, right? I mean the kid has Carol. Why wouldn't this Shelby person put her mother down for that?"

This made no sense. And okay, sure, since I ended up with my fluke billions, I'd had my share of whackos come begging for money. All the guys had. But once I started explaining that I'd set it up in trusts and it wasn't like I had this big pile of liquid cash I could throw around, generally people got the hint. If they didn't, a quick email to my lawyer would get them a cease and desist that sometimes helped them get the hint faster.

"Carol has more medical issues than a doctor magazine. She's not a great choice for a three-year-old."

"And I am?" I shook my head, even though Dad couldn't see me. Wasn't this the whole purpose of foster care? I winced. That...was not the compassionate spirit Jesus wanted us to have. And it definitely didn't align with the whole concept of *the least of these.* "Surely this Shelby had friends? What about the dad? The boy has a dad, right?"

"In prison for second-degree murder. He'll be eligible for parole in about twenty years."

I closed my eyes. This wasn't happening. "Friends? You said she left the boy with a friend. Why can't the friend look after him?"

Dad sighed. "I don't know. I do know you're the one Shelby Ann listed in her will, and there's a lawyer who'll be reaching out to you very soon."

"I don't know anything about kids. What would I do with a kid? He's three? That's still a toddler. Right?" My mind was spinning off in so many directions I couldn't concentrate. What would possess someone to do something like this?

The answer was simple. Money.

Except, for every problem it seemed like money would help, I was discovering there were always new problems that cropped up.

"What about you guys?"

Dad laughed. "You're not serious."

I scrubbed a hand over my face. Maybe I wasn't. But it sure seemed like Mom and Dad would be better equipped to handle this kid than me.

"You know we'd be happy to help. It's a little trickier now that we're down here, though." Mom had taken the phone back, apparently.

And she was right. One of the first things I'd done was set Mom and Dad up in their dream home. That dream home had turned out to be near the beach on the Gulf Coast of Florida. I missed having them nearby, but I didn't begrudge them wanting to leave the DC area.

"You could always come down and stay a bit." Mom continued. "I don't really understand why you're still working."

"I like my job, Mom. You know this. I don't want to sit around doing nothing just because I can." I clicked the remote and turned off the TV. "How long do you think I have to make a decision on this?"

"I imagine the lawyer will get in touch with you tomorrow. There's the welfare of a child at stake here, honey. You have to do the right thing."

I was pretty clear where Mom stood on what that right thing was, but I wasn't convinced.

I made a noncommittal sound. "Love you, Mom."

"Love you, too. Call us when you know more. If you want Dad to go with you to get him, we can figure that out."

The phone call ended and I stared at the blank screen. After a moment, I pulled myself together, scrolled through my contacts, and hit call.

"Tristan Lee."

"Tris, it's Scott."

"Oh, hey man. I didn't look, sorry. What's up?"

I heard Tristan typing in the background and frowned. "Are you still at work?"

"Yeah. I have a motion I have to file tomorrow and I'm behind on it."

Hm. I didn't want to distract him. Like the rest of us, Tristan had kept his job—although he talked about branching out on his own and getting out of corporate law. "Do you know anyone who does family law?"

"Family?" The clicking of the keyboard stopped and the echo disappeared. He must have taken me off speaker. "What's going on?"

I summarized the phone call with my parents, ending with, "I don't know what to do. Or even what my options are. Thus, someone who knows family law."

"Wow."

I waited, but Tristan didn't offer any more thoughts. To be fair, that summed it up well enough. "Yeah."

"I don't know anyone off the top of my head, but I'll ask around. I'm guessing you need someone fast."

"Yeah. Mom guessed the cousin's lawyer would call tomorrow to figure out arrangements." I looked around my apartment's living room and shook my head. Where would I even put a kid? I had a one-bedroom. With an office. At least the couch in there was a pullout.

What was I doing? I didn't want to take on this kid. He wasn't my problem. Just because Shelby Ann decided I had enough money to qualify as guardian didn't mean I was the right choice.

"You're not listening."

"Sorry. Distracted. It's a lot."

Tristan laughed. "Yeah, I'll give you that. I was saying it seemed to me that you had to be willing to take on the kid. So maybe it's as easy as declining. You're going to decline, right?"

I frowned. I wanted to say yes, obviously, because that was the smart, sane thing to do. But Mom's words echoed in my head and I found myself saying, "I don't know."

2

WHITNEY

"No!" Beckett stomped his foot and scowled at me.

I squatted down and rubbed his arms. "Beck, we have to. It's very important."

He shook his head, his eyes filling with tears. "Want Mommy."

"I know, baby." I opened my arms, and it was half a heartbeat before he flung himself into them.

It wasn't his fault Shelby Ann decided to hike a trail that washed out from under her during a freak storm. She'd left him with me—she did that a lot—and Beckett and I had been having a wonderful time. Until a quick weekend turned into a week and a half with tragedy at the end.

"Mommy's not coming home, though. And Mr. Jenkins is going to talk to you about your new home."

Beckett turned his tear-stained face up. "I stay you?"

"I'm working on it, baby."

If I hadn't been determined before, Beckett's plea would have turned the tide. What had Shelby Ann been thinking? Well, I knew what—she'd heard about her long-lost cousin the billionaire and gotten dollar signs in her eyes. Just like her mom. I sighed. Maybe the guy would see reason, and we could figure out a way for me to take on Beckett. I was the next closest thing to family. He belonged with me.

"Come on. Let's get in the car and go see Mr. Jenkins. Okay?"

Lower lip quivering, Beckett nodded.

I scooped him up and settled him on my hip. "Should we get teddy?"

He nodded again, so I detoured to the cot I had set up in the corner of my studio apartment and snagged the well-loved teddy from on top of his pillow.

"All right, bud, let's go." I hooked my purse over my shoulder and checked that the door locked behind us before trekking down the four flights of stairs to the parking lot.

I bit my lip as I settled Beckett in the backseat of my beat-up car. It was a rust bucket that I held together with prayer and bartering with a friendly mechanic who thought he had a chance with me. He didn't. Maybe he even knew it and was being nice, but I wasn't sure about that. Right now, I didn't really care. The car ran—mostly—and it wasn't like I had other options.

I double-checked the five-point harness, then slid behind the wheel. The engine coughed and sputtered out. I laid my head on the steering wheel and breathed in. "Let's pray for the car, Beck. Okay?"

"K!"

For all Beckett knew, this was how people started their cars. It sure seemed like whenever he and I had to go somewhere, it started out like this. Shelby Ann had never been happy about it. She accused me of forcing my beliefs on her son, but she backed off quickly enough when I told her I understood and wouldn't be hurt if she found someone else to watch him. She'd needed me. Beckett needed to know about Jesus.

I cleared my throat. "Dear Jesus, Beckett and I need to get to the lawyer's office. We need the car to get there. Please let it start. And please...have Your hand on this situation."

"'Men!"

"That's right, Beck, Amen." I reached for the key and, after a quick hesitation, gave it a turn. The car sputtered and I gently pumped the gas pedal. It caught! "Oh, thank You, Jesus."

I checked behind me and backed out of the parking spot. Now we just needed to avoid getting lost. I'd been living in the Los Angeles area for close to three years, but since my car didn't really qualify as reliable, I tried to stay close to the apartment if I drove. When I went to auditions, I took the bus. Or sprang for a taxi. All that to say, I wasn't super confident when it came to getting around.

I recited the directions under my breath as we made our way to the lawyer Shelby Ann had used to set up a simple will. I was surprised, honestly, that she'd bothered. Planning ahead wasn't a quality I associated with my friend, but I guess she cared enough about her son to at least make sure he was taken care of. She'd spent a little time in foster care in upper elementary school and, from what I gathered, it hadn't been a great experience. Her mom had done the work and gotten her back, but Shelby Ann had always said that wasn't an option for Beckett. Ever.

Thus, the cousin.

I shook my head. I would have been happy to be named guardian for Beckett. And if I was honest, I was a little hurt that Shelby Ann never even asked.

I looked around at the signs lining the side of the street. There. I signaled and changed lanes, hunching my shoulders at the blast of horns from behind me. I gave the drivers a little wave, then signaled again and turned into the parking lot.

"We're here, Beck."

He didn't answer. I hoped he hadn't fallen asleep. He didn't wake up well after short naps.

I eased the car into a spot and parked, then blew out a breath and shook my hands. I'd been clenching the wheel without realizing it. I grabbed my purse and pushed on my door. Of course, it stuck. I slammed my shoulder against it, and it swung open with a screech.

My face heated as I stepped out and eased it closed. No one was looking, but still. The cars in the lot were all from a different century than mine with their gleaming, glossy paint jobs. What was I doing here? How had Shelby Ann afforded a lawyer with these digs?

I opened the back door and shook my head as my gaze landed on Beckett's sleeping form. I worked the clasp and eased his arms out of the straps. I shifted his heavy little body into my arms and held my breath as his head lolled on my shoulder. He didn't wake. I sent up another quick prayer of thanks, closed his door, and started toward the building entrance.

After what felt like an eternity, I found the right office and eased through the gleaming glass door.

The receptionist's eyebrow arched as she spotted me, but her voice remained professional. "Can I help you?"

"Whitney Hall. I have an appointment."

The woman swiveled to her computer and clicked, then reached for the phone. She spoke quietly on the extension, then replaced the handset. "He'll be right out. You can take a seat if you like."

I eyed the seats. It would be nice to sit, but Beckett would probably wake up. And if he didn't wake when I sat, he surely would when I stood back up. I did walk to the far side of the reception area, bouncing slightly as I moved. Beckett liked the bounce and sway when he was sleeping.

I turned from my study of the framed magazine article

naming the practice one of the best estate firms when the door opened.

"Ms. Hall?" The man in the doorway wore a dark suit with a bright teal tie. He was probably my dad's age, but there wasn't a hint of silver in his dark blond hair.

"That's me. Hi."

"And this is Beckett?"

"Yeah. Yes. He fell asleep in the car on the way over. I'm sorry."

He smiled and shook his head. "Don't worry about it. Why don't we head back to my office and we can talk? I have a sofa you can lay him on, if you think he'll keep resting."

I passed through the door, moving in the direction he gestured. I spotted "Jenkins" on a gold nameplate and turned into the open door. The sofa was a sleek, black leather monstrosity that probably cost more than I made in a year, but maybe Beckett would sleep. It might be easier to have this conversation if he did. I eased him onto the cushion and reached for the throw on the back to drape over him.

Beckett stirred, his mouth moving, and then he found his thumb and sighed.

"Have a seat. I'm Chad Jenkins." He kept his voice low and gestured to the chair across the desk from him. "I'm sorry for your loss."

"Thanks. I'm not sure it's real yet." Honestly, the fact that I still had Beckett was really the only reason I believed Shelby Ann was dead and not just off on another wild-hair adventure. Solo hikes? Sure, she'd do that. But when she decided she was moving to Palm Springs? She took Beck. It lasted all of two weeks before she was back in LA, sleeping on my floor for a few days before she found a more permanent place for her and Beckett.

"Understandable. Shelby Ann's will is very straightforward.

Her personal effects are to go back to her mother, and guardianship of Beckett is assigned to her cousin, Scott Wright. We can work with the courts to have a guardian ad litem do the transfer, as Mr. Wright resides in the Washington, DC, area. Are you willing to continue to house him for another day or two until those arrangements can be made?"

"I am. But isn't there any way he can stay with me? Or that I could at least take him to this cousin? Beckett's comfortable with me. He's never met this cousin—I'm not really sure Shelby Ann has met him, if I'm honest. It just...it's such a bad idea to rip him away from the only people he's ever known."

Mr. Jenkins's face was a study of compassionate concern. "If the child's grandmother was opposed to the placement, I could see how the courts might be willing to overturn a duly executed will. But for a friend? It's unlikely."

I glanced over my shoulder at Beckett and my heart broke. "But, he's just a baby."

"I understand your concern. Tell me about yourself. Perhaps, if I can convince Mr. Wright that you're a viable choice, he'd be interested in relinquishing the child to your care."

I swallowed. It was a chance. But not really. I didn't look good on paper. I knew that. "I'm from Kansas, originally. A small town near Wichita. Which you probably couldn't care less about. Um. We do a big Passion play every year and I've been part of it since I was old enough—and even before then my parents were hauling me around in baby carriers while they worked on it. So, I've always loved theater. It was a natural thing to come to LA and major in undergraduate theater with an acting emphasis. And when I graduated, I stuck around."

"And your work?" His smile was knowing.

I swallowed. "I do a lot of auditions and pick up shifts in a coffee shop and bookstore near my apartment. I'm making it work. He wouldn't go hungry."

Mr. Jenkins shook his head slowly. "I can't even in good conscience recommend you as an alternative. I'm sorry. A child needs a stable home that's able to provide all his necessities."

"What about love? Doesn't he deserve a home that provides that?" I glanced over as Beckett whimpered. I hadn't meant to raise my voice, but I couldn't believe I was about to lose him before I even had a chance to try. "Can't you at least ask?"

Mr. Jenkins drummed his fingers on his desk. "No. But I'll let you ask. I have a few strings I can pull, and I can probably make it so you can fly with Beckett to deliver him to Mr. Wright."

I bit my lip. It wasn't much. In fact, it was hardly anything— all it did was delay the inevitable. But it was still a chance. "All right. I'll take it."

3

SCOTT

"I still can't believe you said yes to this." Cody shook his head and reached across me for the ketchup.

I watched as he squirted a huge pool of the goopy, red grossness on his plate. I faked a shudder. Clowning around was easier than admitting how terrified I was about what was going down in another three hours. I gulped, grateful that I'd convinced my friends to keep to our usual Sunday tradition of church and lunch together. I needed normal before I headed off to the airport to completely change my life.

"Your mom talked you into it, didn't she?" Noah reached across and snagged a fry off Cody's plate, grinning as he shoved it in his mouth over Noah's exclamation.

"Sort of." It was true. Mom was adamant that I was the best option for the kid—Beckett. I was trying to do better about using his name. Not only did it make things feel more real, it reminded me that he was a little boy who lost his mom. "He's three."

"What do you know about three-year-olds?" Noah shook his head. "For real, man. Why can't his grandmother take him?"

"Carol has health problems."

That was the polite way to refer to her many and varied

addictions in public. And she'd been using recreational drugs and alcohol daily in large quantities long enough that her body wasn't in the kind of shape that made caring for a kid a possibility. When I'd pushed, Mom had gone into the details. I hadn't realized. I mean, I didn't know a lot about Aunt Carol to begin with, but it seemed like this was something Mom might have mentioned.

"Ah." Cody made a drinking motion.

I snickered. Leave it to Cody. "You're not wrong. But also some physical stuff. Plus, she's basically my mom's age. I don't think there are many single women in their midfifties who want to start the toddler game when there are other options. I'm giving it a try. It doesn't have to be permanent."

"Pfft." Noah picked up his burger. "You're not going to do that to a kid."

I frowned. "I might. I mean I could. If I'm not the best choice for him...it's not like I have a wife. He's going to spend most of his time at preschool and daycare."

"Aren't they the same thing?" Cody swatted Noah's hand when he reached for another fry. "Why didn't you order your own?"

Noah shrugged and took another bite of his burger.

I sighed and pushed the chicken Caesar wrap around on my plate. It had sounded good—different—when I ordered it. But I couldn't bring myself to eat it. I'd probably be having the same problem if I'd gone with my usual burger. "They are sometimes the same thing. When you realize you're in need of such a thing three weeks after school starts, however, you don't have a ton of options. Also, three is on the young side for preschool, but older for daycare. I've learned entirely too much about this since Tuesday."

"You found somewhere?" Cody pointed a finger at me. "I know. You could quit at Robinson and become a house dad."

Cody and Noah snickered.

My lips twitched but it was hard to find the humor. Mom had suggested the same thing—I didn't really get why she was so weirded out by my decision to keep working just because I had money all of a sudden—and my answer remained the same. "Not happening. I have some leads. I'm taking this week off to try and get it figured out."

"Uh-huh." Cody smirked at me.

My stomach tightened. I reached for my Coke and took a long drink. I'd find something. I had to.

"You could always hire a nanny." Noah was barely managing to hold back his laughter.

"Oooh. A nanny." Cody made the last word into a singsong. "Then you could finally get a date."

"Can one of you remind me why we're friends? I'm not clear on that right now."

Noah snickered. "Sorry, man. You know you'd be ragging on us if the situation was reversed."

"Right? For real you'd never let us live this down. And hey, we're gonna be surrogate uncles, basically. It's kind of our job to be the fun ones."

I ran a hand over my face. They were both correct. I'd be there, front and center, making fun if this were one of them. I'd like to be able to say it was because we had a solid, fun friendship. But right now? "I must be super annoying."

"Aw, man. No." Noah sobered and stared at me. He reached across the table and tapped Cody's arm, his eyebrows lifting. "Why don't we finish eating, I'll text Austin, Wesley, and Tristan, and we can meet up at your place and pray."

And that right there was why we were friends. All six of us. We'd hit it off in college our freshman year and by the time we were juniors, we were living in an on-campus house together. Graduation—and the years following—might have put some distance in there. Some of us went to grad school, that sort of thing. But now we were back. We'd all settled in Old Town so we'd be close—because I'd learned first-hand growing up in the suburban sprawl of DC that if you didn't make an effort, you'd never see friends who didn't live close by. But Old Town was like a small town smack in the middle of the bustle.

I raised my hand to catch the eye of our server and mouthed the word, *Check?*

She nodded.

"Are you gonna eat that?" Cody pointed at my untouched wrap.

"Nah. You want it?" I pushed the plate toward him.

The server brought the check and a box. I took the check—it was my turn—and Cody took the box.

"Let me know how it is." I pulled cash out of my wallet to cover the meal, plus a tip, and dropped it on the table.

"Oh, it's not for me. Have you seen the older homeless woman who's started showing up on the corner right before the entrance to the apartments?"

Had I? I searched through my mind trying to dredge up her face, and came back with a vague recollection. "Maybe?"

Cody pointed at me. "Exactly. Anyway, Megan was talking about her the last time she tagged along with Austin. I guess Megan is trying to get the woman to come in to social services and get some help, but she's resistant. Seems like she'd probably appreciate the meal."

"I imagine so. Should we get her some pie, too?" I waved the server back over and ordered a slice of apple pie to go. The pie there was more of a draw than the regular food, although it wasn't as if the regular food was bad.

Cody and Noah both laughed.

I shrugged. "If she says no to the pie, you can bring it back to my place. I'm sure it'll get eaten. Kids like pie, right?"

"I hope so." Noah slid out of the booth. "But what do I know about kids?"

"Probably about as much as I do." I sighed and followed. I paused and tossed a few more bills on the check to cover the pie, then accepted the container from the server. "Have a good day."

She smiled. "Y'all too."

Cody patted my shoulder as he brushed past, snagging the pie out of my hands. "See you in a few."

We probably should have all carpooled to church, but I liked to drive. Cody and Noah, at least, had shared a ride. That made more sense, seeing as they still roomed together. And as far as they'd said, neither of their moms had started on their cases about buying a house out in the suburbs proper rather than still living like a bachelor.

It didn't mean it hadn't happened, but I suspected they would have said something.

Maybe it was because the two of them worked for a big Christian non-profit? I wasn't sure why that would matter, but I know my mom would probably be able to explain how the fact that they were dedicating their lives to serving Jesus made it all more reasonable for them not to start living like billionaires. I could point out, if I were snarky and willing to risk Mom's wrath, that the Ballentine Coalition was run by a man who had plenty of personal wealth. Maybe he wasn't a billionaire, but he was up there.

I slid behind the wheel of my car. It was new, and a bit of a splurge, but it wasn't a flashy sports car. That was just asking for speeding tickets. No, I'd gone luxury sedan and was fully looking forward to the weather turning cold enough for the heated seats to go on. I already loved the fact that they cooled along with the AC. And it was a quiet, smooth ride.

I glanced at the back seat, then turned fully to check before backing out of my parking spot. It should hold a car seat, no problem.

I frowned. Was I really doing this? Who in their right mind signed up to be a single dad to a kid who wasn't even theirs?

My phone rang and I thumbed the button on the steering wheel to answer. "Hello?"

"Hi, honey. What time does Beckett's flight land?"

"Hi, Mom. I'm good, thanks. How are you?" I smiled to myself, imagining her rolling her eyes at me.

"Sorry, Scott. Hello. I'm well. So's your dad. We're excited. Can you blame us?"

Maybe a little. I still wasn't convinced this was the right thing for either of us. "I guess not. He lands just before four. I'll leave for the airport at three thirty."

"Is that early enough? Won't you need to be there sooner? You don't want him to have to wait. He's three!"

"Mom, chill." The panic in her voice was giving me anxiety. "It's a fifteen-minute drive from my place. I'll park and go in. I'm supposed to meet him just outside security—it's not like I'm allowed to go to the gate. I don't need to be there cooling my heels for an hour."

"I wish you'd go a little sooner. What if they get in early?"

I scoffed. "When do planes ever get in early? Tell you what, I'll check the ETA online and keep an eye on things. If it looks like I need to, I'll go earlier."

She sighed. "That'll work. I'm sorry. It's exciting. It's almost like getting a grandson."

"Except that I skipped over the getting you a daughter-in-law part of things." And all the fun aspects of marriage and having kids. How many virgin single dads were there out in the world?

"Well yes. There's that. But maybe Beckett will help you find a nice girl and you can—"

"Whoa. One major life change at a time, okay, Mom?" I

signaled and changed lanes, heading for the exit that would take me home. "The guys are coming over for a little to pray. You and Dad want to join us? I could set up a video call."

"No, that's okay. We're praying here, for sure. Maybe we can do that video call once you're home with Beckett? If you think he'd be okay with it. Otherwise, give us a call later tonight when you've got him settled. And you know you can call me any time. Right?"

"Yeah, Mom. I know. Thanks. Love you. And Dad." I ended the call after she said goodbye, and finished my drive in silence. It was almost like praying. At least I hoped so. Because if this was the right thing for me to be doing, I definitely was going to need God to help.

A lot.

4

WHITNEY

I held Beckett's hand tightly and pulled our carryon suitcase with my other hand as we shuffled down the aisle of the airplane and out into the jetway.

"You doing okay, bud?"

Beckett turned to look back at me, eyes wide as he nodded.

I smiled.

All things considered, he'd done a great job on a very long plane ride. In some ways, I felt like he'd done better than me. Of course, he didn't have to deal with the crippling anxiety of wondering just what kind of reception we were going to find when we arrived at the airport in DC. As far as Beckett knew, we were coming to meet someone who'd known his mom. I wasn't sure how true that was—Shelby Ann had certainly never mentioned Scott as anything more than her cousin with a lot of cash. At least not within my hearing. But three-year-olds didn't need adults filling their head with more information than they were able to process. At least not in one huge lump.

So. A friend of his mom's. And I was just praying it was true. Because if it was, then surely Scott would understand that

Beckett needed to be with someone who loved him. Meaning me.

I scooted us over to the wall when we got out of the flow of traffic and looked up to scan the signs hanging from the ceiling. I pointed down the hall that seemed to stretch forever. "Baggage claim is this way. Are you still okay to walk or do you need me to carry you?"

Beckett started to walk.

I squeezed his hand and joined him. He'd probably tire out before too long, but I was going to embrace letting him walk for as long as he'd take it. He could get heavy fast.

I kept one eye on the signs as we walked past the other gates. I didn't want to miss a turn and keep Scott waiting longer than necessary. We'd landed five minutes late. In the overall scheme of things, that was nothing, but I didn't like it as a first impression.

"This way." I tugged Beckett's hand so we could turn to follow the signs. And there, straight ahead, were the guarded doors that clearly meant we were leaving the secured gate areas. My stomach clenched and my heart seemed to stop. I forced myself to breathe. This was it.

Mouth dry, I swallowed and looked down at Beckett's deep brown eyes as they stared up at me. He popped his thumb in his mouth and inched closer to my leg.

"You want up?"

He nodded.

I crouched and hefted him onto my hip. He dropped his head onto my shoulder and I could hear the quiet sounds of him sucking his thumb. I should probably tell him to stop—Shelby Ann had broken him of thumb sucking a year ago—but I figured if you lost your mom you got to comfort yourself however you needed. I didn't know a ton about raising a child, but so far, operating on the "how would I want someone to treat me" theory seemed to be working.

"All right, here we go. It's gonna be okay, Beck." I brushed a kiss across his downy black hair and rejoined the foot traffic.

Outside security, I looked around. Scott had said he'd meet us there. We were late, so there was no reason he shouldn't be here. And yet...I didn't see him.

I bit my lip.

Other passengers hurried past, waving and running to embrace family members. Maybe he was meeting us at the baggage claim? Between holding Beckett and pulling the suit-case, I couldn't easily get to my phone to double-check the texts. I started toward the escalators.

"Whitney? Whitney Hall?"

I stopped and turned when I heard my name.

A man jogged over. Where had he been hiding?

"Are you Whitney? I'm Scott Wright." He held out his hand.

I studied the hand a moment before letting go of the suitcase handle and taking it. "That's me. It's nice to meet you. Um. This is weird, but could I see some ID?"

His eyebrows lifted and one corner of his mouth quirked up, but he reached into his front pocket and drew out a wallet. He flipped it open and held it out.

I leaned forward to study the Virginia driver's license. The photo was definitely him. The name lined up. "Thanks."

"Um. Maybe I should see yours? I'd hate to end up with the wrong kid." His chuckle was weak and forced.

I lifted my eyebrows. I guess turnabout was fair play. But really, how many people did he imagine were on this airplane bringing him a child? I worked my purse around so I could reach inside for my wallet and dig out my own license. I offered it to him.

Scott took it and I watched, amused, as he looked between it and me before handing it back. "Nice to meet you, Whitney Hall."

"This is Beckett." I craned my neck to look at the boy and shook my head. "He's asleep. Figures. He wouldn't nap on the plane at all."

"That's okay. Let me get the suitcase and we'll head down to baggage claim. I'm assuming he has more than this?" Scott took the handle of the rolling bag and gestured toward the escalators that would, presumably, take us to get the other one.

"Not a lot, actually, but there's one more suitcase." I wasn't going to mention that it was mine. Everything Beckett owned was in the small bag, and most of what he had was because I'd gone to the store and blown a big chunk of my meager savings to get him clothes that fit.

We joined the crowd that had gathered around the carousel. Checked luggage had already started circling. I scanned them as they passed, looking for my beat-up, leopard print suitcase. I'd found it at the thrift store for six bucks and, since the price was right, I'd bought it. Whatever I'd wanted to keep that I hadn't been able to fit in the suitcases was boxed up and stored with my landlady. She promised she'd mail them as soon as I got her an address. And I'd left her enough money to cover the shipping— and told her she could keep the change—so hopefully she'd actually follow through.

"That one." I pointed as my suitcase started toward us.

Scott laughed, but he wormed his way through the crowd to stand by the conveyor and snagged the bag when it got in reach. He hefted it over the side and set it down. "Oof. What's in here, bricks?"

I shrugged, my face heating. "Some books. Essentials."

"Fair enough. I'm in the hourly lot. It's this way." Scott

paused and looked at me again. "Are you okay with him? If you think the suitcases would be easier, we can switch."

I shook my head. "I've got him. Thanks."

He nodded and grabbed the handle of the smaller bag before starting toward one of the clearly marked exits.

I fell into step behind him. It was a nice view. I probably shouldn't have enjoyed it like I did, but the guy wore jeans like they were made for him. Hadn't Carol said he was a programmer? He didn't fit into the mental picture I'd created when I heard that. Scott Wright was definitely not a grown-up version of Screech. He could even give the grown-up version of Zach a run for his money. And fine, I watched too much *Saved by the Bell*, but insomnia left me craving comforting and familiar, and it was a show I'd watched with my mom when I was little when *she'd* needed something soothing.

We exited into the parking garage, and he jerked his head to the left as he turned. "I'm not far."

I was glad. The day had started to catch up to me now that the adrenaline was wearing off.

Scott stopped at a shiny luxury sedan and opened the trunk. He hefted the suitcases in and turned to look at me. "Do you want to put the backpack in here, too?"

"I'll keep it with me." Maybe that sounded weird. There wasn't anything special in it, but I'd have to jostle Beckett to get it off and it seemed like too much.

"Okay." Scott shut the trunk then came to the back passenger door. "I put the car seat in the center. Everything I read online said it was the safest place. I stopped by the fire department and they checked that it was installed correctly, so it should be good to go."

"Wow." I don't know why I hadn't thought he'd be prepared. I eased through the door, kneeling on the back seat so I could shuffle Beckett into the car seat. It was one of the fancy ones. A far cry from the fifty-dollar version I'd scored with two coupons and a Black Friday sale last year. I wasn't sure there was really much of a difference when it came to keeping Beckett safe, but if Scott wanted to waste his money, I wasn't going to tell him not to.

I double-checked that the straps were tight, but not too tight, and eased back. "I have to say, I'm surprised he didn't wake up."

Scott smiled. "It's nice of you to come all this way for him. When do you head back? I can drop you at a hotel, or whatever."

I closed the car door and flexed my hands a few times at my sides to try to dispel the nerves. "About that."

He cocked his head to the side, frown lines etching into his forehead. "About what?"

"Here's the thing. I was a friend of Shelby Ann's and I love Beckett. That's why she'd leave him with me when she went on her solo adventures." And they happened a lot. More than just hikes. Overnights here and there. But I wasn't going to get into that with him. Not right now. Probably not ever. "I just don't think it's right that they're sending him to you when I'm perfectly willing to keep him. And really, he'd be happier with me."

"He would? You know this for a fact?"

I could hear the ice in his tone. I stiffened. "I know he'll be happy with me. I don't know anything about you."

"That's right. You don't. It's entirely possible he'll be even happier with me than he would be with you. And I have the means to care for him. Do you?"

I shrank a little under his penetrating stare. "I'd make it work."

"Uh-huh." He glanced at the trunk. "That's not all his stuff, is it?"

I shook my head.

He let out his breath in a huff and probably would have said something if his phone hadn't rung. He shot me a fulminating glare before pulling out the phone to check it. "I need to take this. But you and I aren't finished talking."

I chewed my lip as he stalked a few paces away with the phone to his ear. I hadn't really had expectations, but if I had? This had gone much more poorly. Why did it sound like Scott actually wanted Beckett? What single man wanted to become an instadad to his cousin's kid? It didn't make sense.

I leaned over and checked on Beckett. Still sleeping. His thumb was back in his mouth and his head rested against the side of his car seat. A nicer car seat than I'd ever be able to provide. Especially since I'd sold my car before heading out here. The money might just come in handy today, though. If Scott insisted I stay at a hotel, I'd have to either dip into the meager cash the car had gotten me, or pray my credit card had a little extra juice on it.

He wouldn't do that, right? He was a billionaire. There had to be a room somewhere in the back recesses of his mansion I could hole up in for the night.

"Yeah. Thanks. No, I appreciate it. Bye." Scott's tone implied the opposite of his words as he ended the call and shoved his phone back into his pocket. He stared at me a minute then shook his head. "When is your family expecting you back in LA?"

"It's open ended." I twisted my fingers together. I should explain more thoroughly, but I really didn't want to get into it if he was kicking me to the curb. Worst-case scenario? I could head back to Kansas and endure the side-eyed looks of "I told you so" from everyone there.

Scott's mouth tightened. "Your job isn't waiting for you to get back?"

"I'm sort of between things right now. It worked out, since Beckett needed someone to come out here with him."

"I see."

I got the feeling he really did see and that was unnerving. "I can't dump Beckett with some unknown guy and then go away, whistling a happy tune. I can't. The lawyer, Shelby's lawyer, didn't think you'd go for it, but I had to come out and ask in person. I need to be part of his life. He loves me and I love him. I really don't think Shelby Ann would have wanted him to be completely out of my life."

"Right. That's why she made me his guardian."

I blew out a breath. "Yeah, okay. But so you're clear, she only did that after she heard you had money. She was like that."

He nodded. "What is it you do, for a career, out in LA?"

"I'm an actress." My face burned. It sounded so stupid standing there in a parking garage in DC. It's what they said in all the classes—manifest yourself into the career you want or something like that. So I never said I was an aspiring actress. I tried to claim it so that it would be true. It hadn't worked, yet, but I was still giving it a shot.

"Been in anything I'd know?" He didn't even bother to hide his derision.

"Look. I haven't landed any gigs yet, okay? I wait tables, I run errands, sometimes I do food delivery. I make it work. I'd figure out how to provide for Beckett. You don't need to worry about that."

"No, I don't. Because he's staying here with me. He needs a stable home and I can provide that. But..." Scott held up a finger as I opened my mouth to object. "I have a proposition."

"I'm listening." I crossed my arms. He didn't seem like the kind of guy who meant what most of the guys in LA bars meant when they used the word "proposition." And we were in a public place. I could scream. Or run. Or run and scream at the same time if it came to that.

"That phone call was my last lead for a preschool. They're full, but he's on the waiting list. Number twenty-two." He shook his head and his gaze raked over me from head to toe. "How do you feel about being a nanny?"

5

SCOTT

I could have kicked myself the minute the words left my mouth, but the truth was, I was desperate. Prayer with the guys had left me settled. Peaceful. I knew in my heart that taking Beckett on was the thing God wanted me to do right now. So I was confident He'd work out how I was supposed to manage working full time with a toddler.

And that phone call had jarred me. Because, hello? God was supposed to provide care for the kid while I went to work. Which was why, somewhere in my clearly nonfunctional brain, I'd come up with the decision to ask Whitney Hall to be his nanny.

I held my breath. Maybe she'd say no.

Please, Jesus. There has to be another option out there.

"I can do that." She grinned at me, her green eyes lighting up like Christmas. "I don't know a lot about the contract side of things, but I know how to take care of Beckett. This is perfect."

I forced a smile and hoped it didn't look as nauseated as I felt. "Great. Well. Get in the car, then, I guess, and we'll head home."

Home.

I smacked myself in the forehead.

"You okay?" Whitney looked across the top of the car at me, obviously concerned.

"Yeah. Sure. Just...forgot something." I opened my car door and slid behind the wheel. I waited until she was in and buckled up before starting the car. I'd planned to put Beckett in the little office space of my apartment. He was three, so it wasn't like he needed a ton of space. I'd found a toddler bed and dresser and had set it up as best as I could.

"What sorts of things would you want me to do, as a nanny? I mean, obviously take care of Beckett, but I can cook pretty well, so if you don't have other staff that already handles dinner, I don't mind adding that on. I can even do some cleaning. Beckett always helped around my place in LA and thought it was fun. I'm just saying, I don't mind handling some other chores if you need me to."

I looked over at her. She was grinning at me like I'd just given her winning lotto numbers. Who knew, maybe to her this was the same thing. The life of a wannabe actress in Los Angeles had to be pretty tight financially.

"You can have weekends off. I don't work weekends, so I don't mind being in charge those days. I'd already planned on it. And evenings, too. Um. I can help you find a place to stay and figure out transportation."

Her face crumpled.

I fought off the urge to hug her. She was an employee. Nothing more. "What's wrong?"

"I just...you don't want me to live with you? I really won't be extra work for your staff. Promise. And I only need a room. I was in a studio in LA, so it's not like I'm used to having a huge sprawling place of my own. I'd really like to be close to Beckett."

I shook my head. "I don't know why you keep talking about staff. I don't have staff."

"Okay. I guess I just assumed. From what Shelby Ann said—"

"If she got her info from her mom, and really where else would she get it if not Aunt Carol, you have to know it was blown all out of proportion."

I didn't add that I was reasonably sure my own mom had talked it up in an exaggerated way. Mom could get caught up in trying to convince her siblings that she was living a perfect life. She always regretted it. And she was quick to apologize when things got out of hand. Mostly, we'd all learned to roll with it.

I exited the GW Parkway and wound through the streets of Old Town to the high-rise where I lived. I glanced over and, if it hadn't been so awful, I would have laughed at the confusion on Whitney's face.

"Home sweet home." I pulled into my assigned parking spot and shut off the engine. "I'll get the bags if you can grab Beckett."

She stared at me for a moment before unbuckling her seat-belt and pushing open her door. Whitney moved slowly, like she was dazed.

Yeah, well, welcome to my world. It was only going to get worse when she saw the apartment I had. Not a studio, but not palatial splendor like she was clearly expecting, either.

I waited while she undid the five-point harness and jiggled Beckett out of his seat, then hoisted him into her arms. She bumped the door closed with her hip and looked at me.

I smiled, hoping it'd be reassuring. "The elevators are this way."

I watched her as we made our way through the understated elegance of the lobby to the bank of elevators.

Beckett had awakened and was rubbing his eyes, a tiny, sleepy scowl etched on his face.

My heart melted. He was cute. If nothing else, I had to give him that. And I was going to find a way to make it work and give him the kind of life he deserved. It wasn't his fault his mom died.

The elevator came and we loaded on.

"Wanna push the button, Beckett?" I pointed to the one for my floor.

He nodded and leaned out, away from Whitney, to poke the circle. He had to try twice before he mashed it hard enough to get it to light up.

The trip was short and smooth. So why was my heart beginning to race as we stepped into the carpeted hallway?

I cleared my throat. "This way."

Whitney looked around her. I tried to imagine what she must be thinking, but came up blank. I didn't know her. I didn't know what her expectations were. Well, other than that I lived in a mansion with staff.

I snorted quietly and came to a stop in front of my apartment door. I unlocked it and gestured for her to go in ahead of me, then dragged the suitcases in, leaving them in the hall beside the front door. I made sure it was closed and flipped the deadbolt.

"So. Um. I was planning to put Beckett in that little room on the left. It's an office, technically, but I figured it'd work for a while. He's small…" I trailed off.

Whitney just stood there staring at me.

"What?" I wanted to cross my arms so I forced myself to put my hands in my pockets instead. Casual. Friendly.

"You live in an *apartment*?"

I couldn't have stopped the laugh if I tried. She sounded so completely appalled, like it was a crime against humanity for me to have a modest home that met my needs.

"I do, in fact, live in an apartment. As you see." I offered a tight smile. "Obviously, now that I've got Beckett, I'll need to think about finding a home sooner rather than later, but like I said he's small. There's time." I looked at Beckett and grinned. "What you think, buddy?"

Beckett buried his face in Whitney's neck.

So...not the best response ever, but at least he didn't start screaming.

"Come on, I'll show you your room. Do you like *Cars*?" I'd found matching linens online featuring the grinning red racecar. And okay, from what I could find out, it was an older movie, but who didn't love the idea of talking cars? I scooted past them to the door of what would now be Beckett's room and went in ahead of them.

Whitney hesitated in the doorway, her gaze flitting all around.

Beckett squirmed in her arms. She set him down almost robotically.

He made a beeline to the small bookshelf that had bins for toys on the bottom and books on the top. He reached for a bin, then stopped and looked up at me.

I nodded, squatting down beside him. "Go ahead. Those are for you."

Beckett pulled the bin out and plopped on his butt as it came free. He scurried back up on his knees and peered down into the bin before grinning and reaching in for toy cars that matched the bedding. With one grasped in each hand, he started zooming them on the area rug. Conveniently, the rug had roads, buildings, parking areas. Honestly? I'd had a lot of fun outfitting the room.

It was nice to see that, at least for now, Beckett seemed pleased.

Whitney's arms were crossed. She looked uncertain, bordering on scared.

"Why don't you come into the kitchen? I can fix you a snack, or I guess it's almost dinnertime. We could figure that out.

Maybe a drink?" I cut my words off as I got precariously close to babbling. And I wasn't a babbler.

Whitney nodded.

I slid past her, ignoring the electricity that seemed to crackle in the air when I was close to her. I wasn't going to think about it. More than likely, it was just because I was in this bizarre situation and once we got all the kinks worked out and a schedule arranged, everything would go back to normal.

"Have a seat if you want. I have some sodas or apple juice. The water in the fridge door is filtered and cold. No alcohol—it's never been my thing and even if it was, I don't really think it's appropriate around little kids."

"I don't drink." Whitney studied one of the stools at my island for a moment before climbing onto one. "Soda, I guess, if you have something without caffeine?"

"Sprite okay?"

"Sure."

I grabbed a can out of the fridge, then decided that sounded as good as anything and snagged another for myself. I set hers in front of her and stayed on the other side of the island, leaning back against the counter. "I guess this isn't what you expected."

"Not so much."

I popped the top of my soda. I took a sip, then set it on the counter beside me. "I'm rolling with the changes as best I can, you know? I'm not sure what to do about you, though. I don't think there are any vacancies in the building right now. Maybe there are some in the other two buildings that make up the complex. I should get online and we can check that out."

"I can't afford to live here." Whitney blew out a breath, and it set her bangs flying off her forehead. "Or did you miss the struggling-actress part of my job history? Everything I own is basically in those suitcases. Minus a couple of boxes my landlady is holding for me."

"Yeah, okay, but it's not like I won't pay you for taking care of Beckett. I don't mind covering the deposit on an apartment for you as part of everything. Call it a hiring bonus." I shrugged. This was the least of my worries right now. If it was a problem that money could solve? It was an easy to solve problem.

"I don't think he should be alone with you. I need to be here. Full time." She'd sat up straighter, almost like she was steeling herself to get the words out.

I frowned. "That's ridiculous. He's my responsibility. Of course he'll be here with me."

"I should be here." She stabbed at the counter with her finger.

I gestured to the living space. "This is what there is. Where, exactly, were you thinking you'd fit? I'm not giving up my room. Beckett deserves to have his own space not be shoved into the corner somewhere. And that doesn't even address the impropriety of you living with me."

"Impropriety? Did we time travel back to the eighteen hundreds without me realizing? I'm the nanny. It's my *job* to be available to my charge."

I snickered. Charge. Talk about time travel. "I'm pretty sure there are nannies who show up for work in the morning and leave at dinner. Maybe there's a different word for them, but that's kind of what I need here. I don't need someone living here to take care of Beckett."

"Don't you?" She crossed her arms again.

There had to be something wrong with me, because I kind of liked her attitude. I liked that she didn't just shrink and crawl away. Even if it was super annoying that she wanted to fight me on this.

I raked my hand through my hair and stalked over to the floor-to-ceiling windows that made up the far wall of my living area. What was the right thing here? "Beckett is the priority."

"I agree." Her tone had softened. There was also a hint of surprise in there that had me wanting to roll my eyes. Did she honestly think I didn't get that?

"I really think," she said, "and I promise I'm not saying it because it also happens to align with what I've already said—that he's going to do better if I'm here twenty-four seven. He's had a big loss followed by a major change. I'm the only thing he has left that's familiar."

I closed my eyes, hating that she had a point. "Okay. You're right. I hope you like pullout sofas."

"I'm sure it'll be fine."

I turned back to look at her. She'd gotten off the stool and taken a few steps closer. I pointed at the sleeper sofa I'd pulled out of the office as part of getting it ready for Beckett. I'd shoved it in the corner against the wall, since there really wasn't a better place to put it in here.

Her eyebrows lifted and she crossed to it. She sat and bounced a little before shrugging. "Like I said, it'll be fine. This is still better than what I had in LA."

I smiled. "Aspiring actress" wasn't something that made the big bucks. Or even the medium ones. "I can try to figure out a way to give you some privacy."

"I wouldn't say no, but I understand it'll take some time. It's not a big deal." She stood and rubbed her hands on her legs. "I could always move it into the room with Beckett."

"I'd rather you didn't. He needs his own space."

She frowned but didn't reply.

I could see she didn't agree, but I was also glad she was willing to let it go. For now. I got the clear impression it was a "for now" situation.

I cleared my throat. "It's almost time for dinner. Although maybe you two aren't hungry yet?"

"There wasn't anything good on the plane. Eating isn't a bad idea."

Score one for me. "Not a bad idea" was pretty high praise coming from Whitney.

"Does Beckett like pizza?"

"He's three. Of course he does. He's not a huge fan of pepperoni, but he likes sausage and doesn't mind vegetables."

That was surprising. Then again, it wasn't like I knew Shelby Ann well enough to have opinions on her parenting. I could only base my thoughts on my impression of her from things Mom told me. And all of that was secondhand, having first come through Aunt Carol.

"I'm going to double-check with him. Not because I don't believe you. I do. But I want him to know I care about his opinions."

Whitney gave me that measuring look tinged with surprise again as I passed her.

Well fine, she didn't know me. I didn't know her. But clearly, we'd both jumped to some conclusions without a complete set of information. I wasn't going to let that change how I interacted with the kid, though.

I paused in the doorway and watched him as he continued zooming cars on the rug. He'd pulled out several more of the characters and had them lined up or parked in various spots around the scene. But what struck me was how quiet he was.

The cars raced on the track, but there were no accompanying zooming noises.

I frowned. That was probably a bad thing. Did I need to hook him up with some kind of therapy? Did that even exist for three-year-olds? I'd worry about that later.

I knocked on the door frame. "Hey, Beckett."

Beckett stopped driving and looked up.

I smiled and moved closer, then squatted down so I was at his level. "You like pizza?"

He nodded vigorously.

"Excellent. I thought I'd have them bring us some for dinner. That sound good?"

Another nod.

"Anything special you don't like on it?"

"Peroni." His whisper was nearly inaudible.

"Got it. No pepperoni. You like mushrooms? Sausage?"

More nods.

"All right, that's what I'll get. What do you say to some ice cream for after?"

Beckett's eyes widened and he grinned.

"I'll take that as a yes. It'll be a little while. Feel free to stay here and play or you can explore the rest of the apartment. Whatever you want. I'm around if you need something. I'm Scott, by the way." I hesitated then stood. I didn't want to crowd or overload the kid. All of this was overwhelming for me, I couldn't fathom what it would be like for a kid.

I headed back to the living room.

Whitney was standing at the windows looking out, but she turned when I came back.

"He's good with sausage and mushrooms, so hopefully you are, too?"

She laughed. "Sounds good."

"I'll get that ordered, along with ice cream for after, and then I can bring the suitcases in here and we can rearrange. Maybe find a way to get you settled."

"Thanks."

I studied her for a moment before turning away. I was also going to have to reach out to Mom's real estate agent friend. If Whitney was determined to be a live-in nanny, we were going to need more space.

6

WHITNEY

I glanced over at Scott as he pulled up along the curb in front of a four-story townhome near the waterfront.

"Nice." He angled his head to the side and looked up, nodding. "So far, so good."

"Why are we here?" I glanced at Beckett in the backseat. He was clutching a toy car in each hand and grinning. He always had liked car rides.

"We're meeting the listing agent to look around inside. Online it seems perfect, but I can't bring myself to buy a house without walking through it."

I blinked. "You're just going to buy a house? Like it's no big deal?"

"Yeah. We need more space. I know it's only been two days, but I can tell you're miserable on that pullout. Plus, I'm fairly certain my lease wouldn't stand up to three people living in a one-bedroom for very long. I have friendly neighbors, but it's asking a lot." He shrugged. "All signs point to a house."

"Or townhouse, in this case." I wrinkled my nose. It was absolutely not the kind of place I imagined him buying. Maybe that was prejudice on my part, but billionaire equaled mansion in my mind. Something with a lot of marble. Probably columns. With the option of cherubs painted on the ceilings.

"I want to stay in Old Town. Detached housing would mean moving further out." He frowned. "I guess I could have looked at that, but I like my commute. I like knowing my friends are all nearby. I like being able to walk to the water and the shops. It's homey here. Let's look. If it's terrible, I'll rethink."

I got out of the car and opened the passenger door to release Beckett. I shouldn't have said anything. I needed to keep quiet in general. It was his house. His money. And honestly, I should just be grateful that he was looking for something that would allow me to have my own room, because he wasn't wrong. I was miserable.

I'd thought living in a studio apartment had prepared me so it wouldn't be a big deal to be on a sleeper sofa in the living room. Boy, was I wrong. A studio with just me was still private. A couch in the living room with two other people living there? That was the opposite.

"Come on, Beck. We get to go inside and look around. Won't that be fun?"

He held up his cars and shot me a questioning glance.

"Yep. Bring the cars. But don't drive them on any of the stuff in there, okay?" Was someone still living there? Maybe bringing a toddler along to a showing was a bad plan.

I took Beckett's hand and helped him jump down out of the car. We walked to the stairs leading up to the front door where Scott waited.

"Ready? I texted Lorelai. She's already inside. I guess she parked in the garage and came in the back." Scott shrugged and pointed up the stairs. "Let's head up and in."

Since Beckett was slower on the steps, I let Scott go ahead of us. Did it snow a lot? Would it be annoying to have to climb stairs to get into the house? The ground level must be the garage. Maybe some storage? How many cars would it hold?

I didn't have a car. Yet. But I would need one. I dreaded talking to Scott about that, but I'd have to. Right now, and I knew because I'd logged in first thing this morning to check, I had exactly six hundred thirty-two dollars and twelve cents to my name. That was not going to help me score a ride. He'd said he'd be willing to advance me an apartment deposit. Maybe that would also translate to a car. Especially since I really only needed it to take Beckett places as part of my job.

Scott pushed open the front door.

I helped Beckett over the threshold and followed, then closed the door behind me.

"Lorelai?" Scott called out as he headed up three more steps that took him out of the little entry hall, past the kitchen, and into the dining area.

"Right here." A statuesque blonde strolled in from the open doors at the far side of the living space. She was probably pushing fifty, but she was stunning.

I glanced down at my jeans and T-shirt and wished I'd worn something nicer. Wished I had something nicer to have even considered wearing.

Scott held out his hand.

The woman took it, then pulled him close and brushed an air kiss to each of his cheeks. "I'm so glad you called me. I just knew this house was for you the minute I saw the listing. It's three bedrooms. There's a one-car garage below and room for a second car outside but the deck makes a sort of carport-like shelter. The laundry is downstairs as well. Here on the main, it's the kitchen, dining, living, and a powder room."

I watched as she gestured to each area when she named it. The fact that I could stand just inside the front door and see everything there was to see, spoke for itself. It was small. Sure, bigger than his apartment, but why would Scott be looking at this place? There had to be houses—actual houses that didn't share walls with other houses—that he could afford. Didn't there?

Scott gestured for me and Beckett to join him by the dining table. "This is Beckett. He's my cousin's son, but he'll be living with me full time."

I gave Lorelai credit for crouching down, despite her killer skirted suit, and making eye contact with Beck. "Hi there, little man. You want to go upstairs and see the bedrooms?"

Beckett's eyes were wide and his hand tightened on mine.

Lorelai looked up at me with a warm smile. "Are you Scott's cousin?"

"Oh. No. That was Shelby Ann. I'm the nanny." I could have kicked myself. That was about as lame an introduction as stuttering out something vapid about carrying a watermelon. "I was Shelby Ann's best friend."

"How lovely." Lorelai's gaze cut to Scott and took on a measuring glint.

I fought a wince. I was just here for Beckett. I wasn't trying to catch the eye of some rich guy and bag me a husband. Was that what everyone was going to think?

"I'd like to go up." Scott broke what was rapidly turning into an awkward silence. He held out a hand to Beckett. "Want to come, bud? Maybe you can help me choose the best bedroom for you."

I'm not sure who was more surprised of the three of us when Beckett slipped his hand into Scott's and dropped mine. I stopped myself from clinging. This was good. It was right. I wanted Beckett to bond with Scott.

I'd probably have to keep reminding myself of that, but in my head, I knew it was a good thing, even if my heart was slow to catch up.

"Shall we join them?" Lorelai gestured to the stairs that Beckett and Scott were already halfway up.

"Sure. Thanks." I ran my hand over the smooth wood railing as I climbed. "You didn't mention the price with your spiel. Maybe Scott already knows, but I'm just curious."

Lorelai chuckled. "It was in the listing I emailed, but it's not a secret. It's a steal for this area, honestly. The sellers are motivated, so they set it at one point two, but I'm fairly confident I can get them down a solid one."

"One point two?" I paused on the landing and looked at Lorelai. She couldn't mean million dollars. Except that was the only kind of dollar amounts people said that way. For this?

"Right?" Either she didn't understand that I was appalled or she was a great actress. "I sold a unit two streets over last week for almost twice that. And here you've got water views. Like I said, a steal."

Numb, I could only nod.

I finished climbing the stairs and hesitated on the landing, listening for Beckett.

Lorelai stopped beside me and gestured to the doorways on either side. "Two bedrooms with a Jack and Jill bath between them. One has a lovely wall of built-ins, so it could be an office if the owners didn't need a third bedroom."

I stepped through the nearest doorway. I'd chosen the room with the bookshelves, as it happened. The bottom was cabinets, so at least there was good storage. Honestly, this would make a great room for Beckett. He could put his toys in the cupboards, have all his books out, and still have a good-sized room for sleeping and playing. And the space would grow with him.

My heart gave a little pang at the thought of him growing. Was I going to be able to be there to watch that? I wanted it more than I'd realized.

Giggling drew my attention and I followed the sounds

through a generous bathroom to the other bedroom across the hall. Scott had hiked Beckett up on his hip and they were laughing together at something out the window.

"Ducks!" Beckett pressed his hand to the glass.

I smiled and joined them. There were, in fact, ducks. They were waddling across a brick courtyard near the river.

"Did you see the other bedroom? I think he might like it even better."

Scott's gaze was warm when he met mine. "Not yet. We got distracted by the ducks. This is a good space though, don't you think?"

"It is." I could make it work, for sure. And sharing a bathroom with Beckett wouldn't be a problem. Not now, at least. When he was older...well, would I still be his nanny then? Would he need me when he started school full time? Even if Beckett did, would Scott agree?

I pushed my worries aside. Dad always got on my case for borrowing trouble. I considered it more working to be prepared, but whatever. Right now, I wasn't going to be able to answer any of the questions, so I was better off leaving them in the back of my mind to simmer.

"Say bye to the ducks, Beck, and let's go look at the other room, okay?"

I bit my lip when Beckett reverted to a nod. He exclamation over the birds had been the first word I'd heard from him today. He hadn't completely stopped talking, but he was definitely quieter than I was used to. I was worried. But a little internet searching had convinced me it could just be because of the changes. So I was going to give it a little more time before I mentioned it to Scott.

I went back out and joined Lorelai by the stairs that continued up to the top level.

"You can head up and see the master, if you want. It has the whole top floor." Lorelai's voice oozed excitement.

It probably was exciting. Especially if you were the one who'd end up in that spacious retreat. And that was not going to be me. But I was still curious, so I started up the steps. I'd made it to the landing when I heard the rest of them coming up behind.

"As you can see, it's a restful, open space. You can easily fit a king-size bed and still have plenty of room for a sitting area or a workspace if you're using all the bedrooms. The bathroom is divine. There's a deep jetted tub, separate steam shower, and double sinks. Plus the walk-in closet and dressing area." Lorelai's eyes gleamed as she described the luxury suite. "I'll head back down to the main floor. You join me whenever you're ready."

I hovered by the stairs as Scott, with Beckett still ensconced on his hip, wandered through the area. He let out a low whistle when he went in the bathroom. "You've got to see this."

I really didn't want to. I'd have tub envy. I knew I would. But maybe he'd let the nanny borrow his tub every now and then if I promised to clean it really well afterward.

Despite my misgivings, I followed him into the space. And okay, wow. Talk about posh. "Nice. That tub."

Scott laughed. "Leave it to a woman."

"I've known men who take baths."

"Men in LA."

"Well, yes. Because that's where I lived."

"Uh-huh."

I frowned. "What's that mean?"

He shrugged. "I just don't associate the LA crowd as the pinnacle of masculinity."

I cocked my head to the side and took in his lean, tending-toward-skinny, frame. Granted, I'd always liked the geeky, studious sort, but he didn't need to know that. "Which you are?"

He shrugged again. "I don't swim around in jetted tubs. I'm saying it counts for something."

"Whatever." I cast one more glance at the drool-inducing tub, then forced myself to walk over to look at the oversized shower before heading into the walk-in closet and dressing area. The whole top level was probably the size of his apartment. It was like a self-contained piece of heaven.

"What do you think?"

I turned and found Scott watching me.

"I don't know how to answer that. Did you see it's one point two million dollars? *Million*. For, how big is this place, a thousand square feet?"

"About twenty-two hundred, actually. And yeah, it's a steal." I must have looked dumbfounded because he laughed and added, "Location, location, location."

"It feels like a lot, but it's your money."

His lips twitched into an almost-smile. "Other than the price, any objections?"

"No. The bedrooms look fine. I don't mind sharing a bathroom with Beckett and I'll be close if he needs me. I wish there was a yard." I was surprised by that. There wasn't a hint of grass anywhere. I'd assumed there would be something in the back, but that was an alleyway for all the garage entrances.

"There's a park about a block down." He pulled his lower lip between his teeth. "Do you think we should look for something else that has grass? It's not unheard of, but maybe not near the water."

Beckett squirmed and Scott set him down. Beckett ran over and grabbed my hand, tugging slightly. I leaned down so he could whisper in my ear, but he just wanted to rest his head on my shoulder.

I held him close and let him snuggle in while I sorted through my thoughts. He hadn't had grassy space to run and play in LA, outside of parks, either. So really, why would it matter here? Was my hesitation simply because I couldn't get over the price tag?

"If you like it, you should buy it. It solves the immediate space issue and the rest will work itself out. Beckett loves going to the park." I laughed when Beckett nodded vigorously. "See?"

"All right. Let's go down and make Lorelai's day." Scott gestured for me to go first.

I held Beckett as we tromped down two flights of stairs. I looked around the main living area again and tried to wrap my head around the fact that this tiny house cost so much.

"I want it," Scott said. "Let's make an offer."

Lorelai beamed. "I knew you would. The paperwork shouldn't take too long."

"What if Beckett and I wandered down to that park you mentioned?" I didn't need to be here for paperwork. And Beckett wouldn't want to hang out if it was going to take more than five minutes.

"That's a great idea. I'll drive down and pick you up when we're finished here." Scott pulled out one of the dining room chairs.

"Come on, Beckett. Let's go see if we can find a slide." If it was my house, I'd be looking for something with a yard and no shared walls. But it wasn't. And this was a much better solution for me than Scott sticking me in a different apartment somewhere nearby.

I'd promised Shelby Ann I'd take care of her son. I was going to do whatever it took to keep that promise.

7

SCOTT

I pulled into the garage of my new townhome and shut off the engine with a relieved sigh. The last two and a half weeks while we went through home inspections and all the other things that had to happen to close had felt longer than necessary. A one-bedroom apartment—even one with an added-on office space that could function as a bedroom—did not work for three people.

Especially when one of the three was incredibly stubborn.

I'd offered to put Whitney up in a hotel until we could close. Honestly, it was the most reasonable solution. She'd have space of her own, and Beckett and I could get used to the rhythm of being together on our own in the evenings.

She'd refused.

I'd moved to suggesting more strongly, and she'd dug her heels in. And fine, maybe—and in my head, I emphasized the maybe part because I wasn't convinced—she had a point. This was a lot of change for the kid. But he was going to have to adjust at some point. I wasn't going to be employing a nanny for the rest of his days. Beckett was three. That meant I had, at a maximum, two years that I had to deal with Whitney Hall being in my life. And I was going to shorten that if I could find a preschool that had room for Beckett.

All in all, I was glad Lorelai had managed to swing closing in less than the thirty days the owners had originally wanted. She'd probably helped avoid a murder.

I rolled my eyes and pushed open the car door. Maybe that was a little dramatic, but Whitney Hall was on my last nerve. And I suspected I was going to be in for a fight when she and Beckett got back from the field trip I'd insisted on for moving day.

I grabbed my backpack off the passenger seat, closed the car door, and dug in my pocket for the key that would let me in through the ground-level door.

I didn't try to stop the grin that formed as I entered and looked around the laundry-slash-mudroom space. It wasn't exciting, but it was mine. I headed up the stairs, my grin widening as I made it to the main living area.

I'd hired an organizing and decorating company to unpack and get everything set up. Moving was the world's worst activity. Maybe money couldn't buy happiness, but in this case, it sure bought some convenience. The furniture from the apartment fit well in the living room. There'd been enough space that the pullout sofa could be arranged with the rest of the seating and not look crammed in. It wasn't going to function as a guest room when my parents came to visit—and Mom was determined to make that happen soon—but there were hotels and B&Bs within walking distance and we'd figure it out.

My phone rang. I laughed as I saw Mom's face on the screen. "Hi, Mom. I was just thinking about you."

"Good things, I hope."

I chuckled. "You know it. Want to switch to a video call and I can give you the grand tour?"

"Why do you think I'm calling? I've been watching the clock

all day waiting for you to be home. I'm hanging up, call me on that app thingy."

I chuckled and ended the call. App thingy. I guess I should be glad she knew how to use it, even if she didn't know what it was called. I tapped to initiate a video call.

"Hi, honey." She cocked her head to the side and looked at me with a smile. "You're still handsome. Turn the camera around and let me see your house."

I couldn't stop the laugh, but I did go ahead and flip the camera around. "This is the living room."

"It's good. All your furniture fits. Too bad."

"Why is that bad?"

"Because it's bachelor furniture and I was hoping you'd have to get something that had some style."

"Hey. The decorators complimented me on my furniture and said it was easy to coordinate with."

"Yes, honey, that's because you paid them." Mom sighed. "I like the art they chose at least. And the rug."

I hadn't actually noticed the rug. I looked down. "It's nice. Here, they had to buy a dining room set."

I turned so she could see into the dining area and the brand-new table and chairs. They'd sent me three options while I was at work. It had been easy to settle on the wood with simple, straight lines.

"Ooh. Mission style. It's classic and very you. And it goes with your man furniture, but see how nicely they've dressed it up? It's homey. Let me see the kitchen."

I showed her the stairs down to the front door then turned into the kitchen. "It's nothing special, but it has everything I could need. And they put my dishes away, so that's one less chore to have to deal with."

"Speaking of chores, are you going to keep your cleaning service?"

"I was planning on it. Why? Should I not?" I flipped the camera back around so I could see Mom's face. "Why wouldn't I?"

"Beckett should have chores."

"He's three, Mom. I kind of figured his chores would be stuff like picking up his toys and helping with the dishes. Three-year-olds can't vacuum or clean a toilet, can they?"

I was admittedly out of my depth on this, and certainly willing to listen to Mom's ideas. But it wasn't like I had any memory of doing heavy chores when I was a kid. Clean up after myself? Yes. Beyond that? Even though we hadn't been wealthy, Mom had always found room in the budget for a cleaning service once a month.

"Those are good places to start. You'll want to increase them as he gets older so he learns how to do all the things that go into having a home."

I bit back a smart reply about how well that had worked for me. The truth was, in a pinch, I could probably keep my house clean. I'd hate every minute of it, but I could do it.

"Start teaching him to cook, too. He can start making his own breakfast if it's simple. And he can stir and measure with you when you make dinner. Don't eat out for every meal, okay? You don't want him growing up thinking that there's always going to be magic piles of money around."

"Even though there probably will be?" I winked.

Hopefully, Mom knew I was teasing. She didn't completely approve of the fact that I had all this money, so I'd put her in charge of making sure I gave a lot of it away. And she did a good job. The thing was, once I had money? It was a lot easier to keep making more of it. Dad was in charge of that side of things, since it gave him a chance to play around in the stock market.

"Even though." Mom shook her head. "Speaking of that, there's a young couple at our church who is feeling God calling them to full-time mission work in Thailand. He'll teach English and she's got a degree in engineering with an emphasis on renewable energy sources, so she'll probably do something over there with infrastructure development. I was thinking the foundation could take on a part of their monthly support."

"Sounds good. Just a part?" I didn't imagine it was very much. "Why not all of it?"

"Because it's important for missionaries to have a broad support base. It's good for them to visit churches and explain what they're doing and show people a new side of mission work. And also, I think it's good for them to do the work of raising support. They'll appreciate it more. But I do think we should help."

"Absolutely. You know you don't have to get permission."

"I do. But I like you to know what your money is doing, too. You need to be able to talk about it." Mom's voice held a tiny reprimand.

That made sense. I flipped the camera back around and headed toward the stairs. "Let's go up and I'll show you the rest."

I went up both flights. It was easier to start at the top and work my way back down. I put my hand on the handle of the door I'd had added at the top of the stairs into the master. "This is supposed to be the master, but it makes more sense to turn it into the nanny's suite."

"Are you sure? You won't have a nanny forever."

I nodded, even though she couldn't see me and pushed open the door. "I thought about that, but none of the modifications I made take away from this as a master suite when I get to that point. I added the door—and I probably would have wanted that anyway—and then this wet bar area so she has a little kitchenette."

The carpenters had done a nice job adding built-ins along one whole wall, turning the corner into the aforementioned wet bar. I opened the cabinet that hid a half-height fridge. The door next to it disguised a drawer-style dishwasher. "There wasn't a way to hide the sink, but it's not ridiculous to consider it like a wet bar. Resale-wise, I don't think it'll be a problem. I put in a microwave, as you see, and figured one of those induction burners would do if she needed a stove. And she's welcome to have whatever other plug-in appliances she wants."

"What about an oven?"

I laughed. "If she needs an oven, she'll have to come downstairs. I can only do so much. I didn't want it to be a full-on separate apartment. I'd like to get up here myself once we're done needing a nanny."

"We." Mom sighed. "I like the sound of that. I'm glad you've embraced taking care of Beckett. It's not his fault he's in this predicament."

"No. It's not. And he's a fun kid. That said." I flipped the camera around again so I could see Mom's face. "Is it unusual for him to not talk very much? It seems...off."

Mom's eyebrows lifted. "It is. It could be trauma. Or it could be more. What did the nanny say?"

"I haven't asked her about it yet. I wanted to know if it was normal first."

Mom shook her head. "I know you did a search online, why are you asking me?"

"You have actual experience?" I gave her my best effort at wheedling little boy, but she'd grown immune to that a long time ago.

Mom just laughed. "Take him to the doctor. Now that you've got the housing situation settled, it's not unreasonable to start setting up those relationships. Doctor. Dentist. That's probably a good place to start."

"All right." I added those to my mental to-do list and flipped the camera around again. "This is the rest of her space. I got the bedroom furniture, and she'll have to deal with it, because I like it and it'll be mine eventually. But if she wants to get different linens, I don't mind changing that."

Mom made a noise I took as positive and I started back down the stairs. "This is my room. It's all my old bedroom furniture. The room's about the same size, so it wasn't a big deal. The closet is smaller, but I never filled up the walk-in closet in my apartment anyway."

"It's nice. Homey. And you'll share a bathroom with Beckett?"

"Yeah, it's through here." I walked to the door in my bedroom that connected to the bathroom. It was a good-sized space, too. The double sinks would make it easy to separate his stuff from mine. "I'm hoping sharing won't be too bad. There was only one bathroom in the apartment and we made it work."

"You'll be fine. People didn't used to have seventeen bathrooms in their houses."

I laughed. Two and a half was a far cry from seventeen, but I took her point. I went into Beckett's room. "I told the decorators to have fun. Looks like they did."

"Oh, Scott. This is a dream."

Mom wasn't wrong. The animated car theme I'd started with in the apartment had expanded, but it wasn't overwhelming. It was just fun. The road-and-track rug was larger, taking up the half of the room by the built-ins. I'd added a few more toys as well. They were probably—hopefully—in bins hidden in the bottom of the breakfronts.

"I think he'll like it. He seems pretty into the cars, even sleeps with them."

"You did that. I was so worried you'd bruise a rib rolling over on one of them. Or the action figures that you switched to as you got older. You never did, though. He won't either. I can't wait to meet him in person. When can we come?"

I went out into the hallway and back downstairs. When I was on the couch, I flipped the camera back so I was looking at Mom. "Any time. You see I don't really have a guest room though. I thought about keeping the apartment, but that seemed silly. So unless you want the pullout sofa—"

"We do not."

I laughed. "Didn't figure you would. Let me check what the B&B down the street has open and get back to you with dates."

"I can do that. I'll let you know."

"Let me buy your tickets, okay?" The guys and I had talked about going in on a fractional ownership of a private jet together. Maybe now was the time to pull that trigger. We were due to have poker night here on Friday, I'd bring it up.

"We have money."

"I know. But why should you spend it on this?" I shrugged.

"We'll see. I'll get you dates and we'll figure out the details. Have you heard from Carol?"

I shook my head. "I've been expecting her to get in touch, but nope. I thought about reaching out—should I?"

Mom sighed. "I'll do it. She made such a stink about missing Beckett at first, but now I'm beginning to wonder how real it was. Maybe ask the nanny—what's her name again?"

"Whitney."

"Right. Whitney. Ask her if she's heard anything. I don't know how well she knew Carol for all she was Shelby Ann's friend."

I hadn't gotten the impression that Whitney knew Carol at all. "I'll ask. It's not like Shelby Ann lived anywhere near Carol."

"True. And still, she's Beckett's grandmother. If she wants to see him, I feel like we need to facilitate it."

"Hey, I'm fine with it. You know that."

"I do." Mom glanced over her shoulder then looked back

and rolled her eyes with a grin. "I need to run. Your father can't find his glasses."

"Tell him to check the top of his head."

Mom laughed with me. "First place I'll look, believe me. Love you."

"Love you, too." I ended the video call and checked the time. Beckett and Whitney should be home before too much longer, which meant I should get dinner figured out. I couldn't deal with another night of super healthy food. That seemed to be Whitney's specialty. Maybe it was what she preferred. Maybe she was just determined to make sure Beckett had the best possible nutrition. But I didn't think it would kill any of us to spend a night or two eating chicken nuggets and mac and cheese. It didn't have to be fancy.

I pushed myself to my feet and went into the kitchen to consider the options. Whitney couldn't object if I already had it going when they got home.

That was something I was learning. When it came to Whitney, it was better to act first and stand strong until she decided to deal. The woman had her own ideas about everything.

She drove me crazy.

8

WHITNEY

"Can I speak to you in the living room for a minute?" I hovered in the doorway of the kitchen, frowning.

Scott glanced over, eyebrows raised, then turned and poured milk into the bowl in front of Beckett. "Get started on that, bud. I'll be right back."

I stalked to the living room, crossing to stand at the French doors that led out to the deck.

"What's up?"

I turned in time to see Scott tucking his hands in the pockets of his khakis. I cleared my throat. "I'm unclear what's going on here."

"Um. Beckett and I are eating breakfast before we head to church. It's Sunday. For me, that means church. And I think Beckett will enjoy it, too. They've got a great children's program and I've already got him registered."

"I'm not sure he's ready for that." I'd taken him to my church in LA when I could, but it was a small, friendly place. I'd looked up the church Scott named as his online. Small did not describe it. "I can just keep him home or go along and hang out—"

"No. He's going to be fine. It's the weekend, which is your time off. We talked about that."

"Well, you talked about it. I don't remember agreeing. I really think—"

"That it's my call." He crossed his arms. "Look, I'm sorry. I don't want it to be like this, but you're my employee. And I appreciate the help, believe me, but you're off on the weekends. If it's going to be a problem for you to remember that? We can discuss finding you an apartment nearby again."

My throat felt like it was closing and I struggled to get my lungs to take in air. I wanted to argue. Shelby Ann had been my best friend. I'd known Beckett since he was born—had, in fact, been there to take him home from the hospital with his mom since his sperm donor had ghosted as soon as he realized Shelby Ann wasn't going to have an abortion. And then, apparently, he'd ended up in prison for the rest of his life.

Beckett was more to me than a nannying charge. And I wanted to keep it that way.

So I took a deep breath and swallowed back all the words that I wanted to spew and simply nodded.

Scott's posture relaxed some. "Did you get a chance to double-check that your salary was deposited correctly?"

I nodded again. I'd logged on to my banking app that morning. I'd been half-tempted to talk to him about that, too. The amount was more than seemed reasonable. Sure, he had the money, but that didn't mean he had to pay me outrageously. Especially since he was also providing me with room and board. "Thanks."

"It would probably be good for you to look for a car of your own. I'm happy to help with that, if you want, but I know sometimes people like to do it themselves."

I bit my lip. It would be good to have a car, but I didn't know the first thing about buying one. The rust bucket I'd had in LA had started as a used car Dad bought me in high school. "I'll see what I can do. I appreciate the offer. I guess I'll let you get back to breakfast."

Scott smiled. "Have a good Sunday."

"Yeah, thanks. You, too." I'd been half-hoping he'd invite me to church with them. Although I guess that was far-fetched given how adamant he'd been about how this was his time.

I trudged upstairs—all the way upstairs—to the top floor. It was nice of him to have given me this space of my own. I was probably going to have to remind myself of that six or seven hundred times. A day.

I wanted to be on the same level as Beckett.

I wanted to be there if he woke up at night and needed something. Or someone.

I rubbed right over my heart and flopped into an overstuffed chair that I'd put near the big windows looking out over the street that ran in front of the house. I didn't consciously realize what I was doing until the phone was ringing on the other end.

"Whitney? What a nice surprise. How are you, honey?"

My eyes filled. "Hi Mom. I'm okay I guess."

"Hmm. That's not convincing. Hang on a second. Let me tell your father to go on to church without me."

"No. Mom, don't do that. I didn't think about the time. Call me when you get home and you're done with lunch."

"Are you sure? It's no problem."

"I'm sure." I tried to brighten my voice. "Then I can talk to Dad, too. I need his advice anyway."

"Well, he'll love that. I'll talk to you soon. Love you."

"Love you, too." I ended the call and sighed. Everyone was going to church. I ought to figure out where I was going to go. It wasn't that I didn't want to attend, I'd just thought I was doing the right thing for Beckett by limiting the new experiences that got thrown at him all at once.

Maybe I was wrong.

I pressed the heels of my hands to my eyes. Maybe I was wrong about all of this and I should just head back home.

Except, of course, I wasn't sure where that was anymore.

And this was dumb.

I opened a browser on my phone and navigated to the website of Mom and Dad's church in Kansas. They weren't a huge congregation, but they'd always embraced new technology as soon as it was available. Even when I was young, the services were replayed on the local public access TV station or available on a CD. Now? It was online all the way.

Although maybe the public access was still going on so that older members didn't have to learn something new.

I didn't sing along, and my mind wandered a little during the sermon, but by the closing prayer, I felt a little better. Smoother around the edges.

Mom wouldn't call for another couple of hours though, and suddenly it felt as if the walls were closing in on me.

I'd go for a walk. Get some air. See what the historic downtown area of Old Town was like on a Sunday morning.

Resolved, I found my sneakers and a purse that I could wear crossbody so I didn't have to worry about it while I walked, and headed out, careful to lock the front door.

I only got lost twice.

It shouldn't have been possible. All I had to do was follow the waterfront south until I hit the main shopping area, but I'd jumped the gun and turned into a neighborhood that had a lot of dead-end streets. But now I was here and I couldn't stop my smile.

It was charming.

So many people walked along the sidewalks on both sides of the cobblestone streets. It was a gorgeous day—warmer than I'd expected seeing as it was just now October—and we were all taking advantage.

I slowed as I passed shop windows. I didn't need trinkets from Ireland, although there was a gorgeous fisherman's sweater in the window that called to me. A few doors down though, I was halfway through the bookstore door before I'd consciously decided to turn in.

"Hi there. Welcome to Portable Magic. Let me know if I can help you find something." The woman leaning against the counter looked about my age.

"Thanks. I like the shop name. Stephen King, right?"

The woman's eyebrows lifted and she grinned. "You're one of the few people who have pegged it. You must be a true book lover."

"To the bones." The boxes my LA landlady was hopefully shipping to me this week were, primarily, books. And even those were a pared-down version of what I would love to have. "I've been surviving with my e-reader lately. It's not the same."

She laughed and came around the counter with her hand out. "I like you. I'm Megan Campbell. This was my grandma's shop, but she retired, so now it's mine. I'm only really here on the weekends, though."

"You're not the manager?"

Megan shook her head. "I wish. It's a great job for someone with a husband who can support the home. It's not so much a living wage otherwise. So for now, I'm stuck using my degree working for the city as a social worker."

"That doesn't sound too bad."

She waggled her hand side to side. "Some days yes. Some days no. I like when I can help people. I don't love the bureaucracy."

"Makes sense. I'm Whitney, by the way."

"Nice to meet you." She cocked her head to the side and studied me.

I struggled not to squirm.

"Are you a nanny?"

"Um. Yes?"

Megan grinned. "Small world. My brother, Austin, is friends with Scott."

"Oh." I wasn't sure what else to say. I'd been doing a little reading on nannying—it seemed like a good idea to know how most people expected the job to be done. It wasn't like I was an official nanny from an agency. I was just someone who loved a little boy and wanted to make sure he was being well cared for.

"I think it's great. I was a little worried about Scott and a three-year-old. Not because Scott's a bad guy, mind you, but I don't think he's had anything to do with a toddler since he was one himself."

I chuckled. "You wouldn't know to see him with Beckett. He's a natural."

"Yeah?" Something gleamed in Megan's eyes.

Oh, boy. I really didn't want to deal with jealous girlfriends. Though if she was Scott's girlfriend, she probably would have led with that, not the brother's friend thing. So...wannabe girl-friend? That seemed worse somehow.

I cleared my throat. "Is it okay if I look around?"

"Oh. Of course! Sorry. Do you have a favorite genre? I can point you in the right direction."

"I'm kind of eclectic." I shrugged.

People either got it or the didn't. Mom had hooked me on romance when I was a teen. Anything to keep me from getting lost in the dystopian fantasy that seemed so popular with my peers but inevitably left me depressed for weeks after reading it. Dad had steered me toward sci-fi. And I'd found I loved every-thing else in between.

Megan's eyes lit up. "Yeah? Me, too. I can't wait to see what you choose!"

I offered a small smile and started toward the first set of bookcases. These appeared to be local-interest type things. Colonial history—fiction and non—cookbooks. The kind of thing tourists would want as a souvenir.

I wrinkled my nose and kept walking.

I found the science fiction and trailed my fingers over familiar spines, pausing when I found a title I didn't recognize. I pulled it out and tucked it under my arm. I made my way through the small shop and by the time I got back to the front, I had six paperbacks.

"You weren't kidding." Megan looked through the pile that I set on the counter. "Oh, I loved this one. Have you read more by her? I love dual timeline stories and I never thought I would."

"Right? I thought the same thing when I tried the first book by her, but my friend was adamant that I'd love it and she wasn't wrong. I just wish she wrote faster."

"Yes!" Megan rang up the stack, pausing at the space Marine volume. She looked up at me. "Really?"

"Really. It's a great series. I'm impressed that you have indie authors."

"Grandma's a big proponent of stocking what sells. She doesn't care who published it if it's a good story."

"I think I'd like your grandma." I tried not to cringe when I saw the total. I'd just been paid and my bank account currently had more money in it than...ever. I wasn't going to spend it in one place, but six books weren't going to break my budget. I handed Megan my credit card.

Megan swiped the card and gave it back. "Whitney Hall, I'm glad you stopped by. I'm here a lot of evenings and most weekends. I hope you'll come back."

It was my turn to study her, and I made a snap decision. It

wasn't risky, because my parents had always told me people who loved books were generally good people. "Do you have any evenings free?"

"Yeah. I come to the shop even if I'm not scheduled. I live with my brother and it's good to get out of the house sometimes. Plus it makes me feel closer to Grandma since she packed up and moved to Florida."

"Want to grab dinner sometime? It might be later than a usual meal—I need to wait until Scott's home and taking charge of Beckett." I forced myself to stop talking. I was babbling. But I found the prospect of a new friend exciting.

"Late works. The day job doesn't always end at five." Megan grabbed one of the store cards out of a holder by the register and wrote on the back of it. "Here's my number. Text me, okay? Girlfriends are hard to come by these days."

"Tell me about it." I grinned and pocketed the card before reaching for the bag of my books. "I'm glad I stopped in."

"Me, too."

Smiling, I stepped out of the shop and continued down the tree-lined sidewalk. Some of the restaurants and cafés had outdoor seating that I skirted around. I was tempted to stop for a bite to eat, but I had food at home.

And if that wasn't the most grown-up thought.

I stopped and turned around. The little café I'd just passed had looked casual. And the scents wafting through the door were incredible.

I strode back toward it and through the door, then stopped at the hostess stand. It wasn't crowded—there were plenty of patrons, but not a line. My chances of scoring a table seemed pretty good.

"How many?" The hostess looked bored. Her gaze kept dipping to her cellphone that was propped next to the seating chart on her podium.

"Just one. Can I sit outside?"

She shrugged. "Sure. It'll be faster if you order at the counter if you want to do that. Melissa is supposed to be covering the outside tables today, but…"

I laughed. She shouldn't share so much information, but I'd been there with coworkers who were unreliable and left me to take the customer abuse from their unwillingness to do their job. "I'll do that. Thanks."

I ordered French onion soup and a small salad at the counter, then let them talk me into their house-made pineapple fresca. I wasn't sure how well pineapple was going to mix with the soup, but I had stomach medication at home if it came to that.

I took the table number out with me to the little fenced-off seating on the sidewalk and snagged a small table under the shade of one of the trees planted along the curb. I got out the space Marines, tucked the rest of the books by my feet, and settled in.

Maybe having weekends off wasn't going to be so bad after all.

9

SCOTT

"Hey, darlin'. Who's your little friend?" With a smile, Sylvia, our usual server for lunch after church, set a coloring sheet and three crayons in front of Beckett.

"This is Beckett. He's my..." I didn't know what to call him. He was my cousin's son. Which made him some kind of cousin to me. But I was in charge of him now, for good. So not really my son, but also that wasn't wrong. "Nephew."

Cody and Noah rolled their eyes.

I shrugged. No one had asked me what our relationship was, and I needed something better than a ridiculous "it's complicated."

"Nice. Are you visiting for a while?"

Beckett just stared at her.

"He's living with me now. For good." I sensed Beckett relax at my words. Poor kid. I patted his leg under the table. "So you'll be seeing him every Sunday with the rest of us."

"How nice." Sylvia actually appeared to beam.

Who knew she liked kids? I didn't know why she wouldn't, of course. We saw her weekly for lunch after church and that was it. For all I knew, she had sixteen grandchildren that she doted on daily.

"What can I get you to drink?"

I froze. This was harder than it should be. I'd already become dependent on Whitney, and that had to end. "He'll have milk. I'd like a Coke."

"Coke for me." Cody leaned forward to see around Noah. "And a water? I'm only having one soda, no matter how much I beg."

Sylvia laughed. "Got it. And you?"

Noah sighed. "Half tea, half lemonade."

"Arnold Palmer. Sure. Sweet or unsweet tea?"

"I'll live on the edge and choose sweet. Thanks." Noah flashed a grin.

"I'll get those right out to you. Back in a sec."

I watched her leave then shifted to look at Beckett. "Any thoughts on what you'd like for lunch, bud? They have pictures on the back here."

I reached for the coloring sheet and flipped it over to show the kid food options. Beckett's eyes grew large and he smiled and tapped the bowl of macaroni and cheese.

"Great choice." I read the information on the menu then scanned for the pictures of the sides and pointed. "Apple slices, fries, or broccoli?"

"Broccoli?" Noah wrinkled his nose. "What kid is going to choose that? They only put that on there to make moms happy."

I glared across the table at him. What if Beckett liked the stuff? Just because I agreed with Noah didn't mean Beckett had to. "It's okay if you like the trees, dude. They make you grow strong and healthy. So do the apples. And I'll probably get fries with mine, so you could have some of those if you chose one of the two healthy sides."

Cody snorted and shook his head.

I glanced over. "What?"

"I didn't realize bribery was an inherent skill that came with parenthood is all."

Yeah, well, neither did I. And I probably would have been fine with him choosing the fries if I hadn't already started hearing Whitney in my head chastising me for letting him. So this way, he could choose the apples and still get fries and everyone won.

Beckett frowned thoughtfully at the paper before tapping the ice cream sundae at the bottom of the page.

I grinned. "Yeah, I'd go for that, too. But you have to pick and eat one of these first. If you're still hungry though? I'll totally get you the ice cream."

Beckett turned his quiet gaze up at me then nodded once and tapped the broccoli.

"Trees it is. You're on your way to being stronger and healthier than Noah over there. Good job, man."

"Hey. I'm strong and healthy." Noah lowered the menu. "Just for that, I'm getting a side salad."

"I don't think it counts if you drown it in ranch." Cody jabbed his elbow into Noah's side.

"Baby steps. We can't all be perfect like you."

"Well, at least you finally admit it." Cody set his menu down. "I am *not* getting a salad, but I am getting green beans with my meatloaf and none of you are going to tell me how unhealthy those options are when served from here. Okay?"

"Deal." I blew out a breath. My usual was a fried chicken sandwich with french fries. There was nothing healthy about any of it, except the lettuce and tomato that I always pulled off and left on the plate. "I guess I'll give the grilled chicken a shot. But I'm getting the fries because I promised to share."

"Seems legit." Noah leaned back as Sylvia arrived with our drinks.

She set them on the table before pulling a pad out of her apron pocket. "Are you ready?"

We rattled off our orders and she headed back to the kitchen without any comment. She had to be laughing to herself though, because we were absolutely not her healthiest customers.

"We're getting Friday poker back on the schedule now that you're all moved in, right?" Cody tapped his fork to line it up with his knife.

I nodded. "I have it on the schedule. I'll put it in the group text to remind everyone though. Beckett likes pizza, so he's in, too."

"Yeah? Are you going to beat us all at cards?" Noah smiled at Beckett, who shrank against me and buried his face in my arm. "Aw."

"He's a little shy sometimes. It's okay. He'll warm up." I shifted so my arm was around him and gave his arm a rub. It was a strange feeling to have this little body snuggled against me. I liked it. "I was going to ask on Friday, but maybe it's better to talk to you two now and we can toss it into the chat, too, if you're in."

"Well, now I'm curious." Cody reached for his Coke and took a long drink.

"Remember when we first realized just how well our strategy had paid off and we were throwing around all the crazy ideas of what to do with some of the money?"

"Sure. I'm still seriously considering that Mediterranean cruise. It looks amazing." Noah reached for his glass. He frowned at it. "Does this have caffeine? I'm trying to cut back so that's why I didn't get a Coke. But tea has caffeine, doesn't it?"

I laughed. "Yep. The lemonade doesn't though, so it's probably a little less?"

"Better than nothing, I guess." He took a drink and wrinkled his nose. "Ugh. Why do people drink that?"

"You've never had it before? Dude. Why'd you order it?" Cody clearly was trying to hold in his laughter.

"I don't know. It seemed like a good idea at the time. Are we doing that cruise? Think how fun it'd be."

Noah wasn't wrong. It would be a ton of fun, but I wasn't sure how well toddlers and elite cruises went together. "I might have to punt on that for a while now. But we did talk about going in on a plane. Is that still interesting?"

Noah's eyebrows lifted. "Yeah, man. I'd be in for that. I was thinking Colorado over Christmas break and it'd be fun to be able to fly the whole family out together."

"We'd have to talk about holiday use. I wouldn't mind a beach somewhere and I bet I could talk Mom and Dad into that. Probably my sister and her husband and kids, too." Cody shrugged. "But if we owned it, it's not like we couldn't have it take you all to Colorado then come back here and get me and my family and take us to the Caymans or something."

"Fancy. If you're hitting the Caymans for real, you should invite Austin and Megan. Austin is dying to learn to scuba. I feel like the Caymans would be a good place for that." For that matter, I wouldn't mind Christmas at the beach. Of course, I should plan on Florida if I wanted that. My parents would love to have me and Beckett with them. Maybe we could swing a visit to the famous mouse while we were at it. "Details aside, you think it's worthwhile?"

"I think we should have Austin really look at the numbers and Tristan figure out any potential legal issues." Noah shrugged. "But if they don't find an issue and everyone's in? I'm in."

Cody nodded. "Agree."

"All right. I'll put it in the chat." I frowned. "Or send an email. That's probably better in this case?"

"Either one. If you do the email, you know you need to

mention it in the chat anyway or Austin isn't going to see it for three weeks."

I laughed. Cody wasn't wrong.

I glanced over at Beckett and smiled. He was painstakingly coloring in what looked like a dancing lemon on the front of his kid menu. I was actually pleasantly surprised that he wasn't just scribbling wildly across the front. Not that that would have been bad. It's certainly the only kind of coloring I did, if you asked my mom.

Sylvia showed up with a tray full of food before anyone could start a different conversation. "Here we are, gentlemen. Save room for some dessert. We have apple, pumpkin, and cherry pie today. All made fresh this morning. And the sundaes for kids are honestly pretty good. Melvin makes the ice cream himself, so it's not all ice crystals. I know you boys don't usually get dessert, but kids need sweets. Let me know if you need anything else."

She disappeared before I could say thank you. "I'll pray."

If Cody and Noah were surprised, they kept it under wraps. We always blessed the food, but usually I wasn't the one volunteering to do it. I was trying to make it a habit with Beckett though. I didn't imagine Shelby Ann had been one for praying —and there I went making assumptions about someone I didn't know, who wasn't able to defend herself. *Sorry, Lord. I just want to be a good parent to Beckett.*

I took Beckett's hand and my heart felt funny as his little fingers curled around mine. I started to pray.

10

WHITNEY

The little bell on the door jingled when I pushed it open. Megan glanced over from behind the counter and grinned.

"About time! I was beginning to wonder if you were ditching me."

I laughed. "No chance. I've been looking forward to helping you decorate the store for Halloween for the last week."

"Things settling in at home?"

"Yes. You were right. We just needed to find our rhythm, I guess. I still don't love his rules, but as his mom made clear when they were visiting, I'm the hired help."

Megan scoffed. "I don't believe that for a minute. I've met Scott's parents and they're wonderful. Tell me exactly what she said."

I frowned. I didn't remember the exact words. And okay, fine, maybe I read a lot more into them than she'd intended, but I didn't understand why nobody seemed to care about my existing relationship with Beckett.

"That's about what I thought." Megan's smile was gentle. "Look, I get it. You knew Beckett's mom and you're protective.

That's not necessarily a bad thing. But you need to let Scott figure out how to make it work as his guardian long term, too. You see that, right?"

"I guess." There was a big part of me that was holding out hope that Scott would realize Beckett was too much work and he'd give up. Then I could swoop in and save the day. Except, of course, at this point I wasn't sure how we'd live. Being gone from LA for over a month was like a lifetime when you were still pounding the pavement looking for gigs. I'd be starting basically from scratch if I went back. And that left what? Kansas?

Ugh. Not if I could figure out a way around it. The only thing that would entice me back to Kansas was a teaching position at the college, and the drama department only had openings once every billion years, give or take.

"Give it time." Megan came around the counter and rubbed her hands together. "Now, let's get decorating. I pulled the boxes down from the shelves in the storage closet, but some of the stuff is old, so we probably need to toss it."

"Does that mean we get to add new?"

"Maybe?" Megan bit her lower lip. "I guess it depends on the cost. We run pretty close to the line financially. I love the convenience of e-books, so you'll never catch me slamming them, but it's a lot harder to make a living with a bookstore these days than it used to be."

"Sorry."

She shrugged. "It's okay. We've got a good location. Grandma bought the building before the cost of real estate skyrocketed, so it's not like we're going to lose our lease. We get decent foot traffic from tourists. I just wish I could make it a full-time gig instead of something I only work in evenings and weekends. I wish I could afford to hire full-time staff instead of relying on part-timers. I know it's not ideal, but we can't swing all the benefits."

That made sense. I'd been pretty surprised when Scott showed up with an employment contract and health insurance paperwork on Saturday morning. I guess he'd been waiting on his lawyer friend to get everything figure out for him and the guy had brought it to poker on Friday.

"Do the guys play poker every Friday?"

Megan shrugged. "Pretty much. Why?"

"They never invite you?"

She laughed. "No way. It's guys only."

"Typical."

"I don't really want to be invited, either. I imagine they know that. If you wanted to play, you could always ask." Megan arched an eyebrow at me.

I shook my head. If I was part of their friend group, it'd be one thing. But I was staff. Basically a stranger. And I was really only there for Beckett, and that was more because Scott hadn't been able to find daycare and preschool in the week following his notification that Shelby Ann had named him guardian. When it all boiled down, I didn't want to do anything to draw attention to the fact that I wasn't the only option he had.

The bell jingled over the door and I turned in time to see a short redhead hurry in.

"Am I late? I'm late, aren't I?"

Megan laughed. "No, Kayla, you're right on time. Come meet Whitney."

"Hi! You're the nanny. I've heard good things." She clapped her hands with excitement as she looked at the boxes.

"Don't mind her. She's Austin's best friend. They teach together at the same school. And yes, she's been this overexuberant for as long as I've known her." Megan pushed a box toward Kayla. "Pretty sure these are the metallic spiders. You can start with them."

"Are you a math teacher, too?" I didn't know as much about

Scott's friends as I'd like. Because, again, I was just the help. Megan talked like she assumed I was part of the group and as much as I appreciated it, I was often lost.

"Oh, gosh no." Kayla gave a dramatic shiver that started at her head and traveled the whole way to her toes. "I love math entirely too much to try to teach it to kids who are predisposed to hate it because their parents badmouth it constantly."

I blinked. "You love math too much to teach it?"

Kayla nodded emphatically. "It's beautiful, really, once you see it."

Megan's groan interrupted. "Stop. Please, I beg you. I get enough of the language of the spheres talk from Austin. I get it. It's why the two of you are besties, but this is not a math love-in. We're decorating. Remember?"

Kayla rolled her eyes but she pulled the top off the box and peered in. Then she grinned and extracted a wriggly, metallic spider. "Nice. Do I get free rein?"

"Yeah, go nuts." Megan waved at the store.

Kayla hoisted the box to her hip and disappeared into the bookshelves.

I glanced at Megan, eyebrows lifting. "She should teach math."

"Right? But she's a computer science teacher, so really, it's the next best thing. Austin says she gives her students math problems to solve as their programming exercises."

"Diabolical."

Megan laughed. "Basically. I wouldn't want to be in either of their classes, but supposedly Kayla's are the first to fill up."

"Probably because she's perky and adorable." I shook my head and dragged a box across the floor toward me. "Two things I will never be accused of."

"I can hear you two. You know that, right?" Kayla's voice floated over to us.

I flinched and my face heated. "Sorry."

"No, you're fine. Just this store is what, eight hundred square feet? Still, I am both perky and adorable, so it's okay. Keep going."

Megan snorted out a laugh. "We'll add humble to the list."

I looked into the box and brought out rolls of black and orange streamers. "This looks fun. Do you have tape?"

"Check up by the cash register. Where were you going to hang them?"

I pointed at the ceiling. Was there anywhere else for streamers to go? Back in elementary school, I'd perfected the twist that was not too tight and not too loose. I guess we'd see if I still had the touch.

Megan eyed me. "There's a step stool in the back room. I'll grab it."

I carried the streamers with me to the front and slipped behind the checkout counter. It was so organized it was almost painful, but there was, in fact, a full tape dispenser sitting beside a stapler and a full cup of pens and sharp pencils. I snagged the tape and looked up, planning my attack.

"One step ladder." Megan set it down beside me then looked up. "I've never bothered putting them up there. Might be nice."

"Where do you usually put them?" They were streamers. Weren't they supposed to go in swoops across the ceiling?

Megan shrugged. "Down the side of the bookcases mostly."

"There's probably enough in the box, you can still do that."

"I just might. But for now, I'm going to do the window display. If you need a hand with that, holler."

Kayla, empty box dangling from one hand, wandered out of the stacks. "Spiders deployed. Now what?"

"That was fast." I scooted the step ladder over a little and started up, both rolls of streamers in my hand.

"I guess we can add 'efficient' to my list of virtues." Kayla grinned. "You need help?"

I shook my head. "Don't think so."

"Get the box of pumpkins. You can put those around next." Megan gestured vaguely to where the boxes of decorations had been piled. "Or look around and see what grabs your fancy."

"Can do." Kayla sighed. "I love it in here."

"And that's why we're friends." Megan chuckled. "Because the affection you feel for my brother is definitely a check in the negative column."

"Whatever." Kayla shook her head. "He's a great guy. Have you met Austin yet, Whitney?"

"Briefly." His was one of the names thrown at me during a hurried round of introductions on poker night. Before I'd been shooed from the room because my workday was over. "He seemed nice."

"Don't let her fool you. He's not. He's annoying." Megan adjusted a stack of books with alternating orange and black spines in the window display. "Thinks he knows everything. Bossy. Just ugh."

"Gosh, it's like you were listening the last time he was complaining to me about you." Kayla laughed, shaking her head. She turned her gaze to me and pointed. "Take my word for it, he's a good guy."

"If you love him so much, why don't you marry him?" Megan's words were mumbled under her breath.

I glanced quickly at Kayla, but if she'd heard Megan's mutter, she didn't let on. I taped the start of the streamers on the ceiling near the front door then started twisting as I climbed down the ladder and moved it so I could attach the swoop. Before I went back up, though, I glanced over to where Kayla had disappeared.

"Psst. Megan."

"What? Why are we whispering?" Megan came over to stand beside me.

"Are Kayla and your brother a thing?"

Megan stifled a laugh. "What? No. Austin is the world's most clueless man and I don't think Kayla's ever going to work up the nerve to do anything about it. They'll just end up circling each other in a nursing home someday."

I grinned at the mental image. "You should give your brother a nudge."

"Me? No. No way. I don't get involved in other people's love lives. Hard rule. You shouldn't either. For your own sanity."

I frowned. She probably wasn't wrong. I couldn't afford to do anything that would make Scott change his mind about keeping me around to help with Beckett. And while I could see Kayla and Austin being a cute couple, I didn't know either of them. Not really. Maybe they were better off friends.

Friends would be a nice place to get to with Scott.

I climbed back up and adjusted the depth of the streamer's scoop before taping it in place.

There was too much on the line for me to consider any sort of romantic relationship right now. Beckett was the priority. But friendship wasn't off the table. And maybe if Scott and I were friends, I'd be able to relax a little and not worry quite so much about whether or not he was going to send me packing.

11

SCOTT

I punched the garage door button and pushed open the door to my car. Today was one of the days when I seriously questioned my decision to keep working for Robinson Enterprises. I didn't need a full-time job. I didn't really need any job, other than for the fact that I thought I'd go insane bouncing around the house all day.

With a sigh, I grabbed my bag and coat, got out of the car, and shut the door before heading into the house. I tossed my coat onto a hook that I'd hung on the wall just inside the garage door, then aimed for the stairs.

Giggles floated down the steps.

I stopped on the stairs and let the sound wash over me. Who knew a child's joy could be so soothing?

Parents, I guess. But I was still new to that gig. I made a mental note to check with Tristan about the adoption process. It didn't feel like it should be taking this long. Beckett's mother was gone. She'd named me legal guardian. Why was it so hard for me to finalize the process?

The laughter trailed off, so I started back up. I just hadn't wanted to interrupt when it was clear Whitney and Beckett were having fun.

On the main floor, I set my bag down beside the banister and looked around.

"You're home."

I turned at the sound of Whitney's voice, finally spotting them at the little table in the kitchen. "Hey, guys."

I headed into the kitchen and grinned at Beckett. He was studiously rolling out lime-green dough, his tongue trapped between his teeth.

I pulled out the chair next to him. "How was your day, Beckett?"

He glanced up, shrugged, and went back to his dough.

I worked to keep my reaction inside. There was no point in getting frustrated with him, but I was worried. I glanced over at Whitney. "Is that good?"

"We went to the park for a while. Had a picnic. Then we spent after-nap time making the salt dough and he's been rolling like a madman since it was ready."

"You made the dough?" Hadn't I bought a big box of the stuff a few weeks ago when she'd mentioned it would be a good sensory activity for him?

"Yeah. It's part of the fun. He likes the tubs, but I thought..." She stopped and pressed her lips together. "Are you mad?"

"No." I shook my head. "No, just wondering."

I added a small smile, hoping that she'd realize I was serious. It felt like I was always stepping wrong with her. She clearly wasn't happy, but I didn't know if it was because of me, Beckett, or something else entirely.

"Okay." Whitney studied me for another few seconds. "Could I talk to you in the living room a minute?"

My eyebrows lifted, but I stood. "Sure."

It felt a little like getting called into the principal's office as I followed her from the kitchen. She was standing by the doors to the deck, arms crossed.

I moistened my lips and gestured toward the couch. "Can I sit?"

"Sure. Yes. Of course." She looked around before dropping into an arm chair. "It's Beckett."

"Is he sick?" He'd looked fine. If he wasn't well, though, she should have called me at work. I could have come home and taken him to an urgent care.

"Not like you mean. I'm worried about his talking, though. In LA he wasn't this quiet. He's never been loud and yammery like you hear people talk about, but when his mom died...I figured it was just that he was processing and he'd bounce back. But it's getting worse."

I'd noticed this. It was on my list to do something about. The problem, of course, was that my list was about six miles long and there didn't seem to be enough hours in the day to tackle even a fraction of it. But I guess this meant I needed to bump that up to the top priority.

"Okay. I wondered what he'd been like before. I guess I'll reach out to his pediatrician and go from there."

Whitney frowned at me. "What's a pediatrician going to do? It's not a physical problem."

"We don't know that. And the little bit of time I've spent trying to research hasn't given me a clear answer between needing a psychiatrist or a speech therapist. Seems like the pediatrician might be able to point me in the right direction."

She trapped her lower lip between her teeth, then nodded. "Okay. I guess that makes sense."

I bit back a snarky response, but it took about all the restraint I had left after my day at work. I spent the whole day biting my tongue; I didn't really love having to do it at home, too.

Especially not because the nanny thought she'd be a better choice for raising Beckett. "Thanks."

Her eyebrows lifted.

I guess I didn't manage to keep all the snark in my head. I offered a tight smile as I stood and started back toward the kitchen. Next up was dinner. I wasn't in the mood to cook, but I also knew I couldn't live on takeout like I'd done when it was just me. If I'd had any doubt about it, Mom had drilled that into me when she and Dad had visited.

I pulled out the chair across from Beckett and sat, watching him while he rolled the dough. After a moment, he paused and looked up at me.

"How do you feel about spaghetti?"

Beckett nodded.

Whitney drew in a sharp breath.

I glanced over. She was standing in the doorway. Why was she following me? "Did you need something?"

"It's just..."

I waited. Was she criticizing my choice of dinner? Really? "Are we out of noodles?"

"No. But you made spaghetti on Monday."

"And?" Was there a rule about only eating pasta once a week I didn't know about? "I'll mix it up and nuke some broccoli to go with it."

"Yum." Beckett's contribution to the conversation was quiet.

I hid a smile. Broccoli wasn't my favorite, but he seemed to like it and vegetables were good things. So I was going to embrace it while I could. Everyone seemed to have opinions about how to raise a child, and they weren't shy about sharing them.

"There are some chicken breasts in the fridge. You could grill them and they'd go nicely with the broccoli." Whitney started toward the fridge. "Beckett likes grilled chicken, right bud?"

Beckett shrugged and turned his attention back to the dough.

I frowned and stood. I pushed the fridge door closed. "Thanks for the tip. But I think tonight's spaghetti. I'll consider the chicken for tomorrow."

"But—"

"Can I see you in the living room a moment?" I fixed her with a stern look before striding from the room. Was there a reason we were moving into the living room for a discussion? She'd started it, and I was going with it, but wasn't it healthy for kids to see adults argue and find a resolution? I had no idea. I'd have to ask Mom. Or get a parenting book. Maybe both.

Whitney crossed her arms and didn't sit.

"I appreciate your concern, but dinner isn't your problem. It's mine. In fact, you're off the clock as soon as I get home."

"I consider it part of my job to look after Beckett's well-being. Things like his nutrition matter."

"But it's not part of your job. At all. Your job is to take care of Beckett while I'm at work. Period. You're not his parent."

She huffed. "Neither are you."

My eyebrows lifted. "No. But I am his legal guardian."

Whitney deflated, but the scowl stayed fixed on her face. "He needs to eat vegetables at every meal."

"Do you eat a vegetable at every meal? What veggie did you have at breakfast today?" It was a trick question. I knew she didn't eat breakfast. She had a cup of coffee—or two—while she tried to get her brain working well enough to form complete sentences. I wasn't judging. That was basically what I did for breakfast most days, too. Although I did sometimes make a smoothie—complete with some vegetables.

"You know what I mean." She cocked her head to the side.

"Not really. You said Beckett needed veggies at every meal. I know he had a bowl of oatmeal for breakfast today. That's something most people consider pretty healthy on its own. He had some orange juice, which is fruit since I buy the good stuff. I'm not sure what he had for lunch, but since you're in charge for that meal, I'm guessing it was full of healthy veggies, right?" I waited for her to answer.

Whitney looked away.

Interesting. "No veggies?"

She sighed and looked back. "Fine. You made your point."

"There's nothing wrong with spaghetti. I will offer some vegetables, but the reality is, the doctor says he's healthy, so I'm not going to stress too much. But I'm not sure how well this is working."

Whitney's eyes widened. "What do you mean?"

"I just—" I broke off and roughed a hand over my face. "I don't need to come home from work and have to fight with someone about decisions that are mine to make. If you're unhappy with the way I'm raising Beckett, the better solution all around is for you to resign. I'd appreciate it if you could work until I found someone else, but I'll understand if you don't want to."

Whitney paled. "That's not—I don't—I'm not unhappy here."

"But you don't like how I'm raising Beckett."

"I didn't say that." She shook her head.

"Not in so many words." I sighed. "And it's getting old. I need a nanny who's going to be helpful. Supportive. And sure, stuff like his communication I need to know about. That's great, and I appreciate you bringing it up. But dinner choices and stuff like that? I don't really need your input there unless I ask."

"Fine."

I caught a glimpse of shiny eyes before she looked away, and my heart sank. I hadn't been trying to make her cry. I just wanted her to back off a little.

"If that's all, I guess I'll go up to my room." Her back was stiff and she wouldn't look in my direction.

I pressed my lips together. "Yeah. Sure. Have a good night."

I watched her march up the stairs and shook my head. How had that conversation ended up like that? Sure, I needed to clarify the employer-employee relationship. But I wasn't trying to be an ogre.

With a sigh, I headed back to the kitchen. Beckett was still happily playing with the dough, seemingly oblivious to the strife around him.

Was that a good thing or a bad one?

"Do you want spaghetti or chicken for dinner?"

Beckett looked up, a tiny frown on his face. His voice was barely audible when he finally spoke. "Ghetti."

I smiled and reach across the table to ruffle his hair. Whitney wasn't going to approve. I couldn't lie and say I didn't care, but I also cared about Beckett's happiness. So tonight, I'd take the win that was within reach. "All right. Spaghetti it is."

12

WHITNEY

I stared at the sludge in the bottom of my coffee cup and wanted to cry. This was my third attempt at making coffee this morning. All of them had turned out bad. Which meant, I guess, that my coffee machine was broken?

I needed coffee.

I glanced down at my pj's. It was Saturday morning. Surely it was acceptable to go down to the kitchen to make coffee—or, better yet, snag a cup of Scott's that he'd already fixed—in pajamas. It wasn't as if they weren't basically leggings and a long-sleeved shirt.

Ugh.

I wasn't changing. If Scott had an issue with it, he could yell at me in the living room again like he had on Thursday night over the spaghetti.

And okay, fine, he didn't yell.

But man, I wished I had more say in things concerning Beckett. It chafed at me quietly in the back of my mind all the time.

I blew out a breath and offered up my disappointment and frustration to Jesus. Again. Because I had to believe that I was here, with Beckett, for a reason. There was no other possible explanation for how quickly and well things had worked out. So, if Jesus put me here, I was going to do what I could to make sure I was living out what He wanted me to do.

It'd be easier when I had coffee.

I carried my sludge-filled mug down the two flights of stairs. On the last step, I stopped, my heart lifting at the sound of Beckett's laughter. Scott's voice, lower and soothing, wasn't loud enough to distinguish words, but whatever he said brought out more peals of laughter from Beck.

It was hard to stay angry at Scott when it was clear he cared about Beckett. Maybe as much as I did.

I crossed to the kitchen and paused in the doorway to clear my throat. "Morning."

Beckett looked over, grinned, and jumped out of his seat. He wrapped his arms around my legs and squeezed tight. His usual morning greeting.

"Morning." Scott stayed seated at the kitchen table. His plate had streaks of syrup on it, the only telltale signs of what must have been a pancake breakfast. "There are a couple left if you want."

"I was actually hoping for coffee." I held out the sludge-filled mug and tipped it so he could see the contents. "I think my machine died."

"Disaster." His smile brought out a tiny dimple in his left cheek. I fought to focus on that and not how well his pajama shirt stretched over his chest. He jerked his head toward the counter. "There's plenty. Help yourself."

"Thanks." I bent and hitched Beckett up onto my hip. He let go of my legs once he realized my intention. Once he was settled, he wrapped his arms around my neck and rested his head on my shoulder. I brushed a kiss across his head as I moved toward the sink.

Scott's hand on my shoulder set little zings of electricity through me. I sent him a questioning glance.

"Why don't you go sit and I'll fix your coffee?"

Why was he being nice? On the other hand, why did it matter? I'd be stupid not to take advantage of it when he offered. "All right. Thanks."

"Sure." Scott took my mug and peered inside. "Gross."

I laughed and settled in one of the chairs at the table, shifting Beckett into my lap. "Yeah. I tried three times."

Scott turned on the sink and scrubbed out my mug. "I'll get you a new machine. Can't have you decaffeinated."

"Horror!" My heart melted as Beckett snuggled back against me. The scent of his baby shampoo filled my nose. Must have been bath night last night. I'd gone out to the bookstore when the guys started showing up for poker night. It was that or hunker down in my attic apartment and listen to the laughter as it drifted up two sets of stairs.

There wasn't much that made me feel left out and unwanted, but being banished to my room during a party was up there.

And okay, fine, Scott probably wouldn't characterize it that way. I was off duty and he probably thought he was being a good boss, making sure I didn't work excessive hours.

Scott set my mug down on the table in front of me. "Sure I can't get you a pancake or two?"

I was about to say I wasn't hungry when my stomach gurgled.

Beckett laughed.

"Uh-oh. Think there's a monster in the kitchen, Beckett?"

Beckett shook his head, still giggling, and shifted. He pressed his nose to my cheek and whispered, "Yummy."

"Really? Better than mine?" I kissed the tip of his nose.

He shrugged.

"Oh, really? Well, then I guess I have to try them." I turned my head to glance at Scott. "Just one, if you're sure you don't mind. Thanks."

"I wouldn't offer if I minded. Butter and syrup?" He stepped to the stove and reached up to one of the cabinets to get down a plate.

I sipped my coffee. I wasn't sure how—or why—he knew how I liked it, but it was perfect. I was going to say just butter, but Becket had already nodded enthusiastically. "If he says I need both, I probably do. Is that why his are better? The toppings?"

Scott chuckled. "I'll take whatever competitive edge I can get. Beckett's a good food critic."

"He knows what he likes, that's for sure." He and I had had a few missteps over the years that I'd been watching him. Shelby Ann never seemed to care if he ate. She gave him what she wanted and if he didn't like it, he didn't eat. I'd asked her once, and she'd said she figured he'd eat if he was hungry. Maybe she was right, but I didn't have the spine to watch him go a whole day without food like she did, so I catered a little. And I learned how to make healthy things taste good enough that he'd tolerate them.

Scott set a plate in front of me and put a fork and knife beside it. "*Bon appetit.*"

"*Merci.*" That was pretty much the end of my French, but Scott didn't say more. I reached around Beckett for my fork and cut off a bite. I barely avoided dripping syrup on us as I moved the bite to my mouth. *Holy sugar, Batman.* I chewed and managed to swallow, then followed up with a big gulp of coffee. "That's...sweet."

Scott pressed his lips together. "You don't like it?"

I glanced down and met Beckett's wide-eyed gaze. Ugh. Now I couldn't admit that, no, I thought it was disgusting. Not when he was looking at me like that. "I just wasn't prepared is all. It's good."

Beckett watched me.

I was going to have to clean my plate, wasn't I? I fought back a sigh and cut another piece with the side of my fork. I shook it over the plate a little to try and dislodge at least some of the syrup before eating it.

At least there was no history of diabetes in my family.

Beckett's still slightly sticky fingers picked at the sleeve of my pajama top. I glanced down at him and smiled. "What's up, bud?"

"Zoo?" His expression was so hopeful, I felt bad that I didn't understand.

I swallowed the pancake and reached for my coffee again.

"Zoo!"

"You're playing zoo after breakfast?" It was the best I had. Scott had purchased practically every toddler-aged Fisher-Price toy on the market, so it wasn't completely out of left field. "Sounds like fun. What animal will you be?"

Beckett shook his head and shot a frustrated frown across the table at Scott.

Scott's shoulders moved like he was sighing, but his face didn't betray any annoyance. "No. Beckett and I are going to the zoo downtown. They should have all the decorations up for Boo at the Zoo. Maybe even some of the trick-or-treat stations. And if not, we still get to see the animals. It seemed like a fun way to spend the day and it's supposed to be almost seventy, so we shouldn't even need to bundle up."

"Oh, fun." I grinned down at Beckett before drinking more coffee. "That's even better. Did you know they have pandas at the zoo in DC?"

Beckett nodded, but he still looked as though something was awry.

"And elephants." Elephants were a favorite of Beckett's, if his insistence on getting to have the toy version was any indication. He liked giraffes, too, but I couldn't remember if the DC zoo had those. Probably better to avoid mentioning them, just in case.

Scott made a pretty decent elephant impression.

Beckett and I both laughed.

"I should probably get out of your way if you're heading downtown. Have fun." I started to shift Beckett to the chair beside me, but he clung on. "Hey, what's this?"

He shook his head forcefully and gripped my arms. His eyes filled and his voice came out as a half-cry. "Zoo!"

"Right. You're going to the zoo with Scott."

"No. You."

I winced. Oh. "Beckett. I—"

"That's a great idea, bud. I should have thought of it." Scott met my gaze. "Can you come?"

And now I was torn. On the one hand, I'd love to go to the zoo with Beckett. It was something I'd been working to figure out the logistics of for a couple of weeks. On the other hand? Going with Scott seemed like a recipe for disaster.

"We don't want to mess with your plans, though." Scott reached over and ruffled Beckett's hair.

"I don't have any plans." I blurted the words before I could think better of it. But they were true. "You really don't mind if I tag along?"

Scott shook his head.

"Okay. Thanks. That sounds fun." Becket was bouncing in excitement on my lap. It solidified my thoughts that the decision was right. Despite my misgivings. I drank more coffee and ignored the barely touched pancake on the plate in front of me. "Maybe I'll snag a quick refill on my coffee and head up to get ready. When did you want to leave?"

"I have a car coming for us in about ninety minutes." Scott

frowned. "You should finish your pancake. There's a lot of walking at the zoo. On a hill."

Beckett picked up my fork and offered it to me. Syrup dripped off the tines. I managed a weak smile. "Right. Thanks."

"I'll top up your coffee." Scott reached for my mug as he stood. "Then you and I should go get dressed too, okay, Beckett?"

Beckett nodded and slipped off my lap. He padded out of the kitchen. I watched until he disappeared up the first few stairs. "You're sure you don't mind me coming?"

"I'm sure. And Beckett's excited. I'd only mind if you felt like we were forcing you to do something you didn't want to do."

"No. I like hanging out with Beckett. You know that. But I'm also just the hired help. I'd hate to impinge on your family time." I hated the snarkiness in my tone, but he'd hurt me. As much as I was working on getting over it, it was still there.

Scott closed his eyes. "I'm sorry. This is new for all of us. I'm doing my best, even if it's not enough."

I took my mug when he offered it and sipped. "You're doing a good job."

His eyebrows lifted.

My heart sank. "I guess I'm sorry, too. I didn't mean to imply you weren't doing enough."

He gave a weak smile. "Thanks. Finish that pancake. I'll know if you don't."

I laughed. Maybe he would.

I watched Scott leave the kitchen and squashed the errant thought that checkered flannel pajama pants were a good look for him. Just because we were—maybe—making our way toward a cordial relationship, I wasn't opening the door to more. Not that he was likely to even be interested in more. He certainly hadn't given any indication of that.

I sighed at the pancake. It was too late to try and scrape off the excess syrup. It had been sitting long enough that it had soaked in more of the maple stickiness than I would have thought possible.

Blech.

I cut what was left in half, folded it over, and shoved the enormous section into my mouth. I chewed quickly and washed it down with coffee.

Beckett thought these were better than mine?

I shook my head. Poor kid had no taste.

13

SCOTT

"Thanks. I'll text you when we're about thirty minutes from wanting to head home."

"Very good. Enjoy your day." The driver smiled at me and pulled out into the DC traffic.

I glanced at Whitney where she stood by the large letters spelling out "zoo" at the main entrance to the Smithsonian Zoo. She held Beckett's hand as he hopped from one foot to the other in front of one of the big o's. She cared for him, that much was obvious anytime I saw the two of them together. I just wished I knew if there was a better way to handle things than what I was doing.

"You guys ready? What are we going to see first?" I closed the gap between us and reached for Beckett's other hand.

"Panda!" Beckett shouted.

I grinned, not just at his exuberance, but for the fact that he'd been loud and clear. Maybe we wouldn't need that doctor appointment after all. "I'm in. Work for you, Whitney?"

"Absolutely. Not every zoo has a panda. In fact, I'm not sure I've ever seen them in person. I do like the videos on YouTube where the panda keeper has to move the babies around while she's cleaning the enclosure or putting out food. It looks like fun."

I laughed. "I've seen those. We should look them up when we get home. You'd love them, Beckett."

The little boy nodded, then tugged my hand toward the entrance to the zoo. There was a steady stream of people heading in—was it going to be crowded? Maybe I hadn't thought this through as well as I hoped. But it wasn't like I could go during the week. Or, well, I could. I could take a day off and we could make a field trip of it, but that seemed irresponsible.

On the flip side, if I had too many more days like the ones this past week, maybe I'd quit and move into consulting like people kept expecting me to.

I sighed.

"Everything okay?"

I glanced over at Whitney. She looked concerned.

I forced a smile. "Yeah, sorry. I'm good. Just got lost in thoughts about work there for a minute."

"Never think about work on Saturday. It's a bad plan." She chuckled before glancing down at her phone then back up. Whitney pointed to a sign. "I think we turn here for the best route to the pandas."

"You've got a map on your phone?"

"Yeah, there's an app." She shrugged. "Seemed like a good thing to have."

Of course there was an app. Everything had an app. "Good call. I'll let you lead."

Whitney flashed a grin. "You could always download the app."

I shook my head. I did not need an app for the zoo. Not when this was liable to be the one time I came here. "I trust you."

We walked down the path, following the flow of people. The

panda house was apparently a popular place. We split from the main paved walkway to a branch leading down, past the outside area for the pandas on the right and tons of panda facts on signs on the wall to the left.

Whitney paused to read them all to Beckett. I lifted him up to my shoulders so he could look for the animals.

There was a bit of a line. It was moving though.

"Where?" Beckett patted my head.

"Not sure, bud. Maybe they're inside? See that big building —that's all part of the exhibit."

It was going to be frustrating for all of us if we didn't get to see the pandas. Beckett seemed to have latched on to the idea and I hated to have to disappoint him.

"Oh! Look!" Whitney patted Beckett's leg, her fingers accidentally brushing my cheek. I clenched my jaw at the inconvenient sizzle her touch left behind.

"Where?" I squinted, trying to follow the direction she was pointing.

"Up that tree, there's a red panda. Which is actually not a panda. Or even a bear, according to the sign. But it's pretty." Whitney stood close, still touching Beckett's leg. "Do you see it?"

I felt him move and glanced at Whitney. "Can he?"

"He nodded."

"Thanks." That was good. The line was moving again. "Ready to go?"

"Yeah. I think the red panda's asleep."

"Probably nocturnal." I felt like most zoo animals were. It was certainly the memory I had from my visits as a kid. Sleeping animals. Or hiding ones. And the few that were awake were completely disinterested in the crowds around them. Of course, they probably just wanted to be out in the wild, not cooped up to be ogled, regardless of how good the living circumstances were. God hadn't created animals so people could put them behind bars. "Here we go, let's bring you down, Beckett."

I shifted Beckett to my hip so we could get through the doorway of the panda house. To the right were floor-to-ceiling glass walls providing a view of the indoor portion of the enclosure. There were huge fake rocks—they had to be fake—and panda-sized doorways between the rooms.

"Look, Beckett." Whitney pointed again. "In the doorway toward the back of that room. You see the panda?"

I laughed. It wasn't a whole panda. Just a panda rear-end. "It's just his butt."

Beckett giggled.

Whitney shot me an annoyed glance. "Really?"

"What? I'm not wrong."

She shook her head and muttered something that sounded like, "Boys."

I shrugged. It had made Beckett laugh, so I was taking the win. "Maybe we can see the rest of him in the next room."

We slid along the hallway with the crowd, studying the enclosures for more signs of the black and white bears.

Beckett pointed.

I angled my head to try and see what he did. There was a tiny hint of white fur poking out from behind the giant rock structure in this room. "Good eye, Beck."

"Where?" Whitney leaned close.

I breathed in and could have kicked myself. I knew better. She smelled like flowers, and her scent was one that would linger in every one of my senses for hours now that it was there, making me want to get to know her better. And the worst thing was that it would never work. She was the *nanny*. I was her boss. Talk about inappropriate.

My voice was gruff when I finally managed words. "There's a little puff of white on the lower left side peeking out."

"Oh wow. That's...not a lot of panda." Whitney frowned.

We continued moving with the rest of the crowd to the third viewing area. This one didn't have any animals that I could see, but I paused and waited while Beckett moved his head from side to side, scanning.

Whitney wandered to the opposite wall.

I shouldn't have been watching her, but I also couldn't stop myself. What was it about her? I sighed and looked down, meeting Beckett's gaze. "Ready, bud?"

He nodded.

I crossed to where Whitney was reading about the pandas and how they'd come to be at the zoo in DC. "Anything amazing?"

"It's kind of interesting, but no. We can go. I'm bummed we didn't get to see more of them."

"Yeah. Maybe we'll have better luck with the other animals. Where should we go next?" I gestured to her phone. "What's closest?"

With a laugh, Whitney unlocked her phone and looked at the zoo map. "Hmm. Looks like we can pass by some bison on our way to the elephants. Does that sound fun?"

"Fants!"

I chuckled. "Sounds like a win. Can you walk a little now, Beckett?"

He squirmed in my arms, and I took it as assent, letting him down to the ground. I kept hold of his hand. Whitney took his other hand and we exited the panda house.

Did we look like a family to the people around us? I ignored the little pang in my chest at the thought. Yes, I wanted a wife and kids. I had since college. But, so far at least, that hadn't seemed to be in God's plans. Well, until He dropped Beckett in my lap. And okay, I hadn't exactly accepted that graciously, but now? I was definitely on board.

Would having a child make finding a wife even harder?

I glanced over at Whitney.

No. That was a bad plan. I'd hired her to take care of Beckett while I worked. She loved him, no question, but she also didn't think I should be his parent. She'd come out here originally to convince me to give up guardianship. It'd be smart for me to remember that.

No matter how much I was attracted to her.

Besides, it was entirely possible she didn't feel the same way. Probable, even. Look how she seemed to fight me on every single thing.

The bison were standing around chewing. We paused and looked at them, but Beckett was almost immediately tugging on my hand to get us going again. It was hard for a bison to compete with an elephant.

When we reached the elephant building, I pulled open the door and winced when the smell billowed out.

Whitney blanched. "Oh. Wow."

"Maybe we'll get used to it. Come on." I waved her through the door. Beckett followed. I took one last big breath of fresh air and brought up the rear.

If nothing else, the authentic smells of the animal areas ought to keep me from imagining this was a romantic date.

"Do you want to watch the movie with us?" I glanced at Whitney and then toward the living room. We'd walked every inch of the zoo's paths, taking turns carrying Beckett when his legs needed a rest. Beckett had napped on the drive home and awakened refreshed and ready to scarf down the burgers we'd picked up on the way.

Now, after a shower and change into pajamas, we were going to watch *The Jungle Book*. The old, cartoon version.

Whitney had been with us for most of the day. There was no reason she had to leave now.

"Oh. I..." She trailed off and bit her lip.

I glanced down at Beckett's hopeful expression. "Please?"

"Okay." She ruffled Beckett's hair before heading into the living room and settling on the couch. Beckett ran after her and crawled into her lap.

I grabbed the remote before sitting on the other end of the couch and propping my feet on the coffee table. I didn't think Beckett was going to make it through the whole movie, but his nap in the car might have made it possible. I guess we'd see. "Here we go."

The movie started, and I found my attention wandering to Whitney and Beckett. It wasn't as if I hadn't seen this movie a hundred times in my own childhood. And there was something compelling about the two of them together. Whitney obviously loved him. And he, just as obviously, returned the feelings.

Was I doing the wrong thing by insisting on keeping guardianship? And pursuing adoption? I rubbed my forehead, trying to get at the ache that was forming. I was praying—that was the biggest piece of advice Mom and Dad had given me about being a parent: pray. A lot. But even with all that, I wasn't getting clear answers. I was listening—or at least I thought I was—and I just hoped that God would close doors that I wasn't meant to go through if nothing else.

King Louie had just started to sing about wanting to be just like the man cub when Whitney's fingers brushed my arm.

I looked over.

"He's out." She pointed to Beckett. His head was in her lap, and he was making quiet snuffles in his sleep.

"I'll take him up." I stood. I was able to slide one arm under his knees. But the top half...I took a deep breath before sliding my arm under Beckett's shoulders. I glanced at Whitney and our eyes locked. My mouth went dry. She had to feel it, didn't she? I leaned forward as if drawn by an invisible wire. Her eyes widened and her mouth opened on a quick inhale of breath.

I gave myself a firm mental kick and tore my gaze away from Whitney's lips. I gently eased Beckett into my arms and straightened before heading toward the stairs.

I wanted to look over my shoulder, but I didn't.

Kissing Whitney would be a mistake. A huge one. If she wasn't interested, I'd be looking at possible sexual harassment charges. If she was...well, that was almost as bad. Because she was my employee. Beckett's nanny. The only real stability the boy had in his life right now.

I shook my head as I reached the top of the stairs and went into Beckett's room. I frowned. I didn't want to wake him.

After a moment of thought, I made my way into the bathroom we shared. I set his feet on the ground, still supporting his weight, and eased down his pajama pants, grateful they had an elastic waist, then quickly arranged him on the toilet seat.

"Scott?" Beckett's voice was thick with slumber. His eyes stayed closed.

"Yeah, buddy. I'm right here. Go potty, okay?" I kept my voice low, praying he'd stay as close to asleep as possible.

"Love you."

Everything in me warmed. It was the first time he'd said it. Maybe having his defenses lowered in sleep made it possible. "I love you, too, Beckett."

He'd finished going to the bathroom, so I got his pajama bottoms up as high on his legs as I could before tugging him gently to his feet so I could get them the rest of the way up. Then I lifted him. Beckett's arms slid around my neck. I kissed his head and went back to his bed. He could skip his teeth one night. It probably wasn't the end of the world.

I tucked him in and double-checked that his nightlight was glowing in the corner across the room. I kissed his head one more time. "Good night. I love you."

He didn't respond. He was already deeply asleep again. I pulled his bedroom door closed behind me and headed back downstairs to clean up the kitchen and maybe spend a little time on the Xbox.

When I reached the bottom step, I stopped. Whitney was curled up on the couch, still watching the movie. I figured she would have headed upstairs. I glanced over at the kitchen. There wasn't much of a mess. And it would all still be there tomorrow.

I made my way back to the couch and sat beside her.

Whitney glanced over, smiling. "I haven't seen this in ages. Do you mind if I finish?"

"No. Of course not." She could stream it in her room, but I wasn't about to mention that. I shifted, getting more comfortable, and put my feet on the coffee table. My hand brushed her arm. Did she feel it, too?

We sat like that—close but not quite touching—as the rest of the movie played out. It was nice. Nicer than I'd thought possible. And it made me wish, just a little, that all my reasons for not even considering getting involved with Whitney weren't valid.

But they were. And I needed to remember that.

When the movie ended, Whitney stretched both arms above her head then turned to look at me. "That was fun. Maybe it's weird to watch an old cartoon without Beckett, but it was a nice change."

I nodded. It wasn't going to be something I did regularly, but I could sort of see her point. Still, all things considered, I probably would have gone for Jason Bourne or Jack Ryan if I'd been given a choice. "I'm glad you joined us at the zoo today."

She angled her head to the side. "I appreciate you asking. I have to admit I was surprised. You're pretty strict about my working hours."

"Strict?" I bobbed my head from side to side as I considered her word choice. "Yeah, I guess that works as well as any other word. I just don't want to take advantage. You should have your own life, you know?"

"I guess. I'm mostly concerned about Beckett though."

"I get that. But what would you have done if I'd agreed to let you keep him? You wouldn't be with him twenty-four seven then, either. You'd have to work. He'd probably be in preschool or daycare. Something, right?" Really, when I looked at it, Whitney and Beckett were both better off with our current arrangement. Especially Beckett. I was confident keeping some consistency in his world was the right thing.

Whitney closed her eyes. "You're right. Honestly, I probably would have moved home to Kansas."

"Your family's there?"

"Yeah. They're great. And they would absolutely love Beckett like he was their own. But Gilead, Kansas, pretty much epito-mizes small town, and I was the stereotypical couldn't-wait-to-get-out teenager. Still kind of am. Minus the teenager thing."

I laughed. "It's funny. I grew up here—well, my parents lived in Fairfax, but the DC area. When I got out of college and came back, I was craving a little bit of that small town feel. It's why I rented in Old Town."

"It is kind of the best of both worlds. I love that we can walk almost anywhere we need to go. Beckett loves the park. And the river." Whitney sighed. "But it's really not the same, because I know there's also a whole other world fifteen or twenty minutes away in the car. And that's the difference. Fifteen minutes outside of Gilead? All you have is fields. Miles and miles of them."

I tried to picture it. Even the smaller town where my college was had been close-ish to civilization. "I can see how that could get boring. Why LA though?"

"The one amazing thing about Gilead is our annual Passion play." I must have given her a blank look because she chuckled quietly before continuing. "They're done around Easter. It's the story of Christ's triumphal entry, trial, death, and resurrection. Like a Christmas cantata, but for Easter."

"Okay. I guess I don't see how that had you running off to California."

"I was part of that play basically my whole life. The acting bug is a real thing. I thought I'd head to college out there and then take Hollywood by storm. Just like every other semi-talented kid from the middle of farm country." She shrugged. "I got some callbacks, but never got cast. I don't know if I would have kept at it."

I wasn't sure what to say to that. She sounded disheartened. It probably wouldn't cheer her up to hear anything about the probability of making it big in Hollywood. "Did you have a plan B?"

"I wasn't there yet. Probably still would have involved Kansas. They have the play every year. There are a handful of paid jobs involved with it. Competition is stiff, but my family is involved. Maybe that would have helped." Whitney shrugged, then covered a yawn. "I guess maybe I'll head up. Thanks again. I had a surprisingly good time."

Ouch.

I stood at the same time she did, and the motion brought us closer. Even with my psyche still on fire from her burn, I was tempted to lean forward and see what would happen if my lips brushed hers.

I forced myself to look away from her lips and met her gaze. I wasn't sure what I read there, but it sparked the tiniest flicker of hope in my chest.

She licked her lips. "I...good night."

"Night." I watched as she stepped back and hurried up the stairs. She paused on the landing and cast a fleeting glance over her shoulder before disappearing.

I blew out a breath.

I knew it was a bad idea.

I knew it couldn't work.

Except...maybe it could?

14

WHITNEY

I slid into the booth beside Kayla, glanced across the room at where the guys were sitting, and then frowned at Megan. "You're sure the guys aren't going to mind that we're eating here?"

Megan rolled her eyes and pushed a menu across the table at me. "Please. They don't own the diner. It's good food and close to church."

I couldn't attest to the first one yet, but it smelled promising. And it definitely was close to the church that Megan had talked me into trying. I'd been streaming church from home still, unwilling to branch out on my own and try to find something local. "Thanks for inviting me."

Kayla bounced in her seat, making me go up and down, too. "I'm glad you could come. So's she. I like this church. And it's so close! Why have I been driving to Springfield every week?"

Megan chuckled. "I don't know. I've invited you probably a hundred times."

"Hyperbole. But also valid." Kayla shrugged and picked up her menu. "Ooh! A Reuben. That was easy."

I looked at the menu. I did like a good Reuben—and this one

wasn't some weird turkey thing that I kept running into in LA Seriously, who made a Reuben with turkey? Give me corned beef or don't bother. "Yeah. I think I'm in for that, too. Are their fries any good?"

Megan grinned. "They're good. Do you seriously eat fries? And you still look like that? Maybe I hate you."

I laughed. "I don't eat them every day. But weight has never been my struggle. Sorry?"

"Yeah, yeah. I guess I have to forgive you since I decided I liked you before I found that out. But too many more of those horrible flaws and we're going to have a talk." Megan slapped her menu on the table. "Dang it. Now I'm eating a Reuben and fries, too, and I'd been telling myself all morning I was going to get a salad."

I wrinkled my nose. "You can eat a salad at home. Why would anyone pay to eat a salad in a restaurant? I've never understood that."

"Of course you haven't." Kayla shook her head. "Although, Megan also has put me on notice about my fry eating, so maybe you and I don't get to talk about salads."

"Exactly." Megan pointed across the table at us, her expression stern for a few heartbeats before she burst into laughter.

"Well, that's a lovely sound." The waitress appeared at our table, pad in hand. "What can I get you ladies?"

"We're all having Reubens. With fries. And I'll live on the edge and get a Coke." I grinned and glanced at Kayla.

"I'm not that brave. Just water for me."

Megan frowned. "Unsweet tea. Can I get some of the pink fake sugar?"

"Sure, hon. I'll get those right in." The waitress turned and started toward the kitchen, stopping at two tables on the way.

I watched her go and jolted when my gaze met Scott's. I quickly turned back to our little group.

Megan's eyebrows lifted. "Well, well, well. That was interesting."

"Oh man. I missed it. What?" Kayla craned her neck around. "Oh hey, we can see the guys from here."

Megan snickered. "Exactly. And Scott and Whitney here just had a moment."

"Oh really?" Kayla drew out the last word like a playground taunt. She clasped her hands together and propped them under her chin. "Do tell. Spare no details."

"There's nothing to tell." I stared down at the table as my cheeks burned. Whatever shade of red they were had to be giving the impression that I was lying. But it was true! There was absolutely nothing going on between Scott and me. The heated tension after the movie last night had clearly all been in my head, and thankfully I'd been smart enough to go upstairs before I did something stupid.

Like kiss him.

That would have been a terrible idea. Horrible.

Also possibly amazing.

"Uh-huh." Megan waited until I looked up. She shook her head. "Not buying it. Are you buying, Kayla?"

"Nope. I need deets. It's been so long since I went on a date, I'm not sure I even remember what kind of details you might have to share."

I couldn't stop my chuckle. "Why do I doubt that? Look at you, you're adorable."

Kayla sighed. "I hate that word. That and cute. No one wants to date cute and adorable. They want to...I don't know...buy me a lollipop and send me to summer camp."

Megan snickered. "Stop it. You could date."

"Nope. The few who are willing to settle for cute all run away when they realize I'm smart." Kayla shrugged. "Anyway, we're not talking about me."

It had been worth a try. I was given a momentary reprieve by the arrival of our drinks and an assurance that our food would be right up. This time, I didn't watch the waitress, even though I really would have loved to see Beckett. "There's nothing to tell."

"But do you want there to be something to tell?" Megan leaned forward, almost knocking her tea over.

"No. That would be dumb. He's my *boss*. Talk about off-limits. All I want to is to be able to watch Beckett. He's who matters." I needed to keep my eyes on that simple fact and not let my imagination run away with the impossible.

"Beckett's adorable. Is he trick or treating next week?" Kayla fished the lemon out of her water, squeezed it, then dropped it back in before stirring her drink with her straw. "You have to take him around the shops. They have the best treats. The bakery gives out cookies. What did you get this year, Megan?"

Megan frowned, like she didn't want to let go of the Scott conversation, but thankfully she relented. "Popcorn balls from across the street and little keychain-sized coloring books."

"That beats a candy bar any day. I guess I need to figure out what he wants for his costume." Even though I'd helped Megan and Kayla decorate the shop, I hadn't really pieced together that it was nearing Halloween. After that, it wouldn't be long before Thanksgiving. Then Christmas. Then New Year's. And then, work on the Passion play back home would be kicking into high gear, with the opening performance on Ash Wednesday.

"And your own." Kayla nodded to emphasize her words. "If you're taking a kiddo around, you should dress up, too. I always wear some kind of costume to school if Halloween is on a weekday."

"Your students are probably all in love with you." I looked over at her. "Do you get mistaken for one of them?"

"Not as much anymore, thankfully." Kayla gave a dramatic shudder. "My first two years though? Ugh."

Megan grinned. "Isn't that how you and Austin got to be friends?"

"It definitely factored in. He came to my rescue a few times." Kayla sighed. "Anyway, this year I'm going as Jen Barber from *The IT Crowd*."

Megan and I exchanged a look. At least she looked as confused as I felt.

"Oh, please." Kayla groaned. "You've never seen it, either? Do yourself a favor and find it on Netflix. It's hilarious. British, so maybe a little on the not kid friendly scale, but still hilarious."

"I'll take your word for it." Megan waited while our Reubens were delivered and we assured the waitress that we were set. "It sounds like something Austin would like."

"He does." Kayla shook her head. "You know it's not against the law for you to like something your brother enjoys, right? He's not a complete nerd."

"Uhhh. Beg to disagree there." Megan grinned and popped a fry in her mouth.

"I'll pray." Kayla sent Megan an arch look before folding her hands and bowing her head.

I quickly followed suit.

"Dear Jesus, thank You for this food and for friendship. Thank You for a great church service and help us to glorify You in the week ahead. Amen."

"Amen." I reached for half of my sandwich and took a bite. Flavor exploded on my tongue—a mix of sour and sweet and meaty combined. Perfection. "Mmm."

"Yeah?" Kayla picked up her own sandwich and bit in.

"See? I said it was good food." Megan dunked another fry into the small silver cup of ketchup. "You doubted me."

"I didn't doubt the food. I just wasn't sure if Scott was going to think I was following him because I didn't trust him to do a good job with Beckett." I snapped my mouth shut. I hadn't meant to say that. He was my boss, and it wasn't professional to spread around any trouble we might be having.

"Scott's not like that." Megan reached across the table and touched my hand. "I really can't see Scott being like that."

I shrugged. She didn't have to see it. I could attest that it was true. I chanced a glance over my shoulder at the boys' table. Beckett was steadily shoveling broccoli into his mouth. He looked happy, though, and his head moved as if he was following the conversation between the guys. Scott was gesturing animatedly with a forkful of salad while Austin, Cody, and Noah laughed.

Maybe he wasn't upset that I was here after all.

I returned my attention to my food.

"Do you not like working for him?" It was the first time I'd heard Kayla serious, without any hint of her excessive bounciness.

"Oh, no. It's great. Like I said before, it's more about Beckett than anything. I could put up with way more if it meant I got to be with Beckett full time." I forced a smile. "Maybe a nanny isn't something I ever figured I'd be adding to my résumé, but it's not like it's a bad job."

Kayla nodded slowly. "Is Beckett happy?"

That was trickier to answer. My kneejerk answer was yes, of course. But the whole speech thing was making me question it.

"I think so? But he's not talking much—enough that I said something to Scott about it and he's going to talk to the doctor."

"Good." Megan took a bite of her sandwich. "Early intervention is a good thing. Poor kid has had a lot of change and trauma lately."

"I try to talk about Shelby Ann with him and see if I can get him to open up. But I'm starting to realize that this may be the first time he's even had a chance at stability. And that probably did some damage. Even without his mom dying." I reached for my Coke and took a long sip. I'd told Scott, and I stood by it, that Beckett had never been a big chatterbox. But maybe that was because Shelby Ann hadn't been a particularly good mother to start with.

A shadow fell across the table.

I glanced over and my heart took off at a gallop.

"Ladies." Scott grinned. "Enjoying your lunch?"

"We are. Thanks. You?" Megan beamed at him.

I fought the urge to kick her under the table.

"It's delicious as always. What did you think of church, Whitney?" Scott's full attention was on me, waiting for me to answer his question.

"I liked it." Would he be okay with that answer? I still didn't know if he'd be okay with me going to the same place as him and Beckett. I knew he didn't want me working on the weekends. On the other hand, he'd been the one to invite me to the zoo yesterday. Well, after Beckett made him.

"Maybe next week we can carpool." He smiled—it seemed friendly enough—then lifted a hand in a wave. "I'll let you all get back to your lunch."

"Bye. I guess I'll see you at home." I pressed my lips together. Why had I added that last part?

Scott's eyebrows lifted, but he flashed a grin before heading back to his table.

I let out a breath.

"Girlfriend." Kayla drew the word out as she fanned herself with a hand.

"Stop that." I hissed at her and bumped her arm with my elbow. "He'll see you."

"I'm sorry. I can't help it. Is it always like that between you two?" Kayla reached for her drink.

"It's a fair question. Because that chemistry was palpable."

Megan's lips curved. "I'm starting to question all your assertions that you're only there for Beckett."

"Pshh. Please." Was I approaching the "protests too much" line yet? I took a long drink to cool my dry throat. "I won't say I haven't noticed he's easy on the eyes. But come on. He's my boss. And I'm only there because he was desperate."

Megan shook her head. "Nah. Maybe it started out that way, but he could have easily figured something out in the two months you've been here. At this point, if he's keeping you around, it's because he wants you there."

My heart wanted to sing at Megan's words, but it was better to be realistic. Yes, maybe there was some truth there. Or maybe Scott was lazy. Or busy. And since I was being so careful not to rock the boat, he hadn't been pushed into making other arrangements. I'd seen that he was aware of the option when we'd butted heads over Beckett's diet.

So even if Scott was as attracted to me as I was to him, it couldn't go anywhere. Just because something might work didn't mean it was a good idea.

I'd keep repeating that to myself as often as necessary.

15

SCOTT

I knocked on the door to Tristan's condo, then tried the handle. It turned, so I walked in. "Tristan? It's Scott."

"Hey man." Tristan came around the corner and waved me in. "Thanks for coming to me. The others are all on their way. Figured it was easier if we did the paperwork together."

"Works for me." I glanced around, taking in the views of the Potomac from his living room. As a lawyer, Tristan had been the one of us who had easily afforded waterfront before we hit the jackpot in the stock market. "Do you ever think about moving?"

"Move?" He looked like I'd asked about dancing on Broadway. "Why would I do that?"

I laughed. "I don't know. Don't you want a house? Land?"

"Oh, like your amazing yard?"

"Yeah, yeah. Green space is hard to come by in Old Town. Even if you have the money to afford it. I like being near the river, though."

Tristan pulled open the fridge and grabbed two bottles of root beer. "Absolutely. I guess if I had a reason to need a house I'd consider it, but for now? I like the convenience of a condo. No maintenance. Fitness center downstairs. Two pools—one indoor, so I can swim year-round. On-site dry cleaning. And you can't discount the concierge."

I took the bottle when he offered it and twisted off the top before taking a long drink. "All right. You're right."

"You don't miss that from your apartment? That complex has good features."

"No concierge. And only an outdoor pool. But I get your point. I never used them. I think Noah and Cody do."

Tristan laughed. "Do you ask them why they're still rooming together?"

"I haven't. Maybe I should."

"What brought this on?" Tristan gestured vaguely to the living room as he took a seat in a leather recliner.

"My mom's on my case a little about working for Robinson. She doesn't see why I want a job that could give someone else a steady paycheck that I don't need." The phone call with Mom on my drive home from work had been full of suggestions. I couldn't call them complaints. Not completely. But she wanted Beckett and me to come visit and stay for a long visit—her suggestion was to come for Thanksgiving and leave after the New Year—and she hadn't considered work a viable reason to say no.

"I've considered going out on my own." Tristan shrugged and spun his bottle in his hands. "I like knowing someone else is handling all the overhead and digging up clients. I don't think it's wrong to be satisfied with your life just because you have more money available to you."

"Right? I tried explaining to Mom that shifting to consulting would make me even busier. I'd have my actual work, plus I'd have to handle all the business stuff. Doing payroll for Whitney is enough of a pain, thanks."

"How's that working?"

I glanced at Tristan. Something in his voice made me cautious. "Good? Why?"

"No reason."

"Nope. Not buying it. Tell me." I leaned forward and set my bottle on his coffee table. "What's the deal?"

"I don't know, I just figure it has to be weird to have a woman living with you. A hot, single woman. Right upstairs. That's not a problem for you?"

I sighed. "She's my employee. She's Beckett's nanny. I don't think of her as a hot, single woman."

Tristan studied me before he scoffed. "Liar."

"It's true." I held up my hand like I was taking an oath in court. "Or, well, mostly true."

"Aha! I knew it." Two loud bangs on the door were the only warning before the rest of the guys showed up. Tristan pointed at me. "This isn't over."

"What's not over?" Austin headed straight for the fridge for his own bottle of root beer. "Why are there no snacks?"

"Because this will only take a minute." Tristan stood and shook hands with everyone before gesturing to the living room.

"Come on. If Scott's here early and you're already threatening him, there has to be something good going on. Share with the class." Austin plopped next to me on the couch. "It's about the hot nanny, right?"

"Oooh. I bet it is." Noah licked his finger and pretended to make a sizzling sound as he touched my shoulder on his way to a seat. "Have you seen the two of them together? Lunch after church was educational."

"Secret glances across the diner. Then Scott goes over, all casual like, with his voice two octaves deeper, to say 'Hello, ladies.'" Austin snickered. "Megan about split a gut when she was telling me about it at home Sunday afternoon. Like I hadn't seen it with my own eyes. Then Kayla corners me on Monday to try to fish for more details."

I could feel the heat crawling up my neck. "There's nothing going on between me and Whitney. Are we signing papers for this partnership and the plane or what?"

"Testy." Cody exchanged a look with Wes. "Interesting."

"No. It's not interesting." I stood up and paced to the floor-to-ceiling windows that looked over the river before I said something I'd regret. It was just good-natured teasing. I knew that. But I hadn't been sleeping well since Saturday, and Whitney was a lot of the reason for it. I just didn't want to admit it.

"Sorry." Austin was the first to speak.

I turned back and found my friends watching me.

I sighed. "No, I'm sorry. It's just...a lot right now. She came to the zoo with us on Saturday. Beckett wanted her there. And then when we got home, we were all watching a movie and Beck fell asleep and when I got back downstairs there was this moment."

"Oh yeah?" Cody leaned forward. "I love a good moment."

Austin sneered. "You wouldn't know a moment if it bit you on the nose."

"Hey. I date." Cody's face was the picture of shocked injury.

"Yeah? When was your last date? College?" Noah shook his head. "You realize that's ten years now, right?"

Everyone laughed. I joined in, grateful that the attention had shifted away from me and Whitney. I probably should have put something about it in the group text Saturday night. I'd thought about it. Typed it out and deleted it six different times. But I didn't know what to say. Not really. We'd had a moment. I'd almost kissed her. It had seemed like she was open to the idea at the time. And this week, I wasn't sure if she was avoiding me or what, but there was no possibility of a repeat, because she wouldn't stay in the same room with me for more than thirty seconds.

"If we're finished teasing Scott?" Tristan reached for the fat folder that sat on his coffee table. "Let's get this paperwork signed and buy a plane."

"Did we figure out how we're handling who gets to use it?" Austin had his phone in his hand and was scrolling. "If not, I thought I'd suggest adding a shared calendar just for the plane. Then we can all just see what's available. First come, first served?"

I shrugged. "That works for me. Did we decide on how we're handling pilots?"

Noah raised his hand.

I laughed. "Go, nerd."

"Whatever." Noah rolled his eyes and put his hand back down. "I found a company that basically facilitates pilot free-lancing. So they do all the vetting and stuff, and you put in your requests, the type of equipment you have, and then pilots bid on the jobs. I thought it might be a good way to start out. And maybe we'll find a handful we like and can request them directly."

"That seems smarter than paying to have people on the payroll constantly when we aren't going to be using the plane every day." Tristan made a note in his phone. "Can you send me the info? I want to give it a look before signing off."

"Sure. I'll put it in the group chat. Everyone should be happy before we agree." Noah dug his phone out of his pocket and started working on it. After a moment, everyone got a notif-ication on their device. "There."

"Thanks." Tristan cleared his throat. "I sent an email with all the details on insurance, hangar fees, all that jazz that goes beyond the purchase. Please read it. Even if you normally just file stuff I send in an email folder and forget about it. Wesley."

"Hey. I read my email. Most of the time." Wes shrugged.

I laughed along with everyone else. Wes was notorious for

missing emails. He was, in fact, the reason we had a group text going. He paid attention to texts.

"Anyone have other questions?" Tristan passed a thick sheaf of papers that was bristling with tape flags to Austin. "If not, red flags are full signatures on the line with your name typed under it. Pay attention or we have to do this all over again. Yellow flags are initials in the bottom right corner. Green flags need initials on a line in the text."

Sheesh. Why did everything have to be so complicated? The crazy thing was, Tristan loved it. It was good he'd chosen law as his profession. It suited him to the ground.

Cody leaned closer, his voice low. "While we're waiting for that to get around to us, you want to share more about this moment with the nanny?"

I sighed. There was part of me that did. I could use an outside opinion or five. These were my guys. My people. But mostly, it seemed like a bad idea. Not because they'd tease me or make it awkward. They were going to do that anyway. Every chance they got. No, it was more because I knew I needed to get the idea of anything happening between Whitney and me out of my head.

"That's a long pause." Cody cocked his head to the side. "You really like her a lot, don't you?"

"I don't know. I guess. It feels complicated. She's my employee. And Beckett's the one who loses if things don't work out and she leaves. Why risk it?" I ran a hand through my hair. "That's assuming she'd even be interested. I'm not positive that's the case."

"What about the moment?" Cody frowned. "In the vague recesses of my brain where dates happened long ago, I feel like it takes two people to have a moment."

I snickered. "I don't actually believe your last date was in college, you know."

Cody grinned and shrugged. "Might as well have been. Apparently telling women you work for a Christian nonprofit lobbying organization doesn't make them swoon and beg you to take them out."

"Not sure I've ever had that exact response myself." I glanced over as Austin set his pen down and flexed his hand.

Tristan shifted the paperwork to Noah.

"Point being I don't think it should be so hard to decide if she's into you. And if I had to guess, the fact that she's sticking around to be your nanny suggests she probably is."

I shook my head. "Nah. It means she's dedicated to Beckett. She came here to try and get me to give her custody, remember? I kind of think she'd still prefer that outcome."

And that was a problem for me. Would I ever know if Whitney was interested in me, or would I always wonder if she was hedging her bets on a way to stay close to Beckett?

Cody winced. "Sorry, man. I'll pray you get some clarity."

"Thanks. I need it."

"Don't we all?" Austin smiled from across the room. "But I'll pray, too. I'm sure we all will."

"Thanks." My face heated. It wasn't that I'd thought I was having a private conversation with Cody—we were all hanging out in the same room, after all—but the other guys were talking among themselves and I guess I'd figured no one else was paying attention. I should have known better. None of us had done a lot of dating—oh sure, an occasional dinner here or party there, but relationships? Nope.

I'd always told my mom I was too busy to worry about it yet, but the real reason was that I hadn't found someone who made it seem like the hassle would be worthwhile.

Until now.

If I really felt that way about Whitney, maybe I needed to

make a move and see how she felt. Stop trying to dance around and just ask her out.

And if she said no?

I'd like to say she needed me more than I needed her, job-wise, but it wasn't true. Beckett still needed someone to watch him and, since I had Whitney on board, I hadn't bothered staying on top of the preschool situation.

So I'd just have to make sure I didn't mess it up.

Slightly nauseated but also resolved, I watched Noah pass the paperwork off to Wes. Austin was telling a funny story about one of the kids in his AP calculus class. I focused back in.

Eventually, the paperwork made it to me and I worked my way through all the flags, signing and initialing for what felt like forever. When I finished, I pushed the papers back to Tristan.

Tristan tapped them on the table to align the edges and stuck them back into the folder. "That'll do it, guys. I'll get the rest of it going tomorrow. But seriously, read the email I sent, because you all have to transfer money into the partnership account so we have operating expenses on hand. I don't want to have to come begging every month for everyone's portion of the fees. Anyone want to stay for pizza and hang?"

I stood. "I wish I could, but I need to get home. Whitney said it wasn't a problem to work late, but I don't want her to think I'm taking advantage."

Austin stood, too. "I'm also going to call it. I've got exams to grade so I can pass them back on Friday."

Everyone else decided to stay.

I finished my root beer in two long swallows and dropped the bottle in Tristan's recycle bin on my way past. "Night, guys. See you all Friday."

A chorus of goodbyes followed Austin and me to the door. We took the elevator down in companionable silence. In the lobby, Austin started toward the door that led to visitor parking, frowning when I turned toward the main exit.

"Where'd you park?"

"I walked." His expression made me laugh and I shrugged. "Seemed like a good idea at the time. It's only twenty minutes."

Austin jerked his head toward the parking. "Come on, I'll give you a ride. You don't want to keep Whitney, right? I know for a fact she usually spends Wednesday evenings at the bookstore with Megan, and I'm not keen on upsetting my sister. Not while she's still my roommate."

"You say that like that's going to change. You moving out?" I really didn't mind the walk, but I also wasn't going to turn down a ride. Austin wasn't wrong. I did want to get home and relieve Whitney. Plus, if I got home fast, I could take over bedtime and that was something I looked forward to.

"Nah. I'm just saying, if you create problems, I'm the one who has to live with them." Austin clicked his fob to unlock his car.

Laughing, I pulled open the passenger door and climbed in. "I'll keep that in mind. Does this apply across the board or just on Wednesday nights?"

Austin shook his head and started the car.

"Meg's still hanging at the bookstore in the evenings? I kind of figured she'd be too tired after a long day of social work." Austin's sister was a nice woman. She was one who seemed to genuinely care about every case that crossed her desk.

"She is. But she says going to the store helps her feel closer to Grandma. And it's relaxing." Austin shrugged and flicked on his turn signal. "I think she's trying to save money."

"Is the store in trouble?" I frowned. I loved that bookstore—and not just because my friends ran it.

"Not any more than any bookstore in the age of online shopping." Austin pulled up along the curb in front of my house.

"Between you and me, I think she'd rather work there full time. She's burning out already. She cares too much—can't keep her heart separate from the cases."

"So why doesn't she? It's not like you couldn't help her out with money."

Austin scoffed. "Do you know my sister at all?"

"She turned you down."

"Got it in one." Austin held his hands palms up. "I'm not sure what more I can do."

"Gives me something to pray for you. So there's that." I pushed open the car door and got out. "Thanks for the ride. Three minutes in a car is better than a twenty-minute walk."

"Especially when it feels like the weather might have remembered it's October. See you Friday."

I closed the car door and watched as Austin pulled out onto the street, then I headed up the stairs to the main door. Inside, I checked that the door was locked and listened. It was quiet.

"I'm home!" I frowned when I didn't hear any answering call to my yell. Where could they be? I peeked in the kitchen as I passed by. The living room and dining room were tidy and empty.

Had Whitney taken Beckett out for dinner?

That would be fine. I would have appreciated her letting me know first, but it probably wasn't something to quibble over.

I headed upstairs. Beckett's room was empty and a tiny thread of worry wormed its way into my heart. I grabbed my phone and tapped Whitney's contact as I turned and continued up the stairs to her level of the house. I couldn't fathom why they'd hang out in her room, but like taking him to dinner, it wasn't something we'd explicitly discussed one way or the other.

"Hi, Scott." She sounded cheerful and completely unfazed when she answered the call.

"Hi. Where are you?"

"Oh. Did you get home? We're at the bookstore. I can start back now—I guess we lost track of time."

I bit back a sharp retort. There was no reason Beckett couldn't visit the bookstore. I'd given Whitney no instructions whatsoever about the evening. Hoping my voice would come out calm I said, "Sounds good. You had dinner?"

"Before we left. There are some leftovers in the fridge. I wasn't sure if you were eating with your friends. We walked, so we'll be home in about fifteen minutes, okay?"

"Sure. I'll see you then." I ended the call and started back down the stairs. I made it three steps before relief turned my muscles to jelly and I sank to the steps. If there had been any question in my mind about how I felt about Beckett, the last few minutes had wiped them away.

But he was safe. And he was on his way home.

I could eat some dinner before they got here and maybe that would give all the adrenaline in my body time to settle.

16

WHITNEY

alfway home from the bookstore, Beckett needed me to carry him. Which was fine. I loved holding him close and having him snuggle in. He was a fantastic cuddler—always had been. Shelby Ann had called it "wallowing," and not in a positive way. I pushed the thought aside. Whether or not I thought Shelby Ann had been a good mother didn't matter now. She was gone, and I was going to focus on helping Beckett remember the good things about her for as long as I was allowed to have influence in his life.

I trudged up the steps, Beckett heavy in my arms, and fumbled for my keys.

I guess I made a lot of noise, because before I could unlock things, the door opened.

"Thought I heard someone." Scott smiled and stepped forward, reaching for Beckett. "Is he asleep?"

I craned my neck so I could get a glimpse of Beckett's face. "Looks like it. I'm sorry. I should have gotten us home sooner. Megan was reading him books from the children's section, and she has a knack with the voices. We were having so much fun, I lost track of time."

"Don't worry about it." Scott hoisted Beckett while bumping the door closed with his hip. "I'll go get him settled in bed. Could you hang out here though? I wanted to talk to you for a few minutes."

"Sure. Maybe I'll make some cocoa. You want some?" I tried to ignore the nerves churning in my belly. Nothing good ever came from the words "we need to talk," and that was basically what he'd just said.

"Actually yeah, that sounds good. Back in a few." Scott disappeared up the stairs, carrying Beckett.

My breath whooshed out. I pressed a hand to my stomach and closed my eyes. *Please, Jesus, don't let him fire me. I need this job. I need to be close to Beckett. And I know praying isn't supposed to just be gimme gimme, but I really think I'm doing good work here. You can use me.*

I hung my coat on the rack by the door and headed into the kitchen. While I washed my hands, I continued praying, finally working my way around to acknowledging that I really wanted to be where God wanted me. *Even if it means leaving Beckett.*

The whole idea was terrifying. What would I do? I missed acting, but I'd finally accepted I wasn't going to make it in Hollywood. So California was out. I didn't want to move home though, either. Move back in with Mom and Dad in Podunk, Kansas, and try to figure out a way to make a living in a tiny college town with an annual tourist draw? No, thanks.

Sighing, I filled the electric kettle at the tap and plugged it in. I got down two mugs and rooted in the pantry for the fancier cocoa packets. I wanted something a little richer than Swiss Miss, and I'd seen Godiva in there when I looked the other day. Hopefully, it was okay to use them.

I bit my lip and stared at the packets in my hand.

Maybe I'd wait for Scott to get back down here before opening them, just in case he was saving them for a rainy day.

It sure felt like a rainy day to me.

I paced the length of the kitchen, trying to line up my thoughts. I had good arguments for why he should keep me as Beckett's nanny. Of course, I couldn't think of any of them right now.

I dug out my phone and opened a text to my mom.

COULD YOU PRAY FOR ME? SCOTT SAYS HE WANTS TO TALK AFTER BECKETT'S IN BED. I'M NERVOUS.

Mom's reply was nearly instantaneous. OF COURSE I WILL. LOVE YOU. CALL ME AFTER?

LOVE YOU TOO. I WILL.

I slipped my phone back in my pocket. As much as I didn't want to live at home with my parents, it really wasn't because of them. They were great. I just wished they lived somewhere else.

The water in the kettle was ready. I unplugged it and drummed my fingers on the counter. Beckett's bedtime routine was usually pretty complicated, but surely when he was already sleeping, Scott would cut it short.

I took my phone out again and opened Instagram. It was basically the only social media I bothered with. I liked looking at the photos and seeing all the creative things people put together. I had an account purely for browsing. I wasn't trying to establish myself as any kind of influencer, even though it was something they'd suggested in LA.

I wanted to act. I didn't necessarily need to open my life up twenty-four seven for the world's viewing pleasure.

Which was one more reason I wasn't cut out for Hollywood.

Well, it didn't matter. I'd left LA and was here now. And when I took the time to really analyze how I felt about it? I was much more content.

Now I just had to keep praying Scott wasn't about to end that.

"Oh, good, you found the fancy cocoa."

I looked up at Scott's words and hastily clicked off my phone. "I wasn't sure they were okay to use."

"Of course, they are. There's nothing special or off limits in the house." He tilted his head to the side. "Did you think there was?"

I shrugged. In all honesty, I had been operating under the idea that anything I hadn't specifically brought into the house wasn't mine to use without permission. Maybe that was wrong? I stood and moved to the counter so I could dump a packet into each of the mugs I'd gotten out. Then I poured the hot water from the kettle over them. I set the kettle down and moved to get a spoon out of the drawer and bumped into Scott.

His hands came up to my arms. "Whoa. You all right?"

I nodded, my mouth dry. But that was a lie. I wasn't all right. I hadn't really been all right since whatever almost happened after *The Jungle Book* on Saturday. "I need a spoon."

His gaze still holding mine, Scott reached over and opened the silverware drawer to get a spoon. He held it up between us.

Swallowing, I took the spoon and, feeling cowardly, stepped back, broadening the distance between us.

Maybe it wouldn't be such a bad idea for him to fire me after all.

I was pretty sure getting involved with the dad was a no-no for nannies.

At least he wasn't married. Not that I was likely to be interested in someone if they were married. I'd never been one to chase a guy just because he was off limits.

I stirred each mug before handing one to Scott and taking mine back to the kitchen table. Maybe having that solid surface between us would help me remember to keep things professional.

Scott's eyebrows lifted, but he carried his drink to the table and sat across from me. He blew across the top of his mug before sipping. "I had a couple of things I wanted to ask about."

I cradled the cocoa in my hands. The heat was starting to sting my palms, but I relished the sensation. "Okay?"

"First up is Halloween. Beckett has mentioned two or three hundred times that he'd like you to come trick or treating with us." Scott chuckled. "I can't get him to say much, but when he does talk, it's usually about you."

"It's Monday, right? I don't have any other plans."

Scott smiled. "Great. Um. You didn't happen to get him a costume, did you? I'll admit it wasn't even on my radar. We didn't have many kids in the apartments, so I haven't paid attention."

"I'm surprised he didn't tell you all about his Spiderman outfit. We picked it up this afternoon. I also grabbed a bag of candy for us to hand out. Or put on the porch in a bowl if we're going to both be out with Beckett."

I'd kind of assumed Scott would stay at the house and answer the door. It wasn't a fair assumption. Scott was good with Beckett. Involved and interested. There was no reason to think Scott wouldn't want to be part of something like this.

"Spiderman? Nice. I'll have to see if I can come up with a costume that coordinates. You could be Spider Gwen, if you're game. I can dig around online later tonight and see if we're not too late." Scott sipped his cocoa again.

I lifted my drink and breathed in the rich, chocolatey scent before tasting it. Where had the idea of a family costume come from? "I hadn't been planning to dress up, but okay. Do grownups do that here?"

"Yeah, sure. When they have kids to take around. Don't they in LA? Or Kansas?"

I snickered. "Not in Kansas, that's for sure. At least not in Gilead. I'm not sure they even recognize that Halloween exists in

Gilead. And LA? I don't think you'd notice who had a costume on there."

He laughed and it did something crazy to my insides. It wasn't the first time I'd heard him truly let go and laugh with abandon, but he didn't do it often, which was too bad. The sound was rich and full, like the hot chocolate we were both drinking.

"Fair enough. From what I've observed, and I'll grant that I haven't paid a ton of attention so I could be wrong, families around here like to all dress up together." Scott shrugged. "I thought it could be fun."

"You find me a Spider Gwen outfit, I'll wear it." I had no idea what her outfit would be like—hopefully it wasn't anything like Wonder Woman. That would be a little chilly, even though it was still in the low sixties these days.

"You don't know who she is." He wasn't asking—he was asserting it. Defensively.

"Not a clue. But I'll look her up. I know about four super-heroes. Maybe five."

He frowned. "You haven't seen all the movies?"

I shook my head. They'd sounded dumb. Shelby Ann had gone to all of them as they came out, and for the last three years she'd needed a babysitter to do it. I didn't mind. Given the choice between Beckett and a movie? I'd always choose Beckett.

"We should change that. They're good. But we can table that and move on to the next thing. Beckett has an appointment on Tuesday with the doctor, and I think she said something about a speech therapist joining in. Do you want to come?"

I nodded, surprised that he'd asked. I'd gotten the distinct impression that Scott considered the speech thing a problem solely for him to handle. "I'd like that. Thanks."

"No problem. I figure they'll have questions I might not have the best answer to. You spend more time with Beckett on a daily basis." He shrugged. "And if we have to do therapy, more than likely you're going to be the one helping there. It makes sense."

It did make sense when he put it that way, and I was grateful he saw it.

"Okay, now for the last question. What are your Thanksgiving plans?"

Thanksgiving? I blew out a breath. It was probably smart to start thinking about that since we were here at the end of October. Except I had no idea what my plans ought to be. "I don't have any."

"Christmas?"

I shook my head.

Scott frowned. "Don't you want to go home and see your family? You get time off. Or have a vacation with friends? I don't want you to feel like you're trapped here."

"I don't feel like that at all. Did you not need me still?" All of my muscles tensed. Maybe I shouldn't give him that opening. I needed this job. For so many reasons.

"My folks are nagging about me bringing Beckett down to Florida for Thanksgiving. Maybe Christmas, too. Or, if they got their wish, we'd go down and stay for six weeks." My eyes must have bugged out because Scott laughed and held up a hand. "I don't plan to do that. Trust me. I love my folks, but living with them for six weeks is a big no. Honestly, if I went down for a couple of weeks, I'd probably want to rent a house nearby or get a hotel. Everyone does better when they have their space."

Wouldn't he still need me when he was on vacation? Did he really want to try to do everything, all day every day, when he was visiting his parents? Of course, his parents would probably want to pitch in.

I fought a sigh. "You wouldn't want me to come along?"

"I honestly didn't think you'd want to."

I stared into my cocoa. "I like spending my days with Beckett." I glanced up.

Scott was looking at me like I was particularly intriguing.

He nodded once. "Okay. Maybe we'll take a long weekend for Thanksgiving and see how it goes. Then we can reevaluate when it comes to Christmas plans. Assuming you're okay with flying to Florida for Thanksgiving?"

Gee, did I want to go to Florida instead of staying here? Yes. Yes, I did. "Sounds good to me. Are they near the beach?"

"They are, as it happens. I'll make the arrangements. I think I remember Mom saying there's a couple who has a second house they use as a vacation rental. If not, I can figure out a hotel."

"I don't mind staying with your parents, either, if there's room for all of us." I bit my lip. "I might need to get Beckett some new clothes. He doesn't have a swimming suit and I think he may have outgrown the shorts you bought him in September."

"Kid grows like a weed." Scott chuckled. "Definitely go through and see what he's going to need. I'd rather we overpacked than under."

That was the opposite of how I tended to handle trips, but this was Scott's vacation, so I'd roll with it. "We'll have to check the car seat. Or I guess see if the rental car company can provide one. I'm not sure how that works. It feels like it'll be easier to bring our own though, even with baggage claim."

"We'll be taking a private plane, so I'll figure out how that works with luggage, but I'm guessing it's not as inconvenient as commercial." He grinned. "I'll add it to my list to square away. Thanks."

"That's it?" I struggled not to goggle at the idea of a private plane. He rarely acted like a billionaire, so when he did, it threw me.

"Yeah. Unless you had something you needed to talk to me about?"

I shook my head, relief coursing through my veins.

"Okay. Thanks for the cocoa." Scott lifted his mug in a toast as he stood. He walked to the sink and rinsed out the mug before setting in the dishwasher. He turned and looked at me. "Actually, there is one more thing."

"Oh?" The way he looked at me set my heart racing.

"Would you, maybe, want to go out to dinner with me on Saturday? Like a date? I could get a sitter."

My breath caught in my lungs. I guess I hadn't been imagining his interest after all. "Yeah. I'd like that."

17

SCOTT

Butterflies were having a rave in my stomach. I hadn't been this nervous in...ever. I honestly couldn't think of a time when I'd been more antsy. And that included when I broached the idea of investing to the guys, as well as when we realized that it was going to work. It made no sense.

Except maybe it did.

Numbers were predictable. Even if the stock market itself wasn't. And I'd been able to watch the trends and look at history and make tweaks and changes to try and enhance our outcome.

I was pretty sure none of that worked with women.

And Whitney was definitely a woman.

I closed my eyes and swallowed the lump that was trying to form in my throat. I could do this. It wasn't like I never dated. Mom had even nagged me into trying the apps. Those meetups were nowhere near as nerve racking.

Obsessing about it wasn't getting me anywhere though, and Megan would be there to hang out with Beckett any minute.

I studied myself in the mirror one last time. A sweater over a collared shirt was fancier than just the sweater, but not suit and tie. Should I have gone that route? Except I told her nice casual. Ugh.

I turned away from the mirror and headed downstairs.

Beckett glanced away from the TV and smiled, then pointed to his show. I came and sat beside him. A very earnest Mickey was counting ten chickens as they were herded into a corral. I wasn't sure chickens would stay in a corral, but it wasn't as if talking mice were super realistic, and counting skills were a good thing to learn.

"You wanna count with him? One. Two." I looked over at Beckett.

He shook his head.

I sighed quietly. The doctor had referred us to both a child psychiatrist and a speech therapist. I'd already lined up an appointment for a speech therapy eval in the coming week. But apparently mental health practitioners had long waiting lists and we were looking at late January before any of the people on the doctor's referral list would have availability.

Hopefully, the speech therapy would get us where we needed to be and we wouldn't need the other.

I kissed the top of Beckett's head.

He snuggled closer, wedging his head under my arm until I shifted and held him close. He made it clear what he wanted without talking, I had to give him that.

The doorbell rang.

I squeezed Beckett tight before untangling myself from his snuggle. "I'll be right back."

He nodded without taking his eyes off the TV.

Chuckling, I made my way to the front door and opened it. "Hey, Megan. I appreciate this."

"Sure thing. I'm looking forward to more time with Beckett. We had fun on Wednesday night at the bookstore." Megan stepped in and unwound a scarf from her neck before working on the buttons of her long coat. "Temperature dropped. We might actually get something close to fall if this keeps up."

"Maybe. I think the weather app said it was going to hit seventy again tomorrow, though. So, I wouldn't get my hopes up."

Megan groaned.

I took her coat and scarf and hung them on the coat rack by the door. "Come on in. He's watching TV, but you can turn it off after the show's finished and do something else. Or we have some movies he likes. Whatever's easier for you. He already ate, but there are snacks. Anything he wants is fine. His toys are in his room, so that's usually where he plays but if you want to bring them down and play in the living room that's fine."

Megan laughed. "Nervous, Dad?"

I cleared my throat and shrugged. "A little. He doesn't seem to mind. I guess his mom did a lot of dropping him off with other people—but it was mostly Whitney, from what I understand. So this could end up being new. And I feel like I'm imposing on you."

"Pfft. Please. You asked. I said yes. That means I'm here because I want to be. I know how to say no." Megan rubbed her hands together. "I like kids and I'm looking forward to this. Plus, this means you're finally asking Whitney out, which Austin and I agree falls firmly in the 'about time' category."

"I didn't realize my relationship with Whitney was the talk of the town." I hated how stiff my voice sounded, but honestly. Were all my friends talking about me behind my back? Or was it just the ones who knew Whitney, too? Neither option made me happy.

"Oh, come on. Don't be that way." Megan frowned and studied me. "You're mad. I'm sorry. You know I live with my brother. You know we both love you and want good things for you. So you might as well know we agree that Whitney falls into that category, too."

"What category?" Whitney came down the final three steps, wearing a knit dress that reached just below her knees and tall boots that disappeared beneath the hem. A thin belt circled her waist, cinching in and showing off curves that weren't visible in her day-to-day wear.

"Wow." My face heated. I drew in a breath. "You look great."

Whitney's cheeks pinked. "Thanks." She shifted and pinned Megan with her gaze. "I still want to know about my category, though."

"Ugh. You're so obnoxious." Megan rolled her eyes, but she was grinning while she did it. "I was telling Scott that Austin and I both think this is a smart move and about time. Okay? Also I'll expect a full report later."

"Hey." I shook my head. "No way. Dates are private."

Megan laughed. "Keep dreaming. Girls share. Right, Whit?"

"I think I'm going to take the Fifth." Whitney held up her hands. Then she looked at me and cocked her head to the side. "I'm ready if you are."

"I'm ready." I went around the couch and squatted down so I could meet Beckett's eyes. "Whitney and I are going out for a bit. Megan's here to play with you, okay? We'll be back, but probably after you're asleep. I'll still come say goodnight, though, okay?"

Beckett frowned slightly, then he nodded.

It would do. I kissed him on the forehead, then stood. "Night, Beckett. Thanks again, Megan."

I gestured for Whitney to go down the stairs to the garage level ahead of me, then jogged down the stairs to try and reach the door that led out to the garage first.

Whitney grabbed the handle and turned it. "I appreciate the idea, but if I get to a door first, I'm going to open it. Okay?"

"Okay." Mom would kill me. She was a sucker for old-school

chivalry. Dad made it look effortless to somehow always let Mom go first and still beat her to every door. Without elbowing her out of the way or running to get there. Maybe it was a rhythm couples found as they were together longer.

I did go around to the passenger door of the car and open it for her.

Whitney shook her head, smiling, as she climbed in. "Thanks."

I shut the door and went back around to the driver's side and got in. "You really do look nice."

"Thanks. I saw this when I was out shopping with Beckett and couldn't talk myself out of it." Whitney smoothed the dress down her legs. "I never needed something like this in LA. Most of the winter clothes I had in Kansas are either still at my parents or donated."

I punched the button on the remote to open the garage door and, when it was clear, started the car and backed out. "That makes sense. Do you miss Kansas at all?"

"Nope."

"That was fast."

"Yeah, well it's an easy answer for me." Whitney shifted in her seat, angling toward me. "Gilead is a college town. Small, Bible college town. So during the school year, there are more people—students, obviously—and because it's a Bible college, they're pretty well behaved, but we still have the usual stuff that comes with being a college town. Some parents send their kids to try to straighten them out, and those kids make it hard for everyone. And our other claim to fame is this Passion play."

"Tell me about that. I searched online when you first mentioned it and found videos of one in Canada and another in Germany. I guess they're pretty famous." I slowed at the four-way stop that led out of our neighborhood and to the street that would take us into the downtown area. We could have walked, but it was getting colder and it hadn't seemed like the best idea for a date to start out with a fifteen- or twenty-minute walk. Especially when cobblestones entered the picture once we hit the historic district.

"Did you watch either of them? It's just like that. It's a huge production that consumes practically every aspect of town life from September through Easter. And once we hit Ash Wednesday and the performances start, then we're jammed with tourists everywhere you turn." Whitney shuddered. "It's a fishbowl. Either the locals, who have known you since before you were born, are all up in your business, or the tourists are giving patronizing smiles and remarking on how everything is quaint."

I laughed. "I can see how that would get old."

"Some people love it. My parents do. My sister does. It just isn't for me."

That made sense, too. "It's good you figured it out though, instead of languishing there thinking you were doing the right thing."

"Maybe."

I looked over, surprised. "It's not good?"

"No. It is. I just probably didn't pray about the move as much as I should have. I applied to college in LA and as soon as I got accepted, I didn't even consider the other options I had. I had some job options after college, too, that would have taken me out of California, but I was positive I was going to be a light for Jesus in Hollywood. All I ever managed was a billboard for a pawn shop and making friends with Shelby Ann."

"That last one though? That's important." I flicked on my turn signal before pulling into a parking garage at the end of the historic district's main street.

She smiled, her eyes softening. "He's great, isn't he?"

"He is." I was probably more surprised than anyone that I felt that way. I thought back to September when Mom had called to tell me about Beckett, and my response. I wasn't proud of it. And maybe I still had moments of doubt when I wondered if I was really the best choice to be Beckett's permanent caretaker, but I couldn't deny that I loved him. And I'd fight to keep him now, with everything I had.

I found an empty space and parked, then cut the engine. "We have a little walk, but it's not far."

"Where are we going?" Whitney unhooked her seatbelt, then pushed open her door.

I opened my door and got out, waiting as she followed suit. It bothered me a little that she wasn't going to wait while I went around to let her out. On the other hand, maybe it was weird to sit in a car while someone ran around it to open a door she was perfectly able to open? I didn't know. What I did know was that Mom was going to ask if I opened doors and the answer wasn't cut and dry.

When she'd shut her door, I closed mine and clicked "lock" on the key fob. I met her at the back of the car and offered my elbow.

She held my gaze for three heartbeats before sliding her arm through mine. I tucked her hand closer to my body as we started to walk, reveling in the sensation of those tiny points of contact.

"Gadsby's Tavern."

Whitney frowned.

"You asked where we were going. That's where. It's been around since 1770 and the food is delicious. You can't live in Old Town and not go to Gadsby's every now and then. It felt like a good first date." Maybe I'd misjudged. The old brick building was just ahead of us. "Should I have asked what you wanted?"

"No. This is good. I just—Megan talks about this place like it's super fancy. I feel under dressed and I'm worried I'm going to use the wrong fork and mortify you." Nerves sparkled on the edge of her laugh.

"I promise not to be mortified. Or to care which fork you use." I'd just wanted something unique. Memorable. Something we could tell our kids about.

My breath caught for just a second.

When had I gone from asking Whitney out to planning a future with her?

And why did it feel so right?

18

WHITNEY

Gadsby's Tavern. Oh boy. Kayla had been gushing about the Tavern as a date location on Wednesday when I was at the bookstore with Beckett. In Kayla's opinion, it was the place guys took someone they were serious about. She'd seen several proposals there and attended two different wedding receptions held on-site.

Kayla was probably going to freak out when I told her this was where Scott took me on our first date.

Scott reached for the door and pulled it open, then ushered me through. I glanced around and took in the candles flickering on tables in the smaller rooms to the right and left. It was quiet. Subdued. There was a subtle murmur of voices and clinking of silverware.

This place was *fancy*.

I cast a glance at Scott. Was this really what he thought it was going to be?

"Good evening. Welcome to Gadsby's Tavern." The woman behind the hostess stand kept her voice low, almost a purr.

"Reservation for Wright. With a 'w.'" Scott tucked his hands in the pockets of his khakis and looked around.

"Of course. This way." The woman gathered menus from a basket before gliding across the wide-planked wood floor into the small room to our left.

"After you." Scott gestured with his right hand, his left coming to rest briefly in the small of my back.

I hadn't realized he could be suave.

Our table was in the far corner, by a window looking out over the garden. It was empty—though I imagined there were tables set up outside when the weather was nice. In fact, it might be fun to come back in the spring and have lunch out there with Megan and Kayla.

Wait. In the spring?

Would I still be here?

I wanted to be—now more than ever—but the reality was, Scott was my boss. He was Beckett's guardian. And I wasn't doing myself any favors by forgetting that.

"Your server will be right out. Enjoy your meal."

I'd missed the spiel about the specials, if there'd been one, while I was admiring the view.

"This is lovely." I glanced down at the menu, surprised it was still easy to read in the candlelight. "Do you have a recommendation?"

Scott shook his head. "I've only been twice. My parents brought me here on my sixteenth birthday and all the guys came to celebrate our stock market win. But I've never had anything I didn't like."

I looked down at the menu, pleased that this wasn't a place he routinely brought women. Although, routine and women didn't seem to be words that went together when it came to Scott. I'd been living in his house for two months and, as far as I knew, this was the first date he'd been on.

"I'm definitely getting the peanut soup." Scott tapped his menu.

"Really?" I'd seen that and moved right on by. Who put peanuts in soup? This place, apparently. "Why?" was the next question. "It's not weird?"

"A little, maybe. But also delicious. Cody made everyone get some when we were here in May. We all liked it." Scott set the menu down. "You don't have to get some, but I'll let you try mine if you want."

"We'll see." I could probably handle a taste. Maybe.

The server came by, introduced herself, and took our drink orders before fading away.

"So." Scott lined his silverware up on his napkin. "If Shelby Ann hadn't died, would you still be in LA?"

I sighed. "I don't know. Right now? Probably. But in six months? I can admit, now, that I was getting tired of trying to cobble together a living while waiting and hoping I'd get cast in something that would pay me more than exposure."

He chuckled. "I had a guy in college offer to let me build a website for his startup, for exposure. He seemed genuinely confused that I didn't jump at it."

"Right? It's like they don't understand that electricity and food cost money." I definitely didn't miss that. I didn't miss my studio apartment on the edge of a sketchy part of town. Really, when I boiled it down, the only thing I sort of missed was being close to the beach. And I hadn't gone all that often. I always figured there'd be time later. "Realistically, I would have gone home for Christmas and Mom and Dad would have helped me put the realization that I needed something different into words. Then I would have fought that, because I get a little contrary when my parents are right—again—and by spring, barring some kind of miracle that turned into an actual acting job, I would've been trying to figure out where I was going from there."

"Any idea what that would have been?"

I wrinkled my nose. "You sound like my dad. I have a business degree. He pushed for the double major, and since he was paying, I played along. There are probably jobs out there that would use a business degree."

"There are. It's true. Would you enjoy them?"

Would I? I thought back to college and those business classes. I hadn't hated them. "Probably? What about you?"

"What about me?"

The server stopped by our table. She filled our water glasses and brought our sodas. She took our food order before moving off.

"What was your plan B? For that matter, why do you still go work an office job every day? All of you do and I don't get it. I would've hopped a plane and gone exploring."

He laughed. "Thought about it. Even made a few tentative plans—then Beckett showed up on my doorstep."

"Ah."

"Yeah." Scott sipped his soda. "I have time. I just need to figure out how to travel with a kid. Thanksgiving should give me a little bit of insight. And now that we have a plane it opens up more options. As for why I work, I guess I just haven't figured out what else I'd do. I don't want to sit around all day playing Xbox."

"You could start your own company."

"I've thought about that. Sort of. I don't want to have employees and an office building, but I could resign and hang out my shingle as a contractor. Then I'd only work on projects that interested me. And only when I wanted to work."

Sounded pretty perfect to me. I couldn't imagine being an actual billionaire and still going into an office for eight hours a day. "And you're not jumping on this because..."

"I guess I don't like change."

I laughed. "At least you're honest. Although...I could point out that Beckett is a pretty big change you embraced rather fast."

"I guess he is." He leaned back as a different server set his cup of peanut soup in front of him and my salad in front of me. Scott reached across the table and held his hand palm up. "Can we pray?"

I rested my fingers in his and closed my eyes while he said a short blessing for the food. He squeezed my fingers before pulling his hand away.

"You have to try this." Scott dipped his spoon into the peanut soup and held it out, his gaze steady on mine.

It almost felt like a dare. All right. I leaned forward and closed my mouth over the spoon, letting the soup roll around on my palate. I swallowed. "It's peanuty."

He grinned. "That's it?"

"I don't know. It's different. I'm not sold on all the peanuts. There are peanuts in my salad." I shook my head. Peanuts everywhere.

"I guess they were a thing in the 1700s." Scott shrugged and dipped his spoon into the soup. "I like it."

"It's all yours." I collected a bite of my roasted peanut, gruyère, and grape salad. It was interesting, too. Crunchy. Salty. Sweet. "Do you want to try this?"

"Sure."

I frowned at my fork. I'd already used it. Of course, he'd gone on using the spoon I'd sampled from, so maybe he didn't care about germs. I put together a bite with all of the components and held it out for him. I couldn't look away as his lips closed around my fork.

What would it be like if he kissed me?

"That's good, too." Scott leaned back and something in his eyes made me wonder if he was thinking the same thing.

I busied myself putting together another perfect bite, almost as if my life depended on it.

Our conversation stalled as we both focused on eating. It was probably okay—after all, we were there to eat dinner together. But I didn't love the awkwardness that I felt in the air.

I pushed my mostly empty plate away from myself. "Will you go back to Florida for Christmas?"

"I don't know yet. Wes joked about going to the Caymans and learning to scuba and I can't get the idea out of my head. I've never actually gone somewhere for Christmas that wasn't a relative's house, you know? It feels decadent."

"Then you absolutely have to do it."

"I do? Why?" He set his spoon down on the saucer beneath the empty cup.

"Because you're a billionaire and you never do anything crazy. You drive a high-end but still super normal car. You're working forty or fifty hours a week. You live in a townhouse with no yard."

He winced.

I hunched my shoulders. "Sorry. Was that too much? I get that you love Old Town, so it makes sense, but I guess I figured you'd go for something bigger. Even if you stayed in Alexandria, just moved out of Old Town proper."

"It's not too much. I just sound really boring."

"You're not boring. At all. You just don't live like I imagined a billionaire would." Which, fine, my idea of the super-rich came from movies and tabloids, and neither of those were particularly great endorsements.

"Is that bad?"

I looked up and our gazes met. Dang it, I'd hurt his feelings. I reached across the table and rested my fingertips on his hand. "It's not bad. It's arguably really good. It shows character and responsibility."

"There you go, making me boring again."

I didn't feel bad this time, because his lips had curved as he spoke.

"Har har. You're a joker." I shook my head. "All I'm saying is that flying off to the Caribbean for Christmas sounds like something you should do."

"And Beckett? Does he get to go on this vacation with me?" Scott's eyes were dancing.

"I mean, yeah. Of course."

"Ah. And he probably would need his nanny along, right?"

"Duh." I managed to keep a straight face for about six seconds before bursting into laughter that I rapidly squelched.

He chuckled and the movement made me realize I was still touching his hand. I started to withdraw, but he flipped his hand over and caught my fingers.

I didn't mind.

"I guess I'll see if Wes minds some tagalongs. I can't imagine that he would. In fact, Austin and Megan might already be going. We can make it a big thing—rent a huge house somewhere." He squeezed my fingers. "You sure your parents won't mind if you don't come home?"

"My parents?" Where had that come from?

"You mentioned in the car that you usually went home for Christmas. I don't want them to worry."

Ah. He really was a good guy. Not many—any?—of the guys I'd known since college would have let that thought cross their minds, let alone ask about it. "Maybe I can zip out for a long weekend sometime between Thanksgiving and Christmas?"

"Sure. Figure out dates. I can have the plane take you."

"You could come." I wasn't sure why I issued the invitation, but it seemed to surprise him, too.

"Your parents wouldn't mind?"

I shook my head. "No. In fact, I think they'd love to meet you."

I knew my mom would. There was no way I was going to avoid mentioning our date when I called home. And there was no way Mom wasn't going to pick up on how I felt about Scott when I did.

I wouldn't say I was in love with him. It was too soon for that.

But I could definitely see it happening.

19

SCOTT

The food at Gadsby's Tavern had always been good, but as I signed the check, I couldn't help but think it had been even better than usual tonight. It was probably the company.

Once we'd gotten over the awkward break in topic when I'd tasted her salad, conversation had flowed. And I had to give it to her—the idea of Christmas in the Caymans was definitely growing on me.

I set the pen down and checked that I'd put my credit card back in my pocket. "All set?"

"Yes. Thank you for dinner. It was delicious." Whitney scooted her chair back and stood.

"Thanks for coming." I dropped my napkin on the table and followed suit, then reached for her hand.

She laced her fingers through mine the moment our hands touched. I smiled as we walked around the tables in the nearly full dining room, to the front door, and then out into the cool evening air.

I looked over at her. "Are those boots okay for walking?"

She laughed. "Worried?"

I frowned, then the strains of an old country song flitted through my head and I chuckled. "No. Not like that. I'm just not ready to go home yet, and I didn't think past dinner. I wondered if you maybe wanted to walk down to the waterfront?"

"I'd like that."

I grinned and we started down the sidewalk toward the river. There were plenty of people out and about. Not surprising. People from all around came to Old Town on Friday and Saturday nights. The waterfront would probably be even more crowded—although most people would be at the restaurants there and not in Founder's Park.

At least that was what I hoped.

"I get why you like it here." Whitney bumped me with her hip. "It's different than the rest of the area. It feels like a self-contained small town in the south."

"Not too southern." I chuckled. "Around here, people will remind you that Northern Virginia is a separate animal from the rest of the state."

"Boy, will they ever." She sighed. "I already ran into that. But still. The cobblestone streets are a nice touch."

"Unless you're trying to ride your bike. Then they're a literal pain in the rear."

Whitney's laugh seemed to fill all the air around us. "I'll keep that in mind. I was thinking it was time to get Beckett started riding something. Maybe a balance bike. I've been doing some research."

"Tell me about it."

I listened as Whitney launched into an explanation of the difference between balance bikes and regular bikes with training wheels and how different options produced different results in terms of learning to ride independently.

Her treatise took us the rest of the way to the waterfront park and I couldn't help but store a mental picture of her talking passionately in the moonlight. She was beautiful.

"When you've decided on the one you think is best, send me a link and I'll make it happen."

She gave a half laugh. "That sounded a little more like a billionaire."

"What? It's a balance bike. I don't imagine that would break the bank of most middle-class couples even."

"True. I wasn't trying to insult you." She frowned. "But I'll get you a link. He'll need a helmet, too. I'll figure out the sizing there. Maybe I'll get myself a bike. Then, once he's got it down, we could do little rides together."

"That sounds fun. Send me a link for that, too."

She shook her head. "No. I can get my own, but thanks. Maybe I'll use yours in the meantime. It's just sitting there in the garage."

"Yeah. I haven't taken the time to ride lately." I missed it. At the same time, I wasn't sure when I was supposed to work that in. Once I got home, I was on Beckett duty. So hey, bonus, if Whitney got him squared away on his own ride, maybe the three of us could go on little jaunts together.

"You should. I don't mind watching Beckett when you're home from work, if that helps. You know that, right?"

"I do. I don't want to—"

"Take advantage." She cut me off. "I know. But the reality is, I'm the nanny. It's my job. And I like doing it."

I nodded.

We made our way to the edge of the path that ended with a drop to the river. I looked out at the rippling water with the moon shining on it, then turned to face Whitney. "Do you think this can work?"

She had the grace not to play dumb. "I don't know."

"Because you're the nanny."

"Yeah."

"I could fire you."

She whirled, her eyes wide and her head shaking vigorously.

I guess that answered that question. "Kidding."

"Don't joke. Beckett has to come first. No matter what." She gripped my arm. "He's been through so much already."

"You're right." I covered her hand and rubbed. "I still want to try. I feel something here. Something with you. Something I've never felt before."

She swallowed. "Me too."

I searched her face and thought I saw the answer I was looking for. I leaned close, slowly, giving her the chance to step back if I was reading the signals wrong. I slid my hands up her arms, her shoulders, her neck, until my fingers twined in her hair as my lips brushed hers, then settled in for a longer kiss.

Whitney's arms came around me and she moved closer until every touchpoint was on fire.

I wasn't counting seconds or anything, but I knew it was past time to step back. Step away. I forced myself to move my hands to her shoulders. I rubbed gently, easing slowly away from the kiss.

Whitney stepped back and took a deep breath then let it out slowly. "Wow."

I grinned and linked my fingers with hers, tugging her hand up so I could kiss her knuckles. "You can say that again."

"Wow." She laughed and leaned her head against my shoulder. "We can figure this out, Scott."

I kissed the top of her head. "I hope so. Do you want ice cream?"

"You know what? I do. But let's eat it at home."

"Home it is." I gave her hand a little tug as we turned away from the river and headed back toward the parking garage where we'd stashed the car.

"Do you think we'll make it back in time to put Beckett to bed?" She sounded hopeful.

I glanced over at her as we turned the corner on the block where the garage was then fished my phone out of my pocket to check the time. "No. Unless Megan let him stay up super late, he's been in bed for an hour."

"An hour." Whitney's eyebrows lifted. "It's later than I realized."

"Time flies and all that?" I'd certainly lost track of time in that kiss. And dinner at the Tavern always took some time. They didn't rush their meals in colonial days, and Gadsby's continued that tradition.

"Yes. I had fun. You weren't worried, were you?" Whitney stopped by the passenger side of my car.

I opened the door for her with a little shrug. "Maybe a little."

She climbed in the car and I closed the door before rounding the back to get behind the wheel. She leaned over and kissed my cheek. "Well, don't."

I turned my head so our lips met.

The windows were starting to fog when I pulled back.

Whitney grinned and turned to reach for her seatbelt. "I think we have ice cream in the freezer."

"You don't want me to drive somewhere and we can pick it up?" There were a handful of specialty shops that were probably still open. It was late enough there might even be street parking out front.

"Nah. Home sounds good. I wouldn't be sad to take these boots off. And Megan's probably ready to head home, too."

"That's true." I started the car and shifted into Reverse.

It didn't take long to get back. In the garage, I closed the door and cut off the engine. Whitney was already pushing open her door.

I got out and waited with my hand on the doorknob to the

basement entry. When Whitney neared, I slid my arm around her waist and pulled her close. "I'm really glad you agreed to go out with me. Thank you."

She didn't have to tip her head back much to meet my gaze. "I feel like that's my line, but you're welcome."

I chuckled and pushed open the door.

Like seeing her in those boots, following her up the stairs wasn't a hardship the way her knit dress clung in all the right places. And that was definitely not a productive train of thought to follow. Not when Whitney and I shared a home. Because she was my employee.

I blew out a breath.

Exactly how big was the can of worms I'd opened by asking her out?

Was it even possible to put the lid back on now, though?

I didn't have time to think about the answer, because Megan was in the process of clicking off the TV when I reached the top of the steps.

"You're back early." Megan shot me a narrow-eyed look. "I figured you'd go see a late movie or something after you ate."

Whitney laughed. "It's not that early. It's almost nine. Church tomorrow, remember?"

"I remember. I guess I'm glad you do, too. Probably don't need or want a ride this week though?" Megan's gaze moved between me and Whitney.

"I'm happy to have you come with Beckett and me, but it's also fine if you want to continue your girl time." I tucked my hands in my pockets and looked at Whitney.

Indecision flitted across her face. "What if we split the difference? I'll ride with you—because it makes more sense than Megan driving separate from Austin anyway—and we can all sit together."

"That works." Megan uncurled from the sofa and stood,

stretching her arms up over her head. "I'll see you at church then."

"How was Beckett? Any problems?" I wasn't sure about babysitters, but I kind of assumed she would have led with them, had there been any. At the same time, I wanted to know.

"Not one. He's a doll. We played cars in his room and he assured me it was okay if we left a few of them parked at the supermarket on his rug." Megan bit her lip. "So if he was supposed to put everything completely away, that's on me, not him."

I shook my head. "The supermarket parking area is by the wall, right? He won't trip on them if he needs the bathroom and that's my only big requirement. Nothing quite like the prospect of stepping on a car, sliding around, and then cracking your head open when you fall in the middle of the night to make tidying up seem like a good plan."

Whitney smiled at me.

Megan laughed. "Look at you, already a worrywart dad. Who would've guessed?"

I frowned. I wasn't a worry wart. I was just using my brain. But I also didn't feel like picking a fight with Megan. I'd much rather she left for home so Whitney and I could maybe spend a few more minutes together before bed, eating ice cream.

"Let me get your coat for you." I started toward the hall. Megan and Whitney's laughter followed me. And okay, fine, it wasn't a smooth transition, but I didn't want this to turn into an extended party. I slid my wallet out and pulled out two fifties. When Megan joined me by the door, I pressed them into her hand before holding her coat for her.

"You don't need to pay me." She held the money out.

I closed her fingers over the bills. "If you hadn't agreed to watch Beckett, I would've had to find someone else and pay them. At least with you I know he had a good time and was well cared for."

Megan sighed and tucked the money in her pocket. "Okay. But for the record, I don't expect it."

"Noted and appreciated. Tell Austin hey." I unlocked the front door and pulled it open while Megan zipped her coat, collected her purse from the coat rack, and unhooked her keys from the strap.

"Will do. See you tomorrow." She leaned to the side and waved. "Night, Whitney."

"Night."

I watched from the doorway as Megan made her way down to her car. She'd parked on the street a few spaces away from the steps. When she was in and the headlights had come on, I shut and locked the front door, and then turned.

Whitney leaned against the kitchen doorway. She'd taken off her boots and something about her casual bare feet made my mouth water.

"Ice cream?" she said.

I nodded.

She pushed off the wall and went into the kitchen. I followed.

Whitney was poking through the freezer. "Why do you only have vanilla?"

"Is this a trick question?"

She straightened and put her hands on her hips. "No. It's an honest question. Of all the flavors in the world, you have the most boring option available. And not just half of a spare tub that's in there because you had root beer floats or something. You have three containers."

"Sure. Because I don't want to run out. Because vanilla is amazing. It's a blank canvas."

"Exactly." Whitney shook her head. "And I, for one, don't understand why someone would eat canvas."

I snorted out a laugh and strode to the freezer so I could pluck the open container of ice cream from the drawer, then closed it. "Oh ye of little faith. Go sit and let me teach you the ways of ice cream."

"Oh, please." Whitney rolled her eyes, but she did go and drop into a chair at the table. "All right. Astound me."

I shook my head and got down two bowls. I dished two good-sized scoops into each before opening the upper cabinet beside the fridge. I got down a stack of containers and pried open the lids before sprinkling the contents onto the ice cream. Mini chocolate chips. Chopped pecans. Peanut butter cup pieces. That was probably good. I put the lids back on and replaced them in the cupboard before opening the fridge to get out the chocolate syrup and whipped cream. When the ice cream was topped, I put everything away and carried the bowls to the table.

"Voilà!"

Whitney frowned at the bowl before picking up her spoon and poking at the toppings. "It's a sundae."

"It's ice cream the way ice cream was meant to be eaten."

She sighed and dug her spoon into the treat. "Sometimes I don't want a sundae though. I just want a scoop of ice cream. Plain. Unadorned. Easy."

I shook my head. I didn't see the point in paying to have some company mix everything together in a big vat so the toppings all froze into a weird consistency. "This way is better."

"It really isn't." She wrinkled her nose and took a bite.

I watched her chew. "It's good. Admit it."

"I will admit only that you make a very tasty sundae. Which is not the same as having a bowl of ice cream."

I groaned and dug my spoon into my own bowl. "Here I thought you were the perfect woman. I guess it's good to uncover the flaws early so I know if I can live with them. For nickel knowledge, if I were to purchase impure ice cream, what flavor would I be getting?"

"Mint chocolate chip." The look she sent me clearly added on the word, "Duh" at the end.

"Uh-huh. Green or white."

"Please. Green. It's not mint chip if it's white."

I shook my head. I'd never really understood how food coloring made something better, but my dad was the same way. At least she'd be happy with the ice cream offerings at my folks' house when we went down for Thanksgiving. "Noted. Any other major flaws I need to know about before we take this further?"

She laughed, which was what I intended, then she leaned over and—before I could blink—dabbed whipped cream on the tip of my nose. "I think I'm the one who should be asking that."

"Hey." I wiped the cold cream off my nose. "Wow. Gloves are off, is that it?"

Whitney grinned at me.

Heart light, I grinned back.

I skipped down the stairs, working on not being self-conscious. I liked leggings as much as the next girl, but I tended to wear them with a long tunic so they were more like tights. The black and white sweatshirt, complete with a pink and gray spiderweb in the hood, that made up the top half of my costume was not what I considered long.

"There she is, Beck. What do you think?" Scott was garbed in a snug green and gold onesie with metallic claw-ended arms reaching around him from the back.

Beckett grinned, nodding his masked head vigorously while he clutched a bright orange plastic pumpkin in his other hand.

"I know who I am, because you told me and I did a web search. And I know who he is, because who doesn't know Spiderman. But who are you?" I flicked Scott's silver lab-style goggles. "Some kind of mad scientist, obviously."

"Wow. You don't know superheroes at all, do you?"

"Sorry. Hit me up on obscure Bible characters and I'm your gal. Do you know the story of Phinehas and his spear work that ended a plague?" I laughed at Scott's blank look. "Exactly. I know the original superheroes."

"We'll educate you. The movies are fun. And some of the cartoons would be okay for Beckett to watch, too." Scott picked his phone up off the coffee table and slid it into a pocket.

I was a little surprised I couldn't see its outline. I guess his costume wasn't as snug as it looked. Not that I was complaining.

"I thought we'd drive over and park at the end of King. That way we can hit up all the stores without having to walk there and back. And if he still has energy after that, we could go up the block and see what kind of candy our neighbors have. Sound good?"

"Sounds good. Let's go." I should stop being surprised by the thought he put into everything. I might not have started out wanting him to be excited about being a dad, but I couldn't deny that he'd jumped in with both feet and was doing an amazing job.

I smiled, ignoring the pang in my chest. Scott was doing a good job and I needed to accept that. It was a little easier now that he and I were dating. I was starting to see the possibility of a future where neither Scott nor I had to lose out on Beckett.

"Candy?" Beckett held up his bucket then peered into it.

"That's right, bud. Candy. We'll stop at the shops and they'll give us candy—just tonight though, it's not a daily thing. And Miss Megan said the bookstore has some other special goodies for the kids." I looked up at Scott.

He lifted his eyebrows and jerked his head toward the stairs that would take us to the garage.

It seemed silly to drive. Except, of course, that I knew better than to count on Beckett's feet and legs holding out. And there was nothing worse than a tired and cranky three-year-old who absolutely did not want to be walking on his own two feet. So driving it was.

Even if it took longer to get Beckett buckled into his car seat than to get there.

Scott found a spot on the street and parked. "That was a find."

"Definitely. And now? Candy."

"Candy!" Beckett cheered from the backseat.

"He knows he doesn't get to eat it all tonight, right?" Scott's voice was low.

"We talked about it a lot today, so I think so?" I shrugged. As much as I was all in when it came to healthy eating, I didn't really think one day of overindulging on candy was going to ruin anything if that was what ended up happening.

The sun was already beginning to set—the joy of autumn evenings—as we got out of the car and started down the sidewalk. There were other families there with small kids doing the same as us. The stores were decorated, most with their doors propped open to make it easier to go in and out. It was warm enough that it shouldn't cause problems for the people inside.

We walked slowly, keeping a pace that Beckett could manage, stopping at each shop for him to thrust out his bucket. I reminded him he was supposed to say "trick or treat" as well as "thank you," but so far consistency for either one was a challenge. We'd had speech therapy for the first time that morning, and the therapist had done a little work with him on those phrases, but asking for candy wasn't a huge priority in the overall scheme of things.

Before long, we were at the bookstore. Beckett charged in, bucket outstretched, "Treat!"

Scott and I were close behind. He held my hand and I was conscious of a subtle desire to tug it loose, which was ridiculous. Except Megan was watching with eagle eyes from the counter and I could see her brother, Austin, and the rest of Scott's guy group hanging out in the reading lounge, and all of a sudden, it seemed a bit much. Was he really ready for this?

"Hey, guys." Megan's gaze darted down to our hands and

then back up. She met mine and her eyebrows started a spasmodic dance.

I glared and she stopped—hopefully before Scott noticed. "Hi. Yours is the happening place tonight."

Megan grinned. "So far. The kids seem to like the popcorn balls and coloring books we put together. Parents are enjoying the discount coupon."

"Excellent." I glanced over at Scott's friends then back at him. "You should go say hi to the guys. I'll be over in a minute."

Scott frowned. "Are we staying here?"

"For a little." I pointed to where Beckett was hunkered down by the kids' books. "He's happy there. I'll keep an eye on him."

"You could come."

Megan's eyebrows started their crazy wiggling again.

I gave Scott a little push. "Go. I want to talk to Megan."

He squeezed my hand before he let go and headed over to the little conversational area.

I heard his friends greet him, then turned back to Megan and fwapped her arm. "Stop that."

"I can't help it. You're so adorable together." Megan's voice pitched up, ending in a squeak. She leaned across the cashier counter so her face was in mine. "You need to tell me everything."

"There's not a lot to tell." I checked on Beckett quickly, then Scott. "We had dinner, it was good, took a walk, and agreed that we want to see what happens if we give things a shot."

"That's it?" Megan frowned and crossed her arms. "You were holding hands like old pros. Are you sure there aren't any juicy details you're leaving out?"

My face heated and I turned away, hoping she'd think I was just checking on Beckett. I know girlfriends were supposed to share details about everything, but I couldn't force out any words about our kisses. And there had been several. Not just

Saturday night. I'd gone down for coffee on Sunday morning before church and Scott cornered me between the fridge and the counter and...I blew out a breath as the memory brought back all the tingles full force.

"Hmmm."

Megan's utterance had me turning back. I forced a smile. "What?"

"I'm not sure I believe that there's nothing else to tell, but I'll let it go for now. I'll get Kayla to drag it out of you."

"Where is Kayla?"

Megan shook her head. "She's handing out candy at her apartment. Absolutely refuses to believe that it's okay to come to the store and possibly miss one or two trick-or-treaters at home, despite the fact that most of them won't come until after it's dark."

I could see that. Kayla had such a big heart and enthusiastic spirit, she probably gushed over every costume that came to her door. "I bet the families of young kids appreciate her."

"Oh, they do." Megan sighed. "I don't mean to be grumpy. I just could have used the help tonight. That's why Austin and the gang are here, actually. I guilted Austin into coming and I guess he put the word out. My evening clerks both quit yesterday. With no notice. I'm not sure what to do, honestly."

"Oh, no." I bit my lip. Losing the two women who ran the store in the evenings was pretty drastic. "Did they say why?"

"Clara's husband is retiring and they're moving to Florida. I guess I sort of get that. I mean, I would have preferred some notice. I can't imagine they're moving this week, but at least she has a reason. Jillian said she's looking for something full time."

"You said yourself you wish you could offer full time and benefits."

"I know, I know." Megan paused to give treats to some newcomers and encourage them to look around. "But she's *looking*. Why can't she keep working while she looks? Then, at least, she wouldn't be leaving me in the lurch. I don't know what I'm going to do. Well, obviously, I'm going to be heading over here every night after working my own full-time job until I can find someone else. But that's not going to work forever."

"I could help." The words left my mouth before I really thought them through. But they could stand. Scott was home, most days, by five. There was no reason I couldn't head out as soon as he got home. Or, if necessary, I could bring Beckett along. It wasn't as if he minded being in the bookstore.

I looked his way again. He was happily flipping through the pages of a brightly illustrated book.

"What time does your afternoon shift clock out?"

"No. I can't let you do that." Megan shook her head. "I don't think Scott would like it, and I'm not going to alienate him. He's my brother's friend."

"He'll be fine. I can't imagine him minding me wanting to help out my own friend. Although we've already made Thanksgiving plans. And maybe Christmas, come to that, so I couldn't work the holidays." Ugh. Maybe I wasn't as helpful as I thought I could be. "Have you ever considered changing the hours? Making them something that a single employee could handle if they were full time?"

Megan frowned. "It feels like giving up."

I could sort of see that. It would be a change of what had, apparently, been a long-standing set of hours. Hours that had been established by Megan and Austin's grandmother.

"Just a thought. But if not, I can still pitch in for a bit between now and Thanksgiving. That's a couple of weeks, at least. Maybe you can get someone in."

"I might take you up on that, but you'd need to make sure Scott's really all right if you do. Not just as your employer—

because obviously what you do in your free time is fine from that standpoint—but as your boyfriend."

Boyfriend? It was the right term, but it was still startling to me. I wasn't thinking of Scott like that. It didn't feel real enough.

"Yeah, okay. I'll talk to him. But I really can't see why he'd mind for a week or two while you figured things out."

I shrugged and looked over at Beckett again. He'd stopped paging through books and was now stacking them as tall as he could and toppling them over. "Beckett, hon, don't do that."

Beckett looked over at me, his face morphing into a scowl.

"It's bad for the books. Why don't we put them back on the shelf and then we can go get more candy. Okay?" I looked at Megan. "Sorry."

She waved it off. "It's fine. Take your little spider family off for more fun."

Aww. The idea of a spider family made my heart swell. Except... "I don't think Scott's a spider anything."

"Of course not. He's Doc Ock." Megan stared at me, aghast. "You don't know who he is?"

I shrugged. "I'm not really into cartoons."

"Comics." Megan clapped a hand to her chest. "Oh, my word, comics. Not cartoons."

Was there a difference? Apparently, Megan thought so. And maybe everyone else.

"Sorry."

"No. It's fine. You're good. Uncultured, maybe. But I can help with that. We'll schedule some movie nights. I'll talk to Kayla and make a plan. Have fun trick or treating." Megan came from around the desk and patted my shoulder before moving over to the kids shelf and scooping up the books that Beckett had pulled out. She quickly sorted and reshelved them.

I shook my head. She was fast. This really was what Megan

ought to be doing with her life. I wondered, not for the first time, why Austin didn't bankroll the bookstore so she could. Although even as I thought it, I suspected I knew the answer. Megan would say no. She wouldn't take advantage of her brother that way.

And she would absolutely see it as taking advantage, even if he didn't.

I reached for Beckett's hand. "Let's go get Scott and go get more candy. Sound good?"

Beckett nodded.

There was chocolate circling his lips and I smothered a laugh. I hadn't explicitly told him not to eat any of the candy yet —and I clearly hadn't been paying as close attention as I should have been.

"There you are." Scott turned, grinning, and scooped Beckett up. "Looks like someone's been eating chocolate."

"Yummy!"

The guys all laughed. Scott and I joined in.

Scott drilled a finger into Beckett's belly. "No more tonight, okay bud?"

"K." He frowned and offered up his bucket.

Aww. My heart melted. Scott's seemed to as well. He pushed the bucket back. "Nah, bud, you still get to collect it and carry it. Just no more eating, okay?"

Beckett nodded.

Scott turned to look at me. "I take it you're ready to move on?"

"Yeah. He's ready to move. Now I realize that's probably prompted by sugar, but whatever. He was done with the books. And Megan is thoroughly appalled at my lack of comic book knowledge, so I guess my work here is done."

"All right. Come on spider friends, let's hit the street." Scott stood and set Beckett back on his feet. "See you guys around."

"Friday, right?" Austin pointed a finger at Scott.

"For sure, if not before."

Since Scott was holding Beckett's hand and Beckett had his bucket in his other hand, I tucked my hands into the pocket of my hoodie as we left the store. None of the guys were acting weird around me. Did that mean they didn't know about me and Scott? Or maybe they didn't care?

It was tricky, balancing this new relationship with our existing dynamic as employer-employee. A tiny piece of me wondered if I had the skill to avoid wiping out.

21

SCOTT

"Knock, knock. Got a second?"

I spun my office chair around and saw Wesley at the entrance to my cube. We didn't tend to see a ton of each other during the workday, for all we both worked in the same part of Robinson Enterprises. "Yeah, sure. What's up?"

"Actually, do you think you could take a walk? Maybe we could go down to the corner and get coffee?"

I studied Wes for a moment. Something was up. "Sounds like a plan."

I spun back to my computer and locked the screen, then stood. I grabbed my cell off the desk and slid it into my pocket, double-checking that I had my wallet with me, and gestured for him to lead the way. "How's your project going?"

Wes shrugged. "Eh. Good enough, I guess. We're basically in maintenance mode now and they're talking about shifting most of us around to new work. There are some proposals underway, and you saw we just won the big NSA research proposal?"

"Yeah." That had been a big win. "You think you'll get on that?"

"Dunno. I guess we'll see. I have a clearance, so I could." Wes reached the bank of elevators first and pushed the call button.

Most of us had some kind of clearance, but Wes had transferred to Robinson from another Beltway Bandit that had needed—and paid for—a higher clearance. It was a good thing to have around there if someone was looking for job longevity.

The elevator came and we got on with the group of employees who had to be from the social media arm. At least if their clothing was an indication. The folks over at SM tended to dress up just a little bit more than those of us who were never customer facing. But when you worked with social media, I guess it made sense to be selfie-ready at all times.

Or something.

We all got out when the elevator reached the lobby. Thankfully, when Wes and I turned left, the other group headed right.

"Phew."

I laughed. "I was just thinking that. So what's up?"

Wes shoved his hands in his pockets. "Is it wrong if I quit?"

My eyebrows lifted. "Why would it be wrong?"

"I don't know. It feels disloyal somehow. If I didn't have all this money, I'd never consider it, you know? I like my job. Most days. But...do you ever feel like you settled and took the simple path even though it wasn't the right one?"

I bobbed my head from side to side. "I don't know. Maybe sometimes."

Wes reached for the door to the coffee shop and pulled it open. "Really?"

"Yeah. I think that's kind of universal, though." That was what my parents always told me when I was unsettled. "Would you do consulting?"

"What?" Wes looked away from the menu and at me, a slight frown on his face.

"If you quit. Would you come back on a 1099 and just work

on the projects you were interested in?" It was what I kept kicking around in the back of my head. Getting away from the expectations of forty-hour work weeks fifty weeks of the year. I could work on a project, then take a couple months off.

"Oh. No." He moved up to the cashier. "Large mocha please."

Interesting. I waited while he paid then slid forward. "I'll have a medium hazelnut latte with extra whipped cream."

The barista rolled her eyes as she rung up my coffee. What was that about? Couldn't guys like whipped cream? If I was going to pay ten bucks, after tip, for a coffee, I wanted it to be worth my time.

I moved to the other end of the counter to stand beside Wes. "So, not consulting. What would you do?"

Wes looked around the shop before leaning closer. When he spoke, his voice was quiet. "I think I want to open a dive shop."

I blinked. I couldn't have been more surprised, not even if he'd said he wanted to buy a ticket to space. "A dive shop. You don't dive."

"Not yet. But I'm going to learn at Christmas. And if I love it like I think I will? Why not do that for a living?"

My mind whirled. People didn't quit their jobs and open a scuba shop in the suburbs of DC. Or—wait—"Would you move? To somewhere with a beach?"

Wes reached for his coffee when his name was called. "I'll get a table."

I watched him walk off, blowing across the top of his mug. He hadn't answered. Maybe he hadn't thought it through all the way yet. Who decided to quit a job they...well, he at least enjoyed it, right? So they could do something they'd never tried before. That seemed...I didn't like to use the word stupid, but it was the only one I could come up with that fit.

My coffee was finally ready. I offered a tight smile as I

reached for it, then made my way across the shop to the booth Wes had claimed.

"I don't think so." Wes cupped his hands around his coffee mug. "About moving. I feel like it could be done in Old Town. I've done a little research. People dive in the Potomac. There's a quarry out west a ways that's been flooded and it's become a big dive spot, too. And it's not like we're far from Virginia Beach. That's what? Two, three hours?"

"So you'd plan trips as part of it? What else?" Maybe Wes had given this more thought than it seemed like.

"Certification classes. Dive trips. And gear sales." Wes took a long drink of coffee. "I imagine that would keep me busy. It's not like I'd need to be open all day every day."

"That's...wow."

He chuckled. "Erudite as ever."

"It's just a big change from fairly specialized software engineer to retail store owner." I leaned back. "You need to give me a minute to adjust my brain."

"And that's why I'm asking if it'd be wrong. I could probably find something super philanthropic to do with the money. Or my salary from Robinson if I kept working there. Something that wasn't as selfish as making a purely self-serving change like this." Wes frowned at his coffee. "Sometimes I wish you'd never had the idea about the investing. I was okay, you know, before the money."

I blew out a breath. I understood a little of what he was saying—there were definitely pros and cons to the changes since we'd done our experiment with the stock market. "I get that. And I don't think it's an all-or-nothing proposition. There's no reason you can't figure out something good to do with the money and still change careers."

"That's true." Wes rubbed his forehead.

"You want to share what's bringing this on? Something more

than reaching the end of your project?" Because this didn't seem like Wes to me. He'd seemed reserved at every gathering lately, and honestly? I should have approached him about it.

"I don't know. I never loved programming. It was something I could do that wasn't awful that would be a decent living. So I went with it. But now? What's holding me here? Nothing. I don't love it. I don't need the salary. What's wrong with looking around to see if I can't find something fulfilling that also pays the electric bill each month?" Wes sipped his coffee.

Put like that, how could I disagree? "I didn't realize you felt that way."

Wes laughed. "Why would you? It's not like I'm going to be noisy about the fact that I'm just here for a paycheck. And I do like some of it. Just not all the grind. The idea of starting a project from scratch though? Ugh."

I grinned. That was my favorite part. It was when we got into the middle where things were inevitably behind schedule and the client was trying to sneak in new requirements without adding to the budget or timeline that I started to get frustrated. "What kind of timeframe are you thinking?"

"I guess I'd put my notice in this week and offer to stay through mid-December. Then I'd be free when we headed down to the Caymans." Wes tipped his mug back.

"You've been praying about it?"

He nodded. "Yeah. Maybe not as much as I should have been, but some. I'm not getting any indication that it's the wrong move."

"Keep praying. I'll join you. You should tell the rest of the guys—you know we'd all want to pray with you."

"Yeah, I know. I guess I was worried you'd all say I was being immature or self-centered. Or something."

"That's not us, man. We might give you some grief, but only out of love."

Wes snickered. "Yeah, all right. You really don't think it's dumb?"

"I'm dating the nanny, so I'm not sure I qualify as the pinnacle of good sense, but no. I don't."

He grinned. "I'll take it. And for what it's worth, I don't think you and Whitney is a bad thing. From what I've seen of her— admittedly not a lot—she's good for you."

Was she? I wanted that to be the case, but wanting something didn't mean it was true. "You think?"

"Yeah. You don't?" Wes frowned at me.

"I guess part of me wonders if we'd be together at all if not for Beckett."

Wes laughed. "Of course you wouldn't. If not for Beckett, she'd be in California and you never would have met."

"That's a point."

"I guess this is where I ask if you're praying about it."

It was a good reminder. "Some. Not as much as I should. So yeah, I'll do better."

"We should probably get back to work." Wes started to slide out from the booth. "I'll expect to hear from you in the group text."

"Same goes." I stood and collected our mugs. Wes had at least managed to drain his, but I couldn't bring myself to chug the last of mine. Oh well. I set them in the tray on top of the trashcan by the door.

We walked back to the office and rode the elevator up, then parted to head to our separate cubes when we reached our floor. It was going to be strange not having Wes around the office anymore. I didn't see him every day, but we tried to at least eat lunch at the same time a couple times a week.

Of the group of guys, Wes was the most likely to keep to himself. He'd been the first to buy a townhouse so he could live on his own in a more private situation than an apartment. Now, he was the first of us to decide to make a major change because of the money. And, as I absolutely would have expected, he'd kept it to himself until he'd already made up his mind.

I sat back down at my computer and unlocked it. So much change in such a short period of time was starting to weigh on me. A lot of it was good. The money. I couldn't say it was bad. And Mom was doing a lot of good with it—maybe I should talk to the guys about going in together and setting up a joint foundation. Mom would be happy to have an even bigger budget to play with.

Beckett definitely qualified as good. Even though I hadn't wanted to take him on initially. Same with Whitney—as the nanny first, and now? Just thinking of her warmed me through. I had to believe this was all part of God's plan.

I pulled out my phone and asked in the group text about the foundation as well as asking for prayer about my relationship with Whitney. Then I put my phone away and got back to work.

By the time I pulled into the garage after work, I was exhausted and ready for twenty minutes of silence. Maybe even a nap.

I pushed open the door and noise ran into me like a train barreling past. The headache that had been building revved into overdrive. I took a deep breath. It didn't help.

I trudged up the stairs. Beckett's shrieks growing louder as I got closer.

"Beckett, bud, you have to stop." Whitney was sitting on the floor beside the flailing and shrieking toddler. How she heard me coming I had no idea, but she glanced over and managed a tight smile. "Hi. Sorry. He doesn't want to pick up his toys."

I got it. Kids had tantrums. In some ways, maybe it was good that Beckett was settling in enough to behave this normally. But I wished he'd chosen a different day. Or that I'd had a different day.

"Look, Beck, Scott's home."

"No!" And then an ear-piercing shriek that had me clapping my hands over my ears.

"Beckett." All the frustration of my afternoon came out in my voice. I wasn't proud of it, but it put an end to the screaming and kicking.

Beckett hiccuped.

"Stand up. Go upstairs. Put away your toys. Right now."

Beckett looked at me, eyes wide, and a tear plopped on his cheek.

"Come on, Beckett." Whitney held out her hand for Beckett and shot me a fulminating glare. "Let's go upstairs."

Sniffling, Beckett clung to Whitney's hand and the two of them headed upstairs.

"Great. Just great." I muttered and went into the kitchen. Now I was taking out a bad day on an innocent kid.

I rummaged through the bottles of vitamins until I found a pain reliever and shook two into my hand. I swallowed them dry while I got down a glass and filled it with water at the fridge. I drained it and set the glass on the counter, then rested my head against the fridge door.

Dinner.

Everyone needed to eat and it was my job to handle food. Because I'd been a stickler about it at the beginning, so Whitney didn't even offer anymore.

I dragged my phone out of my pocket and opened the app for my favorite pizza place. I tried not to fall back on this often, but there was no way I could do anything else today. If Whitney didn't like it, she could get in line.

And that was unfair. I didn't know that Whitney was going to say anything about it. For all I knew, she had plans tonight. Most Wednesdays she ended up going over to the bookstore to hang out with Megan.

When the order was placed, I looked over toward the stairs and sighed. I should go up and help. Apologize.

Putting it off didn't make any sense, either. My headache had died back down to a quiet roar and the pizza wouldn't be here for at least a half hour.

I pushed off the counter and started up the stairs.

In his room, Beckett was sullenly driving his cars into the bins where they were stored. Whitney was putting books back on the shelf. It looked like a lot of playing had taken place today.

"Good job, Beckett."

He looked up at my words then back to his cars.

I went in and crouched down beside him. "I'm sorry I was loud. I didn't mean to scare you."

Beckett didn't look over.

I sat cross-legged beside him and reached for a car. I put it in a bin, then reached for another. We sat in silence putting cars away for a minute or two, then he crawled into my lap. I pulled him close and rested my cheek on the top of his head and felt a little more of the stress of the day drain away.

"I'm sorry, buddy. I love you."

"Love you, too."

I kissed the top of his head and looked up. My gaze met Whitney's. Did I owe her an apology too? I'd wait until she said something.

"Looks like you have everything under control here." Whitney's voice was stiff. "I guess that means I'm off duty."

"I ordered pizza, if you want to join us for dinner."

"Yum." Beckett's voice was a whisper. I doubted Whitney heard him, but it made me smile. Maybe a bad afternoon at work hadn't completely ruined my standing with him.

She sighed. "Pizza?"

I nodded and tried to think back through recent dinners. We hadn't had pizza in probably a week. Had we? I didn't make a habit of ordering in. We had brunch after church at the diner, but that was our only usual meal out. "It was a day."

"I gathered."

I winced. "Sorry."

She shrugged. "You apologized to Beckett and he seems okay with it. And he cleaned up. So you managed what I didn't."

"Maybe I just gave the last nudge after you laid the groundwork?" It wasn't a competition. "You're doing a great job. You know that, right?"

"Today wasn't fabulous here, either." Whitney pressed the heels of her hands to her eyes. "I was going to head out to the bookstore, but I wouldn't mind a slice of pizza first."

I smiled and was relieved when I saw an answering curve of Whitney's lips. Still holding Beckett, I got to my feet. "Let's go downstairs and wait for the food. You can tell me all about your day."

"Me? Or Beckett?"

"Either one of you. I'm interested in both." I reached out and grabbed her hand, giving it a squeeze before letting go so I could start down the stairs.

Maybe this crisis was averted. Was it always going to be like that though? Would a clash of professional opinions inevitably lead to problems in our personal relationship?

At the bottom of the stairs, I set Beckett down. He scampered into the living room and the little bin of toys there. I turned and watched Whitney come the rest of the way down. I opened my arms.

After a moment's hesitation, she stepped into them and I pulled her close. "Hi."

"Hi. Welcome home."

I chuckled. "Thanks. It's good to be home. Rough day. You, too?"

She nodded.

"Wanna tell me about it?" I leaned back and held her gaze.

She sighed a little and shook her head. "There's not so much to tell. Just three-year-old stubbornness. And he doesn't like speech therapy. It's hard."

Right. That was today. "It went okay?"

"Yeah, I guess. The therapist thought so. There's homework. I thought maybe I could do it during the day once and you could do it in the evenings? That way it's not all just one person."

"That'll work."

Whitney stepped back, out of my embrace, and took my hand. "I put it on the fridge. Why don't I explain it to you?"

I glanced over at Beckett. He was happily driving a dump truck in circles on the coffee table. "Sure."

I followed Whitney into the kitchen, wrapped my arms around her from behind and nuzzled her neck.

"Scott." She ended my name with a breathless laugh as she turned around. Our lips met. And the rest of the day's frustration disappeared.

22

WHITNEY

I stepped into the bookstore and unzipped my coat. "Megan?"

"In the back."

I followed her voice and found her up to her elbows in a box of books just inside the storage room at the back of the shop. "Hey."

"Can you believe next week is Thanksgiving?"

I shook my head. I was actually trying not to think about that. When I'd agreed to go along and spend time in Florida with Scott and Beckett, it hadn't seemed quite as daunting as it did now that the date was looming on the horizon.

"What's that look?" Megan set a stack of books on the floor before flipping the now-empty box over and ripping off the bottom tape so she could flatten it.

"I don't have a look."

"Sure you do. It's the 'I'm meeting my boyfriend's parents and I'm terrified' look." Megan shook her head. "But you've already met them. This shouldn't be scary."

"I met them as the nanny. Not as the girlfriend. Who is still also the nanny." I puffed out my cheeks, then blew out the air. "What am I doing?"

"Pick up a stack of books and follow me." Megan waited until I had books in my arms before collecting her own stack and starting off toward the front of the store. "How are things between you and Scott? Any more freak outs?"

I frowned. I never should have said anything about the one time he raised his voice to Beckett. It was two weeks ago now and Megan still brought it up every time I saw her. "No. He had a bad day and he was quick to apologize and make amends. You don't need to have your social worker hat on. He's fine. Beckett's fine. I'm fine."

"That's a lot of fine." She sent me a long look over her shoulder before she dropped her stack of books on top of a half-height shelf. She gestured for me to put my books down as well. "You were upset. I think it's reasonable for me to follow up."

"I think it's reasonable for you to trust me when I say you don't need to." I set my books down and crossed my arms. It made me look defensive, but I didn't care. She was getting on my nerves. Maybe I shouldn't hang out at the bookstore as much as I had been.

The bells on the door jangled and we both looked over to see Kayla hurry in. "Hey girls. It's actually chilly tonight. I can't believe it."

"Only you would be excited about it getting cold." Megan rolled her eyes.

"I like having seasons." Kayla rubbed her hands together then she frowned. "What's going on?"

"Nothing." I looked over at Megan, who'd said the same thing at the same time.

"Uh-huh. My teacher radar says that's a big fib. Spill it." Kayla wagged a finger between me and Megan, stopping when she got to me. She jabbed her finger in my direction. "Whitney goes first."

I sighed. "It's nothing. I just suggested that Megan could take her social worker hat off and stop acting like Scott was a child abuser and I was enabling him because I had the bad sense to vent my frustration about the one time he lost his patience with Beckett."

Kayla's mouth formed an "O" and she turned to Megan. "You haven't let that go yet?"

"Look, it's all fun and games until the neighbors are filing complaints and CPS is having to step in. I don't think it's wrong for me to express concern about a potentially dangerous situation." Megan crossed her arms.

"Potentially dangerous?" Kayla dismissed that with a wave of her hand and a "Pfft."

I hid a smile.

"You don't—"

"I do, too." Kayla cut Megan off. "And so do you. How long have you known Scott?"

"I don't know, five years. Ish."

Kayla kept her gaze firmly on Megan. "And in that time has he ever done anything that would give you pause when it came to him and kids?"

"No. But it only takes once to—"

Kayla held up her hand. "What's really going on? I don't know one parent who has never raised their voice in a moment of frustration. I don't even know any teachers who have managed to go a school year without that. Heck, I practically yelled at my seniors this afternoon, should I lose my job?"

Megan's shoulders sank. "No. Of course not."

"And Scott?" Kayla cocked her head to the side.

"Is a good guy." Megan blew out a long breath. "I'm sorry."

Kayla reached over and rubbed Megan's arm. "Tell us what's happening."

I gestured to the two stacks of books. "Do you want me to do something with these while you spill?"

Megan pressed fingers to her eyes. "They're the top of the shelf display. I was just going to line them up between bookends."

I got to work setting them up. Since these bookshelves were along the picture glass window at the front of the store, I knew Megan tended to alternate the spines so people could read them inside or out. I followed suit.

Megan slid down the shelf and sat on the floor. "I have a case. The dad—and I hate calling him that—is a textbook abusive alcoholic. His wife covers for him, despite currently having an infected burn on her arm she says is from the stove, and two broken fingers. The burn is circular and the fingers were crushed—probably in a door, according to the doctor. Their son is four and already a frequent-flier at two different ERs. Always with a plausible explanation."

"Must not be too plausible. They're your case." I waited until Megan looked up and I offered a sympathetic smile. "I can't imagine a better person to be on their side."

She sighed and rested her forehead on her knees. "Except that his brother's a lawyer and so they appeared in court all polished talking about persecution by the state, and the judge went on about the overcrowded foster care system and dismissed the case. And now it's just going to be harder to get that little boy the help he needs."

"And his mom." Kayla rubbed Megan's arm. "I'm sorry."

"Me, too." I finished arranging the books and tucked the last bookend—this one shaped like a cat sleeping on a stack of books—under. "I promise you I wouldn't leave Beckett for thirty seconds if Scott was anywhere near that way."

"I know. I do." Megan glanced up. Her eyes were shiny. "I just don't understand why the people who know this little boy and his parents are so willing to turn a blind eye."

I didn't know what to say to that. I was probably guilty of it. Shelby Ann hadn't exactly been the picture of a perfect mother. She hadn't hurt Beckett physically, but she definitely teetered on the edge of neglect. Probably tipped over, if I was honest with myself. Maybe instead of going out of my way to pick up the slack, I should have gotten in touch with the authorities. Would that have been better for Beckett from the beginning?

"I'm sorry I snapped at you. Both of you." Megan pushed herself to her feet. "I don't know how much longer I can keep doing this job, though. Not when it feels like every other case ends the same way."

"Are you sure you can't make the bookstore work for you full time?" Kayla propped her hands on her hips. "Let me see your books."

Megan laughed. "You're welcome to take a look. We run close to the bone. I don't know where another salary—this one with benefits—comes from."

"Would you need it to be another?"

Kayla and Megan both turned to look at me.

Megan spoke first. "What do you mean?"

"Well, if you were full time, and you adjusted the hours of the store, couldn't you do it all?" I bit my lip. "And it's not like you have two of the employees you need right now anyway."

Kayla snickered.

Megan frowned. "You've mentioned adjusting the hours. We've always been open nine to nine."

"Sure. I get that. And change is hard and all that, too. But do people actually come in at nine?" I glanced at Kayla and she gave me a subtle thumbs-up.

"Not really. We don't start to see traffic until eleven most days, according to the logs."

I nodded. "So open at eleven. And do people come in after eight most weeknights?"

"Just you." Megan grinned. "But it's a point. If I did eleven to eight Monday through Thursday and maybe add the extra hour on Friday and Saturday nights. I'd still be closed all day on Sundays. It'd be a long day, but it wouldn't come close to the hours I'm putting in now when you add both jobs together."

"And you'd be doing something you love." Kayla pointed at Megan. "Which makes the time fly, I promise you. I guess the next question is whether or not you can live on what the book-store would pay you. And what to do about health insurance."

"Living isn't an issue. The townhouse was Grandma's, too. She gave it to us. So Austin and I split utilities. I could definitely cover that. And my car and insurance." Megan drummed her fingers on a book. "I need to talk to Austin, I think. He's the math whiz."

"Hey. I like math. I'm good at it, too." Kayla crossed her arms, her mouth morphing into a pout. "I thought I was going to look at your books."

"Maybe the two of you can consult." Megan rolled her eyes.

I laughed. It seemed like Megan took every chance to drop a dig about Kayla and Austin being together. And neither of them seemed to notice. Or if they did, they stayed silent. Was that because there was no possibility of more than friendship there, so it was easier to ignore Megan? Or maybe it was because neither of them wanted to be the first to admit it.

Hmm. I eyed Kayla.

"What?" Kayla brushed at her mouth. "I can't have some-thing on my face. I haven't been eating."

"Nothing. Just thinking." My face heated. Maybe I was doing

that annoying thing people in relationships do when they try to picture everyone around them in one, too.

Which meant I ought to be on the lookout for someone for Megan. Except that I knew basically eight people in the DC area. Scott and his group of guys plus Megan and Kayla. I had to believe if Megan was going to date anyone, it wouldn't be someone from her brother's best friend group.

"Have we talked about Thanksgiving yet? You two know I'm going to Florida—what are your plans?" I crossed the bookstore to the little seating area and dropped into one of the comfy chairs.

Kayla and Megan followed.

Megan took the chair across from me. "Grandma's coming up. Mom and Dad decided Austin and I should host, so they'll be over, too. Should be fun. I enjoy getting a chance to play in the kitchen."

"Got room for one more?" Kayla's words were casual, like she didn't care one way or the other, but I suspected she was hoping the answer would be yes.

"You don't have plans?" Megan sent Kayla a shocked look. "I figured you'd be headed to Mexico or, I don't know, Bora Bora."

Kayla snickered. "Sadly, Bora Bora is not in the cards this year. No, Mom and Dad booked an over-fifty cruise and then were surprised when I said that meant I couldn't join them."

I laughed, but quickly stopped. "You're serious?"

Kayla shrugged. "You'd have to meet my parents. But you never will, because that would mean I was something more than a fulfilled obligation that got in the way of them having fun in their twenties and thirties."

"Ouch." I sometimes got annoyed with my parents—who didn't? But at least I knew they loved me and wanted me home —were disappointed, even, that I wasn't going to be there.

"I'm used to it. Anyway, if you're hanging here, I'm not too proud to beg for an invite. I make a mean sweet potato casserole." Kayla batted her eyes at Megan.

"You don't have to beg. Consider yourself invited. Bring the potatoes, though I can't promise I'm going to try them." Megan wrinkled her nose. "Sweet potatoes are gross."

"What? You're nuts. They're good!" I glanced at Kayla. "Maybe you can stick her serving in a container for me so I can have it when I get back."

"Can do." Kayla grinned and waggled her eyebrows. "When you're back from meeting the parents."

"That's not what this is." I shook my head. "Scott needs me to help with Beckett. That's my job. I'm going as part of my job."

"Uh-huh. Keep saying that." Megan shot me a disgusted look. "If I didn't know better, I'd think you didn't want to meet Scott's folks."

"I've met them. They're nice." I had. They were. And Mrs. Wright had been perfectly cordial to me as the nanny. I wasn't sure if she even knew that my relationship with her son had changed. Scott talked to his parents every week, same as me, but I didn't sit there with him. I had no idea what they knew.

"You're nervous." Megan's words came out like an accusation.

I bristled. "Can you blame me?"

"I guess not. But I think you should talk to Scott about it." Megan pointed at me.

Kayla nodded in agreement with Megan's words.

What was I supposed to say to Scott, though? Still, there was nothing to do. Megan wasn't wrong. I just had to figure out the right words. Scott was a good guy, and I liked having him in my life.

23

SCOTT

I slid my sunglasses on and clicked the unlock button on the fob for our rental car before glancing at Whitney and Beckett. I smiled. "You two ready?"

Whitney glanced down at Beckett, who stood close to her, somewhat behind her legs. "Come on, bud, look at the fun big SUV."

I watched as Whitney opened the back door and helped Beckett climb up. I opened the driver's side door and peeked into the back. The rental company had promised me there'd be a car seat, and there was.

I left Whitney to get him settled and went to the trunk to load our luggage. We were only in Florida for a four-day weekend, so I hadn't anticipated having as much as we did. I was grateful we hadn't had to deal with a commercial airline and their weight limits. Although, as I hefted Whitney's suitcase into the back, I realized maybe those weight limits were good things.

Beckett had a small rolling suitcase of his own. I loaded it next, then tossed my duffel in and closed the gate. I peeked in the window—or tried—as I walked back to the front of the car. The tinting was so dark I couldn't see anything, but when I climbed behind the wheel, Whitney was already settled in the passenger seat and Beckett was strapped in.

"Here we go." I turned on the car and took a minute to ensure my GPS was set to get us to the cottage we'd rented not far from Mom and Dad's house. It shouldn't take too long. Should I have hired a driver? I thought the flexibility of having our own car would be a benefit.

After shifting into drive, I started out of the parking garage. "Do you want music? Or I think there's a DVD player if we need to put something on for Beckett?"

"I think we're okay. If you want music, it's fine, but I don't mind looking out the window." Whitney's smile was tired.

"Hey. You okay?" I reached over and took her hand.

"Nervous, I guess. Things are different from when they visited in September."

I squeezed her fingers before letting go so I could steer with both hands. "You don't have anything to worry about."

"They know I'm coming? You told them, right?" Whitney brushed nervously at her jeans.

"Of course." I'd had several conversations with my parents about Whitney. They knew we were dating. Mom was excited. Dad, well, Dad was Dad. He didn't care, really. He was more excited to see Beckett again. That surprised me, if I was honest, because I didn't consider my dad as someone who was particularly good with kids.

"They're not upset?"

"Whitney." I reached over to touch her leg. "It's going to be okay."

Her eyes were narrow as she gave me a long look. "That didn't answer my question."

I hoped my smile was reassuring. "They're not upset."

"Okay."

She didn't sound like she believed me, but there wasn't

anything I could do about that. She'd have to see what happened herself and maybe we could go from there. I shot up a quick prayer that my parents would be on their best behavior—at least initially. It wasn't going to do anyone any good if I took the time to try to reassure her that everything was going to be fine if my parents said or did something that proved me wrong right out of the gate.

Beckett had drifted off to sleep almost immediately—a combination of it being nearly nap time anyway and an early morning to get to the airport. I couldn't count the road trips I'd been on with my parents growing up that had felt the same as this one. I'd always had a pile of books beside me in the back-seat. As I'd gotten older, that had shifted to include more technology—I'd been a nerd from the beginning—but the books had been a constant. And Mom and Dad? They'd sat up front, listening to music, pointing out the sights, and holding hands.

I glanced over at Whitney before extending my hand across the console that separated us. When her fingers curled lightly around mine, all I could do was think, *Perfect.*

We passed the rest of the drive in what I, at least, thought was companionable silence.

Finally, we made the turn onto a smaller neighborhood road right near the beach. The houses were mostly single-story cottages that looked like they'd been built in the fifties. Most were well maintained, their pastel paint fresh, and white trim gleaming.

The GPS said we'd arrived. I double-checked the address and pulled into the driveway.

"We're here." I probably could have come up with something less inane, but it would have taken some thought.

Whitney glanced over with a smile. "It's adorable."

"Mom said the guy who owns it used to be a missionary. He and his wife live next door." I pointed to the house on the left. I was reasonably certain that was the one Mom had said belonged to the landlord.

"And where do your parents live?" Whitney looked out her window.

"They're about a five-minute drive. Mom wanted something newer—she was worried about maintenance on an older home. Dad is a consummate DIY guy, so if he had a project that needed doing, he'd never hire help. Mom—and I, really—think he's getting too old for major repairs."

"Makes sense." Whitney turned in her seat to look in the back. "He's still sleeping. Do you think I could stay in the car with him while you go get us checked in and all that? I'd love for him to nap as much as he can."

"Definitely." A well-napped Beckett was better than a cranky one any day. "I shouldn't be long."

I leaned across the console and brushed my lips across hers. I felt them curve as she kissed me back. I pulled myself away before I let things get too intense. Now was definitely not the time or the place. "Back in a few."

I hopped out of the SUV, leaned in again to detach my phone from the holder, and swiped open my email as I shut the door. I'd pulled up the confirmation and was scanning to figure out my first step when I heard my name being called.

"Scott? Are you Scott Wright?"

I turned and lifted a hand in greeting. "That's me. You must be Mr. Fitzgerald."

"Call me Dave, though, would you?" The older man strode across the front lawn of the house to the left of where I'd parked. He extended his hand and gave mine a firm shake. "How was the trip down?"

"Pretty good." All things considered, it was probably better than that, but I wasn't going to try to work the fact that we'd flown private into a conversation with a stranger. For all I knew,

Mom and Dad had filled him in on the details of my life already, anyway. "My son fell asleep on the drive from the airport, so Whitney's hanging in the car with him for a bit."

Dave nodded thoughtfully. "I guess it's not too hot for that today."

I'd been a little worried about that myself. All the windows were down and there was a breeze, so it should be fine. And Whitney was a smart woman who would know if she needed to change things. For that matter, I didn't think Beckett would keep sleeping if he started getting uncomfortably hot. "I don't think it'll be long. But if we need to drive around for a bit with the AC on, we'll do that."

"Sounds like a plan. Let's go in and I'll show you the house." Dave started up the driveway to the beach cottage we'd be staying in for our time in Florida. Well, whenever we weren't at Mom and Dad's. I didn't actually think there'd be much time when we were here.

"Appreciate it. I'm surprised you weren't already booked over Thanksgiving."

Dave grinned over his shoulder before turning his attention to unlocking the front door. When he'd pushed it open, he stepped to the side and gestured for me to go in. "Elise wanted me to leave it available, so I had the listing turned off. I guess she's been chatting with your mom in their women's group at church. Your mother's pretty pleased you decided to come down."

I gave a short laugh. That sounded like Mom. "Be sure to tell Elise thanks."

"I will." Dave gestured to the right. "Kitchen's over there. Living area. Bedrooms down the hall. It's pretty straightforward. We have some basics in the fridge and pantry that you're welcome to use. The book on the counter has maps to the nearest supermarket and that sort of thing—pretty sure they do grocery delivery now, too, if you go online. Oh, and the wi-fi password is on the inside cover of the book."

"This is great. Thanks." I looked around and took in the casual, beachy decor. Mom had said it was a popular vacation rental and I could see why. "I'm starting to wish we'd come down for a vacation, not to spend time with my family. I don't imagine we're actually going to be here all that much."

"About that."

I looked at Dave and a tendril of unease began to uncoil in my gut as I took in his expression.

He cleared his throat. "It's none of my business, I'll preface with that, but I happened to be watching out the window for you, so I saw you before you got out of the car."

When I'd kissed Whitney.

Dave tilted his head to one side. "There are only two bedrooms."

"Beckett will sleep in my room. Whitney will have her own. We're both believers, Dave, and committed to keeping our relationship one that honors God." Besides all that, we were both adults. I didn't appreciate this guy feeling like he needed to jump in and question us about something when he and I had just met.

"That's good to hear. I guess my question is whether or not you're committed to keeping your relationship one that doesn't cause others to stumble." He tucked his hands in his pockets. "I'll leave you to think about that. You have the key. My numbers are all in the book. Don't hesitate to reach out if you need something. I hope you enjoy your stay."

With that, Dave strolled out of the house. I stared after him.

I scrubbed my hands over my face, grabbed the house key from the counter, and headed back out to the car.

"Everything all right?" Whitney's voice was low.

I glanced in the back seat. Beckett was still snoozing in his booster. He looked so peaceful.

I climbed behind the wheel. "Yeah. Sure. Let's drive around a little. He's going to sleep longer that way anyway. Then when it's time for him to get up, we can head to my folks' house. That okay?"

Whitney moved her shoulders and I took it for a shrug. She opened her mouth, took a breath, then closed it.

"What?"

"Never mind. You're right that Beckett'll sleep better and longer with the air on. And it's a nice day to drive along the beach."

"Then that's what we'll do." I backed out of the driveway and pointed the car in the opposite direction of my parents' house. Dave probably wasn't the first person to question how things worked with Whitney living in the same space as me. He probably wouldn't be the last, either. But Dave was the first person who'd made it seem like we were doing something bad.

How many others felt that way but kept it to themselves?

How much did I care about the answer?

24

WHITNEY

Being in a new place hadn't seemed to throw Beckett off his schedule in the slightest. I'd heard him crashing around in Scott's room at six and had thrown off the covers and hurried across the hall.

Finger to my lips, I pushed open Scott's bedroom door slightly and gestured for Beckett to come to me.

He grinned, grabbed his stuffed T-rex, and scampered over. He threw his arms around my legs and squeezed, nearly knocking me down. I smothered a laugh and eased Scott's door shut. He'd been acting strangely since we checked in yesterday, and I was going to let him get as much extra sleep as he could.

"Come on, Beck," I whispered and reached for his hand. "What if we make pancakes real fast and then go walk on the beach for a bit?"

Eyes wide, he nodded, clutching Rexy.

We were due back at Scott's parents' house by noon—they apparently liked to eat the big Thanksgiving meal around one thirty rather than for supper like we always had in my family. So we had plenty of time to kill before then.

I set Beckett up with a kid show on my phone, then got out

the makings for pancakes. Thankfully, the pantry staples the rental hosts kept on hand included a mix. I could probably have found a recipe online, but then Beckett would have had to relinquish my phone and I wanted him quiet so Scott could sleep.

In minutes, I had the first circle of batter browning in a pan. By the time the show on my phone shifted into the closing song, I had a nice stack of pancakes on a plate.

"Ready to eat?"

"More!" Beckett clutched the phone.

I sighed and gently pried his fingers off. "Not right now. But we have pancakes. And then the beach, remember?"

His lower lip poked out and he watched my phone as I closed the streaming app and tucked the device in my pocket. I bit my lip. He was either going to pull it together and eat, or he was going to shriek and have a full-blown tantrum. TV in the morning was always a dicey proposition, but it had been the quieter choice.

I transferred a pancake onto a plate, spread some butter on the top and gave it a little splash of syrup before cutting it into squares and sliding it in front of him.

Beckett sniffed once then reached for the fork.

Thank goodness.

With that crisis averted, I fixed myself a pancake and sat beside Beckett. "Did you sleep well?"

He nodded. His cheeks were puffed out with pancake.

I frowned and glanced at his almost empty plate. "Oh man. Chew up what you have before you put anything else in your mouth, okay? I don't want you to choke."

Beckett's little jaw was furiously bouncing up and down, but the contents of his cheeks didn't seem to be diminishing.

What was I supposed to do? I took another bite of my own food and watched him. I gently pressed on his cheek with one finger, hoping maybe some of the food stored there would shift between his teeth so he could get it chewed and swallowed.

"Do you want a glass of milk? Or we might have orange juice?"

The word that he pushed out, along with several chunks of half-mashed pancake, didn't resemble milk at all, so I was going to go with juice. I slid off the chair and hurried to the fridge, turning back to check on him frequently. I really didn't want him to choke. Should I have scooped out some of the pancake?

The thought made me shudder. Just...no. Slimy, half-chewed food all over my fingers? Bleh. Only as a last resort.

I poured a glass of juice and carried it back to the counter. "Take a little sip."

Beckett's syrupy hands reached for the cup and he gulped down a big glug—enough that some escaped out the sides of his mouth.

I reached for the cup and took it back. "Careful."

"Yum." At least his mouth was emptying and he could speak clearly.

"No more of either until you've swallowed everything already in there, okay?" I drilled a finger into his belly.

He giggled before opening his mouth wide to show me.

Thank goodness. "All right. One bite at a time. Got it?"

Beckett put a small square of pancake in his mouth and chewed then reached for the juice. I let him have it and focused on my own breakfast. He didn't have much left to eat after shoveling in so much at once to start out, and I didn't want to be the one holding us up when it came to beach time.

"All done." Beckett set the glass down on the counter with more force than was called for, but it didn't look like it cracked.

I popped my last bite in my mouth. "Me, too. Let's wash our hands and stack our dishes and we'll head across the street to the beach. Okay?"

He nodded.

I scooped him out of his chair and carried him to the kitchen sink. After squirting some soap into his hands and instructing him to rub rub rub, I followed suit. When we both had a good lather going, I flipped on the faucet and we rinsed off. With wet hands, I addressed the syrup and juice on his face.

"Good enough. I'll stack the dishes and we'll go." I set him down on his feet and hurried to do as I'd said. "Ready?"

Beckett frowned at me, but he slid his hand into mine.

We were both barefoot. And in our pj's. But his were shorts and a T-shirt and mine were lounge pants and a tee. I didn't see the need to change into something else just because these happened to have been what we slept in.

I leaned down and whispered conspiratorially, "It's a beach pajama party."

He giggled.

Taking that as assent, I checked that my phone was in my pocket, unlocked the front door, and with Beckett's hand in mine, started down the front steps.

I hoisted him back up to my hip when we got to the street. There was no sense in making him cross the asphalt in his bare feet. I half-wished I hadn't tried it, but rummaging around in my bag for sandals might have awakened Scott and I was trying to give him some rest. Besides, I would have taken them off when we reached the sand anyway.

The path down to the beach was easy to spot and before long, Beckett was running on the wet sand chasing birds. I followed close enough behind him that I could run and grab him away from danger, but he might as well get a chance to play. The birds were fast. It wasn't like he was going to catch one. He seemed completely disinterested in the water.

"Good morning. Out for an early walk?" An older woman called out as she approached from the opposite direction.

"Morning." People here were friendly, it seemed. I glanced at her long enough to offer a quick smile before returning to watching Beckett.

"You must be Whitney. I'm Elise Fitzgerald. You're renting our cottage."

Ah. I put a little more oomph behind my smile. "It's lovely. Thank you. That's Beckett."

Elise turned and looked at Beckett. "He's adorable. I can see why Renee has been so excited about having him visit. But you're just here for the long weekend, is that right?"

Renee was Scott's mom. I vaguely remembered that from when they visited in September. But that had been such a whirl-wind and with all the changes in my life it honestly felt like it was two years ago, not two months. "Yes. This trip. I think we have plans to come for longer around Christmas."

"That'll be lovely. Will you be looking for a place to stay then, too?"

"I'm not sure." Scott and I had left that conversation on pause, waiting to see how this weekend went. I imagined he was considering buying a place near his parents in the long run. It's certainly what I'd do if money weren't an issue. Why not have a vacation home? And it wasn't like he couldn't hook it up with a property manager and rent it out when he wasn't using it. "Beck-ett, stay close."

"Why don't we walk so he can keep running?" Elise gestured in the direction she'd just come from.

"I don't want to keep you—you were heading home." Really, I didn't want to have a conversation with a complete stranger. I'd been looking forward to a quiet morning near the ocean.

"It's no bother. Dave's at home prepping for our Thanksgiv-ing. Only my daughter Azure and her family were able to make the trip this year. She lives in Virginia."

"Oh? Where abouts?" I slowed. Beckett had given up stalking

birds and plopped himself on the sand just out of the reach of the early morning tide. He was using a shell shard to dig in the wet sand by his leg.

"In the southwestern part of the state. You're from up near DC, is that right?"

"That's where Scott lives, yes. I've only been there since September." I definitely didn't consider myself from Northern Virginia. I wasn't sure I ever would. It was a fine place to live—I couldn't complain, really, but it wasn't California. Or Kansas.

Elise nodded.

The pause in the conversation felt awkward. It was probably my turn to say something, but I just wanted her to go and leave me to hang with Beckett. If Elise weren't there, I'd plop down next to him and see if we could try to shape the mound of sand he was creating into something. If he got to pick, it'd probably be a car not a castle, but I wasn't picky.

"You and Dave have other kids?" There. That should get her talking, shouldn't it? Everyone loved to talk about their family.

"Dave never had children, but my kids all love him. I have six others. They're all married and settled at the ranch in Northern New Mexico that my first husband's parents' own. We'll head out that way in December to spend Christmas with everyone on the ranch. Maybe get some skiing in."

My eyebrows lifted. I didn't necessarily associate skiing with New Mexico, but I also wasn't a big fan of the sport. I didn't have the coordination necessary. And there weren't exactly a ton of mountains in Kansas to make practice easy and accessible.

"You don't ski."

She hadn't phrased it as a question, but I shook my head anyway. I reached out and grabbed Beckett's hand before he got the shell shard to his mouth. "Beckett. You know better."

Elise chuckled. "Seems like they always have to try."

"Maybe so, but I'd as soon not explain to Scott why Beckett has sand around his mouth."

"How long have you been married?"

I frowned. "I'm not? I'm Beckett's nanny."

"Oh." Elise pressed her lips together, clearly deep in thought. After a moment, she shook her head. "I must have misheard Dave. How long have you been doing that?"

"Since September." I was dying to ask what she thought she misheard, but I also kind of didn't want to know. In fact, I was reasonably certain I didn't want to know. Even if I was curious.

"Do you like it?"

"I love Beckett, and I love that I get to spend my days taking care of him." It wasn't the most direct answer, but it worked. I couldn't say I loved being a nanny, though. I wouldn't want to do it for just anyone. It wasn't as if I felt like I had some deep calling to raise other people's children for the rest of my life. In fact, I still felt that draw to theater and the assurance that God wanted me to act. I just had to figure out how to do both, because I didn't want to let Beckett go. He needed me.

Elise smiled. I got the feeling she understood some of the things I left unsaid. She rubbed her hands together and glanced at her watch. "Oh, is that the time? Dave's going to send out a search party. I'll let you go. It was nice to meet you. I hope you have a great time while you're here."

"Thanks. Happy Thanksgiving." I waved as Elise turned and hurried down the beach toward the path that would take her to the neighborhood. With a sigh, I got my phone out of my pocket to check the time. It wasn't that late. Just in case, I sent Scott a quick text letting him know where we were. Hopefully, he'd set his phone on "do not disturb" so I didn't undo all my effort to not wake him by letting him know where we were.

I angled myself so I'd be on drier sand, and sat near Beckett.

"Want to make something with all that sand or are you happy scooping?"

Beckett looked at me, his face a picture of concentration. "Scooping."

"Okay. You keep scooping." I tipped my head back and let the cool morning breeze from the water wash over me. All that was missing was Scott. I could picture him here with us. He'd dig in the sand—or maybe he'd be brave enough to take Beckett out into the waves. I sure wasn't. I liked the beach well enough, and I enjoyed wading, but once the water was up past my knees, I was out. People who swam in the ocean confused me.

My phone buzzed in my pocket. I tugged it free and smiled before answering. "Hi, Mom. Happy Thanksgiving."

"You're up. I'm so glad. I was worried I'd wake you. Then I thought no, of course I won't, she's in charge of a three-year-old."

I laughed. "He was up right on time. Doesn't matter that his routine was off yesterday with the trip to Florida."

"How is it?"

I put the phone on speaker and held the microphone toward the water for a few seconds. "Hear that?"

"Bliss. I've got to convince your father to take me to the beach this summer. Maybe we can get down to Galveston."

"I'll try to put a bug in his ear when we come visit." I smiled. Dad would take her once he knew she wanted to go. He was still so ridiculously in love with my mom. Sometimes it was embarrassing. Except also? I wanted that.

"Looking forward to it! It's strange having no one here for Thanksgiving—which you are not allowed to take as me trying to make you feel guilty. It's a statement only. I promise."

"You know me too well. Where'd Wendy and Mark go?" I hadn't talked to my sister in a while. We texted, but she was not on board with me being a live-in nanny for a single man, so things were strained. It absolutely hadn't helped when Scott and I started dating.

Mom sighed. "She still giving you a hard time?"

"She's not wrong. I am, technically, living with a man to whom I'm not married. The fact that we have a perfectly platonic arrangement and I have my own floor of the house that no one ever goes to except me is beside the point. The optics aren't great. I get it."

"So why are you still doing it? Especially now that you and Scott have a relationship?"

I closed my eyes for a minute. When I opened them, my gaze landed on Beckett. He was still studiously scooping the sand out of his hole. "Because Beckett needs me."

"Hmm."

"What's that mean?"

"I just wonder sometimes if he needs you or you need him." Mom cleared her throat. "Anyway. I support your choices, you know that. And I trust you to live your life the way you were raised to live it. It does make me sad that you and your sister are fighting, but you've always gotten over it in the past, so I'm praying that continues."

"Thanks, Mom," I murmured. It wasn't a ringing endorsement. She supported my choices, but didn't approve of them. And maybe approval was too much to ask. I wasn't going to let it matter. Not right now. "So. Wendy?"

"Right. Mark's parents flew in to Wichita. They couldn't be bothered to make the drive out to Gilead, so Wendy, Mark, and the kids drove over."

I winced. Mom was hurt. "Are you sure they knew you'd invited them to stay with you?"

"Oh, I'm sure. I called Carla personally. It's fine. They're used to the city and don't understand why anyone would be happy in a backwater town."

I bristled. "Gilead is hardly backwater."

"I know. I shouldn't have said anything. You know how Mark's parents are. They grate on my last nerves. I don't understand how someone so wonderful came from people like that."

I snickered. It wasn't the first time Mom had said something along those lines. It was unlikely to be the last. Mark really was great, though, and he suited my sister, Wendy, to the ground. "Are the kids excited to see their other grandparents?"

"Of course. Because Mark's parents always bring expensive electronic toys. Wendy said she'd heard Mark trying to talk them out of a Nintendo Switch."

"Aw, they'd have fun with that."

"Each."

"Oh." I bit my lip. "That's probably overkill for a four- and six-year-old."

"Anyway. Mark generally handles his parents and the gifts, so I'm sure this won't be any different. I'm just not used to having a completely empty nest."

"I'm sorry, Mom. I should have come home." I watched as Beckett stood and started kicking the big pile of sand he'd made. I stood and scooted out of the way of the flying grit.

"No. You have your job. I'll be fine. This is how life goes. I'm just a little melancholy. I'm glad both my girls have spread their wings and found their calling."

Her words speared my heart. "About that."

"What?"

"I'm not...I don't..." I broke off and sighed. "I was having another conversation this morning about being a nanny. And it's not my calling. I still feel that nudge to act. But Beckett needs me. I honestly believe that. But now I'm confused."

"I'm sorry, honey." Mom paused and I could tell she was carefully thinking through her response. Which meant it was unlikely to be something I wanted to hear. "I know you say he needs you, but I'm going to encourage you to watch with an open mind and see if it's true or if it's just something you want to be true."

Ouch. "Okay. And then what? What if you're right? Then what do I do?"

"Well. I know you don't have a ton of love for Gilead, but there's an opening at the college. Full time. They want someone with a performing arts degree. Honestly? It sounds like it's tailor-made for you."

"They won't have any trouble filling that, Mom. It's full time? Tenure track? Pfft. It's probably already filled." It wasn't as if teaching positions for performing arts were plentiful.

"They're having trouble. It's been open since mid-August. None of the candidates have been what they're looking for. It's serious enough they've asked the faculty to add it to the prayer lists of their churches."

Something stirred in my heart. It was a lot like longing. "Could you...maybe send me the listing?"

"Of course." Mom sounded confused. "It's on the college website, too, but I'll pop a link in a text. You know I love you, right?"

"I do know that. I love you, too. I should probably get Beckett back to the cottage we're renting and get him cleaned up. I don't want to make us late for Thanksgiving with Scott's folks."

"If they don't love you, there's something wrong with them."

I laughed. "Thanks, Mom. Tell Dad I said hi."

"I will. Can't wait to see you next month."

"Me, too. Bye." I ended the call. For the first time in a long time, I was low-key excited about getting back to Gilead. I didn't want to analyze it much further. Instead, I reached for Beckett's sandy hand. "Let's head back, bud. You're going to need a quick shower before anything else happens today."

He grinned at me, but he didn't object when I started us back toward the house, which was good. My mind was too full of spinning thoughts to do much more than operate on autopilot.

The job had come open in August. Mom hadn't said anything—probably because we'd had too many arguments about Gilead before and she was trying to respect my choices.

It shouldn't matter. I had a job. One I loved. And then there was Scott. Just because—minus being in Kansas—I had a shot at something close to a dream job didn't mean I'd get it. And if I did?

I pinched the bridge of my nose and stopped at the edge of the street. I hiked Beckett up on my hip for the trip across then set him down on the grass. Scott pushed open the screen door and Beckett ran to him. My heart lurched. How was I supposed to choose between a dream job and a dream family?

25

SCOTT

Mom was standing on the front porch when we pulled into the driveway. I laughed and waved at her as she started down the steps to the car. "I guess Mom's excited."

Whitney's smile looked a little sickly.

I rubbed her leg. "Are you okay?"

"Of course. Why wouldn't I be?" She pressed the seatbelt release and pushed open her door.

I wasn't sure why she wouldn't be okay, but it was literally why I asked. If she didn't want to tell me, that was one thing, but she'd been quieter and withdrawn since she and Beckett got back from the beach. Maybe she didn't sleep well. I appreciated that she'd gotten up with Beckett, but I could have done without the extra rest if I'd known it would be a problem for her.

I turned off the engine and got out.

Whitney already had Beckett out of his car seat and perched on her hip.

"There you are! Hi, Beckett. Do you remember me? I'm Renee." Mom had bent down a little so she was at Beckett's eye level.

I held my breath. She and Beckett had gotten along well when Mom and Dad came for their visit in the fall, but it had been a while. Would he remember her?

"Hi!" Beckett held his arms out to my mom.

Mom beamed and reached for him. With Beckett settled on her hip, Mom grinned up at us. "Welcome, Whitney. I'm so glad you could come, too. And of course it's good to see you, Scott."

I chuckled before I glanced at Whitney. She looked unhappy. I crossed to her and took her hand. "Hey. What's going on?"

She shook her head. "It's nothing. Look at him, he's really happy to see her. And do you hear him?"

It took me a minute to realize what she meant. Beckett had started jabbering at Mom. Not his usual one or two words strung together, but a full-on conversation about his trip to the beach. "Wow."

Whitney's gaze was fixed on Mom and Beckett. "I never met Carol—Shelby Ann's mom—but does your mom look like her?"

I pursed my lips. I wouldn't have said so. That said, I wasn't exactly positive I'd know my aunt Carol on the street. "Let's go inside. Maybe we can find a picture."

"You don't know?"

I shook my head. "Mom's side of the family is complicated. We didn't do a lot with them growing up."

Whitney frowned and looked like she was going to say more, but she didn't. I put it aside and we climbed the steps behind Mom and went into the house.

I hadn't spent a ton of time at their house in Florida. I'd pretty much told Mom and Dad to find something they liked and I'd buy it for them. And that was what they'd done. Now, looking around, I approved all over again. They had good taste in homes. Or Mom did. I was fairly certain Dad would have been fine with anything Mom said she wanted.

"Dad's in the great room with the TV on. He might switch

away from pregame nonsense to a parade if you ask nicely." Mom leaned in and nuzzled Beckett's nose with hers. "Beckett and I are going to go check on the rolls. Right?"

"Right! Butter? Rolls need butter." Beckett had taken Mom's face in his hands and was looking at her seriously.

"Lots of butter." Mom laughed as she disappeared into the kitchen with Beckett.

Still holding Whitney's hand, I made my way into the great room. Dad was watching the parade. I chuckled. "Mom said you were watching football."

Dad grinned. "Not on yet. Macy's Parade just started though. You're a little early. Thought you weren't coming until noon or so."

I shrugged. "Everyone was ready and we figured there'd be better snacks here."

Dad's laugh filled the room. "You got that right. But you have to be the one to get her to part with them. I've been asking for twenty minutes and she keeps saying not till you get here."

"I can go." Whitney tugged her hand away. "Maybe she needs some help."

"Nah. You sit yourself down and let the boy go. He's her favorite, anyway." Dad winked at Whitney. "Besides, you're a guest."

"He's not wrong. I'll go. Sit down and get comfortable. I won't be long." I touched her shoulder, hoping it was bolstering, before heading to the kitchen.

I stopped in the doorway of the kitchen. All I could do was grin. Mom and Beckett had their heads together, chattering about the sheet trays full of rolls.

I cleared my throat. "I hate to interrupt, but Dad said something about snacks."

"I wanna snack." Beckett's eyes grew wide. "You give me snack?"

"Of course, sweet boy." Mom turned to the fridge.

"I thought I was your sweet boy." I crossed my arms and arched a brow at Mom.

"You both are." She shook her head, eyes rolling heavenward. "And you can both have a snack."

"Smells divine in here."

Mom's cheeks reddened and she waved away my comment. "It's just the turkey. Get the appetizer platter out of the fridge, would you?"

I did as I was told and pulled open the fridge door. The tray would've been hard to miss. I smiled as I tugged it out and looked under the plastic wrap that covered it. "We're not going to need the turkey. This is a good meal in itself."

"Please. You know how your father is with Thanksgiving food. He'll eat until he's about to cry and then stuff one more bite in for good measure."

I laughed. That had certainly been the tradition as long as I could remember.

"What do you say, Beck? You want to bring the snacks into the room with the TV and watch the parade?"

Beckett glanced between Mom and me. "Nee is coming?"

Mom looked around the kitchen and shrugged. "I can come for a bit, sure. Let's go, champ."

Beckett slipped his hand into Mom's.

I picked up the tray and headed out into the great room. Whitney was tucked onto the far corner of a couch. Dad was kicked back in his recliner with his feet out. I put the tray on the coffee table and carefully removed the plastic. "Snack time."

"Excellent." Dad pushed his footrest down and leaned forward. "Mm. All our favorites, right, Scott?"

"You know it." I sat on the couch where I could reach the tray, and speared an olive and slice of sausage with a toothpick. I glanced over at Whitney. "Can I fix you a little plate?"

She shook her head and uncurled before sliding over to sit beside me. "This looks delicious. Thank you, Mrs. Wright."

"It's Renee, honey. And you're very welcome. What can I get you, Beckett? You see those little smokies there? Those were Scott's favorite when he was about your age."

"Smokies?" Beckett frowned at the tray before tentatively reaching out.

"That's right. Those right there. And maybe some cheese?" Mom loaded up a napkin as she spoke. She set it on the table, lowered herself to the floor with a quiet grunt, then patted the carpet beside her. "Have a seat here by me and give this a try."

Beckett dropped onto the spot she patted and stuffed a sausage in his mouth.

I grinned and did the same. "How's the parade?"

"You missed a really nice marching band. I think they were from Iowa." Whitney stabbed an olive with a toothpick.

She was definitely off, but this probably wasn't the place to try to get her to talk about it. Maybe it was nerves. I reached over and took her hand.

Mom glanced up and caught my eye with a knowing look. "So."

"Leave the boy alone, Renee." Dad cut her off with a laugh. "Whitney's nervous, anyway. Don't make it harder on her."

"You don't need to be nervous. We're so glad you're here." Mom looked at Whitney. "Maybe I should let you help in the kitchen, then you'll see."

Dad chuckled.

I shifted in my seat. "You don't have to, Whit."

"No, that's fine. I'd be happy to help if you could use me." Whitney started to stand.

"We've got a little time yet, but I'll take you up on it when we're ready." Mom smiled gently then looked over at Beckett who was tugging on her sleeve. "What's up, little man?"

"I can have more smokies?"

"You definitely can." Mom snagged several more and put them on Beckett's napkin.

Whitney stiffened and drew in a breath like she was about to speak. I imagined she wasn't happy about the pre-meal snack. It was sometimes a challenge to get Beckett to eat. But, as far as I could tell, if he was going to fill up on sausage, cheese, and maybe some vegetables? It was still a win. I was positive Mom would send leftovers back to the cottage with us later. Beckett could have turkey and mashed potatoes then.

We watched the parade together for about a half hour. We didn't sit in silence or anything—there were oohs and ahhs over the floats, snarky comments by Mom and Dad about the commentators, that kind of thing. In all, it was just like I remembered every Thanksgiving of my life. Except this time, Beckett and Whitney were there. And that made it better. More complete.

I'd never spent much time wondering about a family. I kind of figured if God wanted me to get married and have kids, He'd make it obvious. Dropping Whitney and Beckett into my lap felt pretty obvious to me, once I got over the initial irritation about the change in my routines, at least.

As yet another high school marching band played something heavy on the brass, Mom pushed herself to her feet and glanced at Whitney. "Did you want to help? It's fine if you'd rather stay here."

"I can help!" Beckett jumped up and grasped Mom's hand.

Whitney rose. "I'd be happy to."

They disappeared from the room. It might have been ridiculous, but I missed them.

"So." Dad lowered the volume on the parade with the remote. "You're dating the nanny, eh?"

"Dad." I winced. "Could you not phrase it that way? Her name's Whitney."

Dad chuckled. "Always was easy to get a rise out of you."

I shook my head. "But yes. It's going well, I think. Although... how well do you know the Fitzgeralds?"

"Dave and Elise?" Dad gave a little shrug. "Pretty well, I think. They've been down here two years, I think they said. Your mom and Elise hit it off right away at church. I'd say we spend at least every other Friday night hanging out. Why?"

"Dave said something yesterday." I frowned. I'd been trying not to let his words burrow into my subconsciousness, but I obviously hadn't been successful. "Do you think it's wrong that Whitney and I effectively live together?"

Dad's eyebrows lifted. "I hadn't looked at it that way."

"Right?" I nodded, feeling justified. "She's Beckett's nanny. Nannies tend to live with their charges, right?"

"I'll be honest, I really only have the movies your mom makes me watch to go by. But if they're accurate, then yes."

Ugh. I'd offered to get her her own place at the start. There had been that twinge of conscience that suggested I needed to. But it definitely would have complicated things. I rubbed between my eyes. "Is it a thing that if someone's words make you defensive, you're probably doing something wrong?"

Dad offered a slight smile. "I wouldn't say it's a rule, but it's probably a good idea to spend some time thinking and praying about things."

I sighed. "Yeah. I'm not trying to make people wonder. Part of me feels like if they're getting the wrong idea, it's a 'them problem.' You know?"

"I do. But."

I waited for Dad to continue. He'd done this my whole life— end a sentence like that then wait and collect his thoughts a moment before going on. Especially when it was something he knew I probably wasn't going to like.

Dad cleared his throat. "Are we, as Christians, called to live in a manner that leaves no room for people to have a 'them problem,' as you put it? At least to the best of our ability?"

I knew the answer was yes. Dad's rhetorical questions were almost always answered with yes. "Paul was pretty clear on that."

"He was, wasn't he? Now, of course, you can argue that Paul isn't God."

I gave a short laugh. "Are we doing this, Dad? I don't want to argue the inerrancy of the Bible with you. I believe it's the inspired word of God, okay? I get it. Paul isn't God, but the words he wrote were inspired by God. So yeah. I shouldn't be doing anything that could cause someone else—believer or not—to stumble. Like live with a woman who isn't my wife."

I could say the words, but I had no idea what to do about it.

"If it helps any, which it probably doesn't, it might have been slightly less of a problem when it was clear the two of you had a solely professional relationship. But now that you're dating? You've definitely muddied the waters."

I sighed.

Where did that leave me?

There were all kinds of options, I didn't happen to love any of them, though. I could break up with Whitney. That was an immediate no-go as far as I was concerned. Now that I had her in my life that way? I didn't want to stop.

I could get her her own place. She had a car. She could come over in the morning before I left for work and leave when I got home. More like a babysitter than a nanny. And in reality, maybe it was the best option of those available. Beckett was doing great at night. He rarely had any problems and I was perfectly capable of handling them if he did.

But I'd miss knowing she was there. And lately, she'd hung around with us downstairs after dinner. Like a family.

Maybe she could still do that. She'd just shift from work mode to girlfriend mode when I got home. It wasn't all that different from what she did now. Except she'd have to get in the car and go home at bedtime. Or probably sooner, given that she had to travel.

Owning another townhouse in Old Town wasn't a bad idea. I looked at Dad. "Real estate's a good investment, right?"

"Can be. Depends on the location."

"I was thinking I could see if there was another townhome in our neighborhood."

Dad grinned. "Cut down on her commute as much as possible?"

"Something like that." I still didn't like it. I didn't want to miss out on seeing her bleary-eyed and bed-headed as she poured that first cup of coffee in the morning. I wanted those opportunities to sneak a kiss.

"You know your mom would love to have you and Beckett stay here while you're visiting. We've got the room." There was the tiniest hint of censure in Dad's voice.

"I know. I guess she'll get her way. If I can convince Whitney of it." Mom had been pushing for all of us to stay here. Was it okay because they were chaperones? Probably. But I'd thought Beckett would need a quiet, safe space. He'd enjoyed my parents when they visited, but it was nothing like this. Honestly, if he and I didn't stay here, I wasn't positive I'd be able to get him in the car when it was time to leave. "Or maybe even if I can't. Does Mom look like Aunt Carol?"

Dad chuckled. "Oh, yes. And Shelby Ann looked enough like your mom that the few times we were all together, people thought Shelby Ann was ours."

That probably explained that. Was it a good thing or a bad

one, though? Beckett didn't seem to be confusing them in his head—he called Mom "Nee." Maybe it was simple comfort. "Last question."

"Doesn't have to be unless you're out of them." Dad winked at me. "You know I love giving advice."

It was true. I had a lot of childhood memories of Dad sitting behind a newspaper reading the advice columns and giving his take. I remember his advice often sounding better to my ears, but that could have been because I adored my dad. "Is it weird to you that I keep working for Robinson Enterprises even though I don't need to?"

"What else would you do?"

I pointed at him. "This is my question. I could find things. There's contract work I could chase. I don't have a burning desire to start my own company, but I could. I could help you with the money management."

"Hey. That's my job." Dad grinned. "As long as you're not planning to lie on the beach all day every day. Do you want to work at Robinson?"

That was a question I didn't know how to answer. I didn't mind it. Some days I even enjoyed it. Did I feel like it was fulfilling some great purpose in my life? No.

"That's a lot of silence." Dad cocked his head to the side. "I thought you liked it there."

"I don't not like it."

Dad snorted. "Not quite the same thing."

"I know. But I mean, it's not a *bad* job." I rubbed my hands on my legs. "I guess I need to pray more about that, too."

"Prayer is good. Thinking, too. Because I believe it's important to make sure you aren't changing for the sake of change. If you're content and making a difference, why not stay put? Although I say that and I know your mother would love it if you'd move down here. Seems to me you could do that if you were consulting. If you're the boss, you get to make the work-from-home rule, right?"

I chuckled. "I do. And seeing Beckett here with Mom, I'm tempted. His therapists have been stumped at his lack of progress, and I think they'd be amazed to see him now, jabbering away. Would it be better for him, healthier, if we were down here?"

"I couldn't say."

I glanced at Dad and shook my head a little. He could say. He just wouldn't. Because Dad never liked to pressure anyone to do things unless it was a last resort. "Thanks, Dad."

"My pleasure." Dad glanced over his shoulder toward the kitchen. "Since the ladies seem to be spending a longer time in the kitchen than I imagined, you mind if we switch over to the pregame?"

"I was hoping you'd ask."

26

WHITNEY

"You're back!" Megan darted out from behind the cash register as soon as I stepped through the bookstore door, and pulled me into a tight hug. "How was it? Tell me everything. Start with the plane. I'm so jealous you already got to use it."

I laughed and some of the tension in my shoulders eased. I hadn't realized how badly I needed a friend who just cared about me for me, not because I could do something for her. "Are you in on this big Caymans trip in December? You'll get to fly then, right?"

Megan nodded. "Austin finally wore me down. I don't like asking him to pay for all of this for me."

"But you didn't ask. He offered."

"What are you, an FBI wiretap? Those are his words exactly." Megan shook her head. "So okay, yes. Maybe I'm stubborn about paying my own way on things. I'm working on it. Starting with the trip, yes, and then...he convinced me to give my notice and let him help with the bookstore."

"Really?" I clapped my hands in excitement. "That's fantastic!"

Megan waggled a hand from side to side. "I liked knowing I was helping people."

"You'll find a way to keep helping. I know you." I rubbed her shoulder. "I'm glad you get to go to the Caymans. It wouldn't have been right otherwise."

"Please. Like you're going to notice anyone other than Scott and Beckett." Megan winked. "Now. Stop avoiding the topic and tell me about the plane. And your Thanksgiving."

I smiled. The plane was easy—and fun. The rest of the trip? Well, that was why I was here. I needed to talk to someone about it. Maybe Megan would have some ideas of what to do.

"The plane is amazing. Leather chairs—and not in rows like commercial. They're more like couches or recliners. There are some tables that you can extend between seats, if you arrange them to face each other." I searched my memory for more to tell her, but came up blank. As amazing as the ride had been, it was still a plane. And she'd get to see it when we all went down to the Caribbean at Christmas.

Megan let out a long, satisfied sigh. "That sounds amazing. I can't wait. Are we all going to fit?"

"I can't see it being an issue."

"Excellent. So you flew down and then what?"

I picked up a stack of books from the corner of the shelves, glanced at the titles, and carried them with me to their location. "Scott rented an SUV so we drove to the beach cottage he rented for us to stay in. It wasn't a long drive, but Beckett still fell asleep. He wouldn't settle on the plane. Anyway, I stayed in the car while Scott got us checked in with the owner, then we drove around some while Beck napped, and ended up at a local seafood shack for dinner. We made it an early night."

"Man, I miss the beach. I haven't been in years. And even then, it was just Virginia Beach. Which, don't get me wrong, it's a nice place." Megan shrugged. "But it's not the same as Florida."

"Nothing is." I grinned. Even California beaches were different from Florida.

"And Thanksgiving?"

I finished reshelving the books as I told her about my walk on the beach with Beckett and the day at Scott's parents. Megan made a big deal out of how Beckett came out of his shell and I had to agree, it was amazing. But it also made things harder.

"I know Scott is wondering what to do. Since we got home, Beckett is still talking, but we're both worried he's going to regress. And then what? More therapy? All the doctors? When being near his great-aunt could fix it without that?"

"Oof. That's tough."

It was. "It's worse."

Megan's eyebrows shot up. "How?"

I glanced around. The bookstore was empty, but it never hurt to check. I made my way to one of the overstuffed chairs in the reading area and sat.

Megan followed. "Tell me."

"I was talking to my mom on Thursday morning at the beach. You know my sister's been giving me a hard time about living with Scott? I guess Mom agrees, deep down, even though she's trying to be supportive." I frowned. The words still stung. Scott and I weren't doing anything wrong. Why did it have to be a problem? "And then she tells me there's a job at the Bible college back home that's basically my dream. Or my backup dream."

"Backup dream?"

I chuckled, a little self-conscious. "Sure. My dream dream is movies. But let's be real, that's never going to happen. Backup dream? Teaching acting and being part of the big productions they put on. The Passion play for sure, but the college has two big productions a year in addition to that."

Megan nodded slowly. "You should apply."

"Should I? I just...there's Beckett. And now Scott. It's *Kansas*, Megan. That's not exactly going to lure Scott into wanting to follow me." I sighed. "And it feels like Beckett would be better in Florida, anyway."

"What do you want to do?" Megan waited until I met her gaze. "Deep down."

"I want to apply." I closed my eyes as the words came out. It felt like a betrayal of so much to admit it though. If I got the job, I'd be leaving Scott. Leaving Beckett. And it wasn't like I could ask him to do the long-distance thing. This wasn't a temporary job. It wasn't a situation where we just had to make it a few weeks or months and then we could be together again. I'd be choosing Kansas. For the foreseeable future.

"Then apply. You don't know for sure you'll even get it."

I blew out a breath. "That's true. Should I tell Scott?"

"Hmm. That's trickier."

I could list reasons for both choices. "I should, right? People in relationships tell each other everything. Don't they?"

"Probably, yeah. I just hate to see you cause problems in your relationship and then, worst case scenario, you don't get the job. And then what?"

I let my head drop back against the chair and frowned. This was the circle I'd been trapped in every time I thought about the job possibility. "There might already be problems."

"What do you mean?"

"Scott's been acting weird since Thanksgiving. He and Beckett stayed at his folks' house. Scott dropped me off at the cottage each night and picked me up again in the morning. Now he's looking at real estate in the neighborhood...and I'm pretty sure he's decided I can't live there with them anymore. But he hasn't said anything about it, so I don't know."

"So ask him." Megan crossed her arms. "If he's planning to

kick you out of your home, the least he can do is talk to you about it."

"I guess. I don't really understand why...or maybe I do. I don't know." I looked up and met Megan's gaze. "Do you think it's bad that we're living together?"

Megan's eyebrows disappeared under her bangs. "I never really thought about it."

That was something at least. I felt a little better. Mom's and my sister's comments had lodged in my head. "Not even once Scott and I started dating?"

Megan shook her head. "But now that you mention it, I'm not sure I'll be able to get it out of my head."

"I guess I need to talk to him about it. Get it out in the open."

"Talking is always good. It's the mature, adult thing to do, right?"

I laughed. It was. Megan and I had talked about too many books where the main characters didn't bother to talk out their problems before going nuclear. I had to admit that in this situation, it was still tempting. But no. That wouldn't do at all. "Right. I guess I should mention the job possibility, too. I don't want him to buy another house if I could end up moving back to Kansas before the end of the year anyway."

"Oh, man. I don't like the sound of that. I was all in on the dream job thing until I realized it meant you'd be leaving. I've changed my mind. Don't apply. You probably won't get hired anyway, so why risk disappointment?" Her smile betrayed the words.

I shook my head. "Nope. Too late. You already encouraged me to apply. No going back on it now."

The bell over the door jingled and Megan stood. "Hi. Can I help you find anything?"

My cell started ringing, so I didn't hear the older man's reply. I glanced at the screen before answering. "Hi, Mom. What's up?"

"Whitney? Oh, thank goodness. I don't know what to do."

Everything seemed to freeze for a moment before my heart took off at double-time. "What happened? Is it Dad?"

"No. Your father's fine. He's driving. We're on our way to Wichita. It's your sister."

"Wendy?" My mind was racing and I was trying to stay calm, even as panic tried to crawl up my throat. "Can you take a breath and start again at the beginning?"

Mom's breathing was loud over the phone, but I could tell she was trying to calm down. "Mark and Wendy were on their way home. There was an accident. The State Police called because I was listed in Wendy's phone. Mark is..." Mom's breath hitched. "They had to use the helicopter. I keep thinking of calling Mark's parents to see what they know, but..."

I swallowed the lump in my throat as my mind raced. "What about Wendy and the girls?"

"I don't know. No one was giving us any information over the phone." Mom's breath caught. "I'm praying that means they're maybe not as serious. But the sinking feeling in my stomach says that's dumb."

I closed my eyes and tried to keep from sobbing. "I'll try to get a flight out as soon as I can."

"You will? Oh, honey, thank you. I didn't want to ask. I know you're busy. But I want you home. I know we're going to need you."

"Do you want me to call Mark's mom?" I got along with her better than Mom did—mostly because I didn't have any skin in the game. I wasn't vying for anyone's attention. I was just Wendy's sister.

"Could you?"

"I'll do it right now and call you back. Love you. Tell Dad to be careful."

"I will, honey, thank you."

I ended the call and sat, staring at my phone for a moment. I expected tears. A moment ago I hadn't thought I'd be able to keep them back. But now there was nothing more than my racing heart. I sent my jumbled thoughts heavenward, trusting God to figure out what I was asking for, and scrolled through my contacts until I found Mark's mom. I hit call.

She answered on the second ring, tears drenching her voice. "Whitney?"

"Hi, Mrs. Ericson. Mom called me. I'm going to fly out, but she didn't have much information other than the hospital. Dad's driving them to town right now. Is there any more news?" The words sounded awkward to my ears, but I didn't know how I could have phrased it better.

"They're all in surgery. Mark, Wendy, and both girls. No one is saying anything other than that their injuries are extensive and they'll come out to tell us more when they know more. I overheard someone talking about coding in the helicopter, but I don't..." Her words disappeared into sobs.

Oh, Jesus. I closed my eyes. I didn't know how to finish the prayer. "I'm sorry. I'll be there as soon as I can. I'll let my parents know."

"Okay." The call ended.

I lurched to my feet and headed for the door.

"Whit? Everything okay?"

I shook my head at Megan and waved her off. "I'll text you later. I have to go."

It didn't take long for me to get home. I must have looked a little crazed, because Scott glanced over from where he was relaxing on the couch and then stood. "What happened? Are you all right?"

"I need to get home. My sister and her family are in the hospital. Big wreck. I'm short on details. I need to see when I can get a flight out." I started toward the stairs. I needed to get to my laptop and start looking at the airlines. At least National Airport was close, so I could make something that was leaving soon without too much trouble.

"Let me have the plane take you. I just need to text the guys and make sure no one's using it. I can get a pilot within an hour."

I blinked and turned. I hadn't even thought of asking. I watched as he typed on his phone. It pinged quickly after and he looked up. "We're set. Go pack. I'll get a pilot and take you to the airport."

"You can't take me. I'll call an Uber. You need to stay with Beckett. Or should I take him with me?" I bit my thumbnail as I tried to work out the logistics of handling an active three-year-old while also helping my parents and, hopefully, my sister and her family once they were released from the hospital.

"Don't be silly. I've got him. And I'll call Austin and see if he can grade papers here in case Beckett needs something. You're not taking a rideshare to the airport for something like this. Go pack. Let me handle the details."

I rushed across the room and threw my arms around him. "Thank you."

"You're welcome." He pressed a soft kiss to my lips and then my forehead. "Go pack."

I hurried up the stairs to my room as tears pricked my eyes. I blindly grabbed clothes out of my drawers and stuffed them into my duffel. In the bathroom, I loaded toiletries into my makeup bag and tossed it on top of my clothes, then looked around my room blankly. I was probably forgetting something. Or a lot of things.

My gaze landed on my laptop. That would be useful. As would my Kindle. I grabbed them, having remembered charging cords at the last minute, and added them to the duffel. It would have to do. It wasn't like I couldn't buy whatever I forgot in Kansas.

Or I could live without.

I hefted the bag and headed back downstairs. I stopped on the second floor and tiptoed to Beckett's room, gingerly pushing open the door so I could peek in. He was sprawled in his bed, peacefully sleeping. I set my bag down just outside his room and picked my way carefully across the carpet—they hadn't done the bedtime cleanup routine today, apparently. I gently brushed the hair off his forehead and whispered a kiss across it.

My heart wrenched as I made my way back out to the hall to collect my bag and finish heading downstairs. I didn't like leaving him. It wasn't that Scott wasn't perfectly capable of taking care of him. He was. But I loved Beckett like he was my own.

"Ready?" Scott was waiting at the bottom of the stairs. He reached for my duffel. "Austin should be here any minute and then we can leave. I've got a pilot on the way. She'll probably beat us to the airport."

"Yeah. Please make sure Beckett knows I love him. He can call me—video chat, whatever. Any time. Okay?"

Scott rubbed my arm. "Of course. Don't worry about him. I talked to Mom. After they drop you in Wichita, the plane's going to collect her and bring her and Dad up to help out."

"Oh. That's good." I forced a smile. It was better for Scott, certainly. And Beckett would love having his "Nee" there. But I couldn't help feeling that I was too easily replaced. Which maybe was a good thing. Maybe this was God's way of working things out, although it was a little hard for me to get there when I didn't know what was going on with my sister and her family.

I cleared my throat. "I happened to hear you talking to the real estate lady."

"Oh." Scott winced. "I probably should have talked to you about that first, shouldn't I? I got caught up in the investment side of things. Dave—the cottage owner in Florida? He said a few things that got me thinking. And I talked to my dad, who didn't disagree. Basically, I don't think we should still live together now that we're dating. It sends the wrong signal, you know?"

"My sister has been on my case basically since I took the job, but I've been brushing her off. Turns out my mom agrees, though. I figured something was up when you didn't stay at the cottage anymore."

"I'm sorry." Scott pulled me into his arms. "I've bungled this badly. I should have talked to you in Florida. Forgive me?"

"Yeah. Of course. Just..." I trailed off and took a deep breath. "Maybe hold off on buying another place here. I don't know how long my family's going to need me. And..."

Scott waited, searching my face. I didn't know how to finish the sentence though. After a moment, he gave a single, slow nod. "Oh. I was figuring a week."

I shrugged, helpless to add words to it. A week was a good start, sure, but they didn't bust out the helicopters to the hospital for fun. I had a sinking feeling a week wasn't going to see any of them out of the hospital. "It could be. Or it could be a lot more."

"All right." He pressed his lips together. "Would you mind if my parents stayed in your room?"

"No. Of course not. If they need to box up some of my stuff to make room, whatever, that's fine." It wasn't fine. But none of this was fine. And I didn't know what could ever possibly make it right. I hadn't even mentioned the job. Not that it was my priority right now, but I knew Mom was going to ask me about it. And if we ended up back in Gilead, I'd be interviewing—if they were interested at least. So who was I to say someone else couldn't use my space? Especially when the alternative was a pullout couch in the main living area.

A quiet knock at the door kept Scott from responding.

Which was probably good. He'd say something and I'd have to respond and I was out of words.

"Hey, man. Thanks for this." Scott pulled Austin into a back-slapping hug.

"Please. I can grade papers anywhere." Austin shrugged off the thanks and turned to me. "I'll be praying for your sister."

"Thanks." Maybe Austin's prayers would be more eloquent than the *"please help them"* that was playing on repeat in the back of my brain. "Can you give Megan the basics? I said I'd text her, but it might be tomorrow."

"You got it." Austin headed to the living room and settled on the couch. "Get going. I know where everything I could want is, and if I don't, I'll snoop shamelessly."

Scott laughed. "Help yourself."

I started down the stairs to the garage. Scott had my duffel, and I crossed my arms to keep from feeling like I ought to be doing more than I was.

He was right behind me, reaching around to open the door and then putting my bag in the car while I made my way to the passenger seat and got settled.

"It's going to be okay, Whit." He rubbed my leg before punching the garage door opener and starting the car. "If you need anything, let me know and I'll make it happen. Promise."

I looked at him and tried to smile, but the care and concern on his face pushed my overloaded emotions over the edge, and I burst into tears instead.

I buried my face in my hands and turned toward the window as my shoulders heaved with sobs.

Scott didn't speak. He just backed the car out and took me to meet the plane.

27

SCOTT

I watched from the couch as Beckett made his way sleepily downstairs. Mom and Dad were seated across from me with their coffee. How long would it take him to notice?

"Morning, bud. How'd you sleep?" I smiled, standing as he looked up at me. His gaze darted away and his face split into a grin.

"Nee!" Beckett bolted down the last three stairs and flung himself at Mom.

"Hey there, Beckett." Mom peppered kisses all over his face. "I've been waiting and waiting for you to wake up."

"Was sleepy." He tilted his head then reached up to hold her face in his hands. With a very serious expression, he asked, "Pancakes?"

Mom laughed. "We can do that. If you'll help me in the kitchen."

"I help!" Beckett wiggled off her lap, dropped his teddy and blanket, and zipped toward the kitchen.

Mom shook her head and levered herself up off the couch. "I guess I'm making pancakes. I'm assuming you have what we need?"

"If you're okay with the boxed baking mix."

"Oh, Scott. Really?" Mom frowned at me. "How hard is it to measure flour, baking powder, and sugar?"

I shrugged. "Not hard. This is even easier though."

She made a rude noise and headed into the kitchen.

Dad chuckled. "Don't suppose there's bacon in there they could make, too?"

"Probably." I leaned over and hollered toward the kitchen. "Mom? Dad wants bacon."

"Bacon!" Beckett started chanting.

Dad grinned. "That ought to do it."

"Sounds like." I reached for my coffee mug and sipped. "I really appreciate you coming up."

"You know we're happy to do it. Have you heard anything?"

I shook my head. Whitney had texted me last night when she arrived. I'd already known she'd reached the airport because the pilot had informed me, but I was grateful to place her at the hospital with her family. "Everyone was still in surgery. That didn't seem like a particularly good thing. It'd been hours."

Dad nodded and drank from his mug. "You don't have details on the accident?"

"I did some internet sleuthing. I think I found it—if I did, well, they're going to need a miracle. A semi swerved, overcorrected, and jackknifed. This caused another semi to swerve, but there was nowhere, really, for him to go, so he plowed into the barrier wall, crushing at least two cars in the process."

"Oh wow." Dad covered his mouth.

"Yeah. I almost wish I hadn't gone looking. They have two little girls. The youngest is just a little older than Beckett." I glanced toward the kitchen, my stomach twisting. I couldn't fathom waiting at the hospital if something happened to him. And he'd only been mine for three months. Would it be worse if you'd been the parent all along? Though from what Whitney said, neither her sister nor her brother-in-law were in a place to know yet. "It's tragic."

"That's exactly the word. Is it too soon to check in this morning?"

"Do you think I should?" I'd been planning to give her space and let her take the lead on any contact. I couldn't imagine that she had a lot of bandwidth for keeping me in the loop.

"Definitely. You can let her know you don't need her to reply unless she has time, but I think she'd like to know you care." Dad fixed me with a steady gaze. "You do care, don't you?"

"I do." I already missed her more than I wanted to admit. "I'm not sure how smart it is, though."

"What do you mean? The two of you practically oozed love all over every space you were in at Thanksgiving."

My face heated and I took a long drink of coffee to try and steady. "I fumbled the whole house thing. Just started looking at listings without talking to her about it."

"Scott. You know the key to a good relationship is communication."

"I do. I got caught up in the investment property mindset and forgot I was basically deciding her future home for her. Turns out, her sister had been giving her grief about it for a while, so when we did talk, it didn't go badly, except..."

Dad raised his eyebrows. "Except?"

I sighed. "She asked me to hold off until she knew how long she was going to be gone."

"Makes sense."

I scowled into my coffee. "Does it? Why isn't she just going for a week or so? I need her here, too."

"Scott." Dad's voice was full of censure.

Well, I did need her. And okay, fine, maybe not as much as her family, but didn't her responsibilities here matter at all? And what about us? I hunched my shoulders. "You're right. I'm being selfish. And...I guess it's forcing some decisions I was trying to avoid having to make."

"Your job?" Dad always did see to the heart of the problem.

"Not that I don't think you and Mom can do a bang-up job, but do you want to be here, alone, caring for Beckett all day for an indeterminate period of time?"

Dad chuckled. "Not indeterminate, no. But we can stay for several weeks. Weren't you planning on going to the Caymans for Christmas? That'd be vacation, right?"

The Caymans. Right. I drained my coffee. "It would be. If I go."

"Why wouldn't you go? You've got plans with your friends. I know Beckett would love those beaches and maybe even snorkeling. Although that could be tricky. Maybe a glass bottomed boat?" Dad drummed his fingers on his knee. "There'll be some way to let him see the fish."

The idea of taking him on my own—being the sole caretaker for Beckett on a vacation like that—stole my breath. I relied on Whitney so much. I was fun Dad—not that I didn't set limits or discipline Beckett, but I wasn't there for all the little decisions during the day. Those were all on Whitney. "Dad. I don't know how to do that."

"Whitney's made it easy for you. Now it's time for you to figure it out."

I swallowed. He was right. Even though it was terrifying. I pinched the bridge of my nose. "What would you do, if you were me?"

"Go to the Caymans." Dad grinned. "It sounds like a fun trip. And I'm sure your friends will help you with Beckett."

"They will. I meant about my job. What would you do?" I looked up and held Dad's gaze.

"You've been praying about it?"

"Yeah."

"No specific leading?"

I sighed. Was there? I'd been praying, but not really listening or looking for a response. "Not unless the current situation counts."

Dad chuckled. "It just might. God uses everything for His purposes."

"I should resign, shouldn't I?" The words didn't hurt like I'd expected them to. In fact, they settled around me and felt right. "Spend this time getting the hang of being a dad. Then, in the new year, hopefully when Whitney's back, I could set up a consulting gig. I don't want to sit at home on my hands doing nothing."

"I don't blame you. That wouldn't sit well with me, either."

I smiled. Dad still hadn't retired. Not with everything he did for me to manage my investments and make sure I didn't become someone who blew through billions with nothing to show for it. "Apples and trees, right Dad?"

"Yep. Both trees, in your case. Your mother wants to talk to you about adding some new ministries to your giving while we're up here. She has slides."

I laughed. Knowing Mom, she probably did. "I can't wait."

"Pancakes." Mom hollered from the kitchen.

I stood, grabbing my empty coffee mug. "Sounds like it's time to eat."

Dad grunted a little as he got to his feet. "Smells like it, too."

I walked into the kitchen with Dad at my side and couldn't stop the smile. Beckett was nearly covered in syrup already and happily stuffing bites of pancake into his mouth. Mom was still manning the stove. And there were plates heaped with pancakes and bacon in the center of the kitchen table waiting for us.

I moved to the coffee machine to refill my mug. The only thing missing that would make the scene perfect was Whitney.

We plowed through the food and kept conversation light.

Casual, even. Beckett hadn't mentioned Whitney, and I wasn't sure how to broach the topic. I knew better than to give him too many details—especially when there was so much unknown—but he had to be told something.

After breakfast, Mom and Beckett disappeared upstairs for a wash and to get dressed. Dad and I addressed the dishes and tidied up the kitchen and before I knew it, he'd headed up to join Mom and Beck, and I was alone.

First order of business? I opened the email app on my phone and let work know that I wouldn't be in until later this afternoon. I also told Stephanie that I'd like to talk to her if she had a minute for a face-to-face. She probably wasn't going to like what I had to say, but Dad was right—this was what needed to happen.

With that taken care of, I sank back onto a kitchen chair and opened a text message to Whitney.

Hey. Just touching base. How are you? How are things?

I hit send and waited. Would she be able to get back to me with any speed? I imagined she was doing a lot of sitting around, but maybe she was busy getting things for the rest of the family. That would be like her. Whitney was a doer.

My phone buzzed with an incoming text and I swiped to read it.

Stressed. A little crazy. Can I call? It's a lot to type.

Yes, of course.

After a moment, my phone rang. I answered. "Hey."

"Hi." Whitney sighed. I could hear hospital noises in the background. The PA system was making sounds a lot like the teacher in the Peanuts cartoons and there were bits and pieces of conversations.

"How's your sister and her family? How are your parents? How are *you*?" I probably should have asked about her first. But

I also wanted her to know I cared about the whole situation. She knew that, right?

She sniffled. "Mark didn't make it out of surgery."

"Oh, Whitney." I closed my eyes. I couldn't imagine the heartbreak her sister must be feeling. The whole family. His parents. Hers.

"The girls and Wendy are all in ICU. They're saying..." her voice hitched and she took a deep breath then blew it out, the sound crackling in my ear. "They're saying not to have too much hope. Wendy's in a coma. The girls are being kept under medically. Their bodies look so small and frail in the hospital beds."

I stayed on the line and listened, helplessly, as she sobbed. I didn't know what to say. There were no words that were going to help. No words that could make it better. And I couldn't even hold her and offer a physical shoulder for her to cry on.

After several minutes, she took slow, shuddering breaths. I pictured her wiping her eyes and trying to steady.

"I don't see how I'll be able to get back before the new year. I'm sorry. I know I'm leaving you in the lurch. And Beckett—but I just don't—"

"Whitney, stop. It's okay. You're where you need to be." I was glad I'd already made the decision to leave my job. I probably would have realized it was what I needed to do after this conversation, but would there have been a small part of me that wondered if she forced my hand? Well, now there wouldn't be.

"I've got things handled here. My parents are up and will help while I work out my two weeks—although I'm hoping they'll let me do that from home so I can start getting the hang of Beckett's routine. When you're able to get back here, we'll be happy to have you. Until then? We're going to be okay."

"You quit your job?" She sniffled again. "Because of this?"

"Not because of you. Not at all. But it was confirmation of

what I knew I needed to do." I wished I could see her face. It would help me understand, at least a little, what she was thinking.

"I'm sorry."

"Don't be. This is the right thing for me. And I can't wait until you're back and I can hold you and we can figure out the future." I winced. Maybe that was a little much, but I wanted her to know I missed her. To know she was needed.

"About that." She took a breath and her words came out fast. "I'm thinking of applying for a job at the college back home. It's once in a lifetime and I know I'd kick myself forever if I didn't at least try."

I blinked and tried to process her words. They didn't make any sense, no matter how I played them in my mind. "I don't... you're what?"

"I know this is terrible timing. Megan convinced me I needed to talk to you about it and then my mom called and I had to rush out here, but it's still...I need to do this. I'll always wonder if I don't." Her voice had taken on a pleading edge.

So I said what she needed to hear, even though it couldn't be further from how I felt. "Of course you do. Of course you should. They'd be crazy not to want you."

Her breath whooshed out, crackling in my ear. "You do understand. Thank you. I was so worried. I know a long-distance relationship isn't ideal, but maybe—especially since you won't be working at Robinson anymore—you could come out and stay for a bit, once things settle down."

I swallowed. "Sure. Of course. It's just a short plane ride, right?"

"Exactly." Relief filled her voice. "Thank you. It's a big weight off my mind to know I have your support. Now I can focus on Mom, Dad, Wendy, and the girls."

"As you should." I was numb. Completely numb from head to toe. "I'm praying for you. We all are."

"I can't tell you how much I appreciate that."

"Of course. Let me know if there's any way for me to help—anything at all. I'll let you go, Whitney. Stay in touch though, okay? Please?"

"I will. Thanks for calling, Scott. I miss you."

"I miss you, too." I ended the call and buried my face in my hands.

28

WHITNEY

"Honey. If you need to go home, we understand. It's been two weeks."

I looked at Mom and shook my head. "No. I need to be here."

Mom pressed her lips together and blinked back tears. "If you're sure. I just don't want you to feel like you have to stay if you need to go. Doesn't Scott need you? And Beckett?"

In the two weeks I'd been in Kansas, I'd texted and called Scott multiple times a day. He was supportive. Encouraging. Considerate. And not once had he said anything about needing me back to care for Beckett. Oh, he said he missed me—and I missed him—but apparently, he and his parents were managing just fine. Beckett barely spent two minutes on the phone with me when I tried to speak to him. So no. They didn't need me.

I shook my head. "Everything seems fine there. They'll be heading to the Caymans for Christmas soon, anyway."

"You should go. It's not going to be much of a Christmas here." Mom reached over and took my hand. She gestured to the hospital waiting room with her other hand. "If your sister stays in a coma, we'll just keep on with our vigil here, taking turns to break up the day. You should go be with people your age. With the man you love."

"I don't think we were to 'love' yet, Mom." I had feelings for Scott, absolutely. But love? Wasn't it too soon for that? At this point, we'd probably never get there. "It's easier to split the time in thirds. I'll stay. Wendy's going to need me when she wakes up."

"If." Mom held my gaze until I looked away. She squeezed my hand. "You heard the doctor the same as I did. The longer she stays in the coma, the less likely she is to come out of it. And if she does, and they tell her about Mark and the girls? That could be enough to—"

"Stop. I know. But I'm not giving up. She has to be okay." Maybe I was being stubborn, but I didn't care. Mark's parents had insisted on having a funeral for him and the girls. The three of them had passed in the four days following the accident. Mark's parents had waited a few days to see if Wendy was going to come out of her coma—or add a fourth to the funeral—but when it became clear that she was hanging on in between, they'd pushed for closure and then headed home. Mom and Dad hadn't had the strength or the heart to fight.

I'd tried, but my parents had convinced me it wasn't worth it. In my heart, I'd known they were right, but I still bristled at the injustice of not waiting for Wendy. They'd been cremated. There was no reason to have deprived her of a chance to say goodbye to her family.

"I know she is. I just think we all need to realize that 'okay' may mean she's healed and in Jesus's arms." Mom took a deep breath and turned to stare at the far side of the room. "If she does wake up here, it's going to be so hard for her."

I nodded. That much was true, but I still wanted my sister alive. I wasn't ready to lose her, too.

"If you're sure you don't want to go, I'm not going to push. I love having you here."

I leaned my head on Mom's shoulder. "I want to be here with you and Dad."

Mom patted my cheek. "Have you given any thought to the job?"

"I sent them my résumé."

"You did? When did you do that?"

"Last week." I hadn't heard anything back yet. I was trying not to read into that, but I was beginning to wonder if they'd be in touch before everything at the college shut down for Christmas break. "My friend, Megan, kept nagging me about it. I mostly did it so she'd stop."

"It's good to have friends like that." She sighed. There was an air of sadness wrapped around resignation in the sound. "You're building a life there, in DC."

"I had a life in LA."

Mom shook her head. "I don't think you did. You were trying, sure, but I don't think it ever clicked. Look how fast you turned your back on it."

"Beckett—"

"Would have been fine with Scott. You know that."

"Well, I know it *now*." I couldn't go back in time and second-guess. I was going to stand by my decision. Beckett had needed me.

"I think you probably knew it then. You like it there, though, in DC?"

"I do." I'd liked it right away. Even when I'd been bunking on Scott's couch in his tiny apartment.

"Do you think Scott would want to come out and visit after they're back from the islands? You'd planned to come out, the three of you, this week. Your father and I would love to meet him."

I would certainly have liked to see him. And Beckett. "I'll ask. I imagine Scott will say it depends on how things are here. He wouldn't want to intrude. And it's not like the extended stay hotel is amazing for hosting guests."

Mom smiled. "That's true. I'm hopeful, though, that we'll be home by then. One way or the other."

None of us wanted a lengthy hospital stay. There'd been some talk of having Wendy transferred to the hospital in Gilead, but for now, at least, it was better if she remained here.

The doors leading to the ICU opened and Dad shuffled through. With his shoulders hunched, he looked older than his years, and I realized that this couldn't go on forever. It would be too much for them to bear.

Mom looked up. "How is she?"

"The same. My voice is giving out and I'm a little hungry."

I stood. "Why don't the two of you go get lunch. Leave the hospital campus. I'll take the afternoon shift and catch an Uber back to the hotel. You guys need a break."

"No, baby. That's too long." Dad shook his head.

Mom reached for his hand. I saw her fingers contract as she squeezed it before standing. "If that's what you want, Whitney. Are you sure?"

"I am. You guys go get lunch and then relax at the hotel. I'll be fine. If that changes, I'll call you." I wondered briefly if this was the wrong decision, but then I saw the look my parents exchanged. Hospital vigils were wearing. For all of us. But what alternative was there? None of us were ready to say, "Oh, I guess this is the new normal." And then go home and go about our business. Maybe after a month? I didn't know. All I knew right now was that I saw how hard this was on my parents, and I had the ability to help a little in this moment. So that was what I was going to do.

I gave each of them a tight hug and watched as they made

their way to the elevators. After a deep breath, I collected my things and went through the doors into the ICU. I paused by the hand sanitizer dispenser and rubbed a squirt on my hands and up my arms a little. I was honestly a little surprised that they didn't have more requirements, but I was also grateful. I walked down the hall and around the corner, passing the main nurses station before I reached the "room" where Wendy was.

The glass wall that separated the space from the hall gave no privacy. There was a door, but it was always open. Other than that, the room held a bed, various machines on carts that the nurses and doctors pushed around periodically, and an uncomfortable, straight-backed visitor chair.

I think the idea was that visitors wouldn't hang around for long, but it wasn't a deterrent to my family.

The quiet, steady beep of the monitor was reassuring.

I set my bag beside the chair and sat. "Well, Wendy, what's new?"

I wasn't aware I'd had that tiny shred of hope that she'd open her eyes and fill me in until she didn't. Stupid. I sighed and took her hand. "Dad's been reading to you. He always loved reading aloud, but I think this is starting to wear on him, so you might think about waking up and giving him a break. Neither he nor Mom are young as they used to be."

My phone buzzed in my pocket. I looked at Wendy. "Do you mind if I get that? It's my phone. No? Thanks."

I got my cell and answered. "Megan. Hey."

"Hey yourself. When are you coming home?"

"You ask me that every time we talk. I don't know. I might not be. We talked about the job. You're the one that pushed me to apply."

"I know, I know. I take it back. I miss you."

I smiled. Her words soothed something I hadn't realized was

raw. "I miss you, too. But aren't you heading to the Caymans next week? You'll be fine."

"Yeah, yeah. You should be joining us."

I closed my eyes. I definitely would love to be getting ready to hop on a plane and fly south to white sand and blue water. It beat every aspect of this. But... "I can't. My parents need me here."

"Scott needs you here. Does that matter at all?" Megan's tone was sharp.

I frowned and held the phone away from my ear to scowl at it. I put it back to my ear. "It does. But I think you're wrong. Every time we talk, he's full of how well Beckett is doing. Even the therapist says it's amazing the progress that he's made. And since Scott left Robinson Enterprises, he's there all day. I'd be superfluous."

Megan made a rude noise. "Are you dense?"

"Hey." I huffed out a breath.

"I'm serious. You don't think he's just telling you that so you don't worry? The man loves you. He knows you need to focus on your family. You really think he's going to tell you he's drowning?"

I licked my lips. "Let's back up a little. He doesn't love me."

"Oh my gosh. You *are* dense."

"No. You're a hopeless romantic who's seeing things. We're friends, definitely. And we have chemistry, I won't deny that. But we've barely been dating six weeks. And I've been gone for two of them. It's too soon for the L word." Why did people keep asking me about love? Love in real life didn't work like in the movies. Not that I'd been in love before, but I just didn't believe it was possible for us to be in love. Not yet.

Megan sighed. "Whitney. I don't know what you're expecting here. You said it yourself. You're friends. You have chemistry.

You're both believers, so you have a solid foundation for your relationship. Can you picture a life without him in it?"

I squeezed my eyes shut and tried to imagine the future. It was hard. There was so much in limbo right now. Picturing beyond tomorrow was a challenge. But even then, the knowledge that Scott wouldn't be here was a quiet ache in my spirit. "If I try, really hard."

"And do you like that future?"

"No. But that doesn't mean—"

"Stop. Maybe it's good you have this time apart. You need to figure things out, because if you're simply playing with him like he's a shiny toy? I'm going to be first in line to kick your butt."

"I'm not playing with him. I care about him. A lot." And okay, maybe that was the same thing as loving him. It was less scary, though. Way, way less scary. "And also? This kind of thing has to be mutual."

"It is."

"I know you say that, but he's not making it clear to me, okay? I get not wanting to stress me out, but he's done such a good job at that he's convinced me he doesn't notice I'm gone." I swallowed. "I've been thinking of asking him to box up my stuff and have it shipped to my parents' place."

"No. You have to come back."

I pressed my fingers to my eyes. Why had Megan pushed me to send in that application if she didn't think I should take the job? Mom seemed convinced it was mine if I wanted it. I wasn't going to say no if they offered. "It just makes sense."

"On what planet?" Megan groaned. "Maybe—and I'm stressing that word—*maybe* if you get the job, it makes sense. But even then, I think you should push for Scott to move out there with you. Just don't do anything until you know one way or the other, okay? Scott's not the only one who loves you."

"Aww. I love you, too." I hadn't had a friend like Megan in...ever.

"See? It's not hard."

I laughed. "It's a little different."

"True enough. But I'm telling you, you belong back here. With Scott and Beckett. Help your folks grieve. Be there for your sister. But then come home."

Her words settled on me like a warm blanket. Home. That wasn't Kansas anymore and I should probably admit it. "We'll see."

"All right. I'll catch you later."

I ended the call and slid my phone under my leg before reaching for my sister's hand again. "I'm not sure how much of that you got, but I'll fill you in. I sure could use some of your sisterly advice if you felt like waking up and giving it to me."

One of the nurses knocked on the doorframe before coming in. "Hi. Whitney, right? The sister?"

"That's me." I let go of Wendy's hand and scooted back in my chair as the nurse did whatever checks she needed to do. She wasn't a talker like some of them were, which was fine. It wasn't like I really had much to say right now. My mind was struggling to reconcile Megan's advice.

"Everything seems stable." The nurse smiled.

"I guess that's good?"

"The doctor should be around within the hour."

"Thanks." Even then, I knew I wasn't going to get more than "it looks like" and "we think," because no one actually knew what was going to happen. Wendy had stabilized medically, but she remained in a coma. And I knew—based on the internet searches I hadn't been able to stop myself from doing—that two to three weeks was considered normal for a coma. After that, they started to transition to words like "vegetative state" and the prognosis got a lot bleaker.

"Keep chatting with her. There's all kinds of research that says patients can hear you. She may even remember what you talked to her about as she recovers."

"Thanks." The nurse was practically through the door when I responded, so I wasn't sure if she heard me, but I also couldn't imagine she cared.

"All right, Wendy. I'm serious. I need you to wake up so you can tell me what I'm supposed to do."

29

SCOTT

I kissed Beckett on the head and tiptoed out of the room. He was finally down for his nap and I was seriously tempted to join him. How had Whitney done this all day, every day? It was insane. Fun. Joyful. Rewarding. Yes, absolutely all of those things, but also? Exhausting.

I gave my bedroom a longing stare and forced myself down two flights of stairs to the basement laundry area. At least Beckett had enjoyed the earlier game of carrying everything down. I'd planned to have him help with sorting and getting the washer loaded, but it had been too close to lunch and I could see the mutinous lines of hangry starting to form on his face, so I'd abandoned the plan.

He'd helped me make grilled cheese instead.

Of course, he'd wanted chicken nuggets, but I couldn't choke down another one of those. Possibly in my entire life.

I regretted—oh, how I regretted—sending my parents back home on Saturday. At the time, I'd been sure Beckett and I had hit our stride and would have no trouble. And, okay, fine, we were doing okay. Of course if Mom was here, I could go nap. She'd do the laundry.

Ugh. That probably made me a mama's boy, didn't it?

I tossed clothes into the washer, leaving the dark ones on the floor. We were supposed to fly to the Caymans with the gang on Saturday, which gave me two days to get us ready. Two days counting today, since I doubted very much that I'd be doing anything on Saturday morning other than keeping Beckett from bouncing off the walls.

I added soap and spun the dial to get the machine going then trudged back upstairs. I made the mistake of looking at the kitchen and my shoulders slumped. I should clean it next. How had Whitney done all this? I'd never come home and found the place trashed, but on my own? The house was not living up to the standard of tidy that I wanted. Because who had time.

Deliberately turning my back on the messy kitchen, I headed to the living room and collapsed on the couch with my phone in my hand. Whitney was probably busy. Our calls lately had been short. Almost awkward. I was trying hard not to read too much into it.

Enough. Dithering was dumb and if I wasn't going to clean the kitchen, then I was going to at least spend a few minutes talking to Whitney. I scrolled to her number and hit call.

It rang twice before she picked up. "Scott? Great timing! I was just going to find a quiet place to call you. You'll never believe it—Wendy's awake!"

"That's an amazing answer to prayer." I closed my eyes and offered a quick word of thanksgiving to Jesus for what felt like a miracle. While our conversations may have been short, they were full of her worry about the length of her sister's coma. "How is she?"

Whitney blew out a breath. "Physically? Surprisingly good, considering. They've basically taken her off all her pain meds and she isn't complaining. Mom and Dad are in with her now. They're going to tell her about Mark and the girls."

I winced. "You don't need to be in there, too?"

"They thought it might be easier for her if I wasn't. I don't know—it bothers me, but Mom was pretty insistent. She doesn't get that way often, so we tend to give in when she does." Whitney paused a moment. "How are things there? How's Beckett? You leave Saturday, right? Are you ready?"

I frowned. Was I being oversensitive if I focused on the fact that she hadn't asked about me? Maybe. Still stung. "I miss you."

And that was not at all what I should have blurted out in that moment. I didn't need to look like I was some whiny, needy man who couldn't handle things without her. Even if it was true.

"Aw." She sounded like she was surrounded by cute puppies.

I drummed my fingers on my leg. If I was going to look like a fool, I might as well go all the way. I cleared my throat. "I wish you were coming with us to the beach."

"I know. I wish I was, too. It's just that everything is so up in the air. Now that Wendy's awake, maybe we can get her home to Gilead for whatever the next steps are."

"And then can you start making plans to come home?" I pressed my lips together. I wasn't going to beg her. But I wanted to.

"I...I don't know. I'm sorry."

"No. It's okay. I don't want to add to the stress you're under. I'm sorry." I glanced over at the kitchen. If this conversation was going to go the way all the others had lately, now would be when Whitney would start making noises about needing to let me go. And I'd end up letting her, because what was I supposed to do?

"Are you enjoying not going into the office every day?"

I lifted my eyebrows. Maybe this call would be different. "Mostly. You made it look easy. It isn't."

Whitney chuckled. "Some days it was all I could do to get to naptime."

"Tell me about it. He's up there now, and I'd absolutely be sleeping if there wasn't so much to do to get ready for the trip."

"I'm sorry I'm not there to make it easier. But, well, it's kind of nice to know I'm needed."

"Please tell me you're joking. Of course we need you. We love you. Beckett and I both."

I swallowed. That wasn't quite how I'd imagined telling her I loved her. Of course, I'd been saving the words for a moonlit walk on the beach with the crystal waters of the Caribbean stretched out in front of us. Since she was going to be in Kansas for who knew how long, it was probably time to just let the words out. Even if it made me pathetic.

"What are you saying?" Her voice had gone quiet and had a stillness to it.

"I'm saying I love you, Whitney. Not because you watch Beckett or because you help with chores around the house, but because you fill my life with sunshine even when it's cloudy. Without you here, everything is just a shadow of what it was before you were part of my life. Before you came, I didn't know what I was missing. Now, I don't know how I'm going to manage if I have to go back." I bit my lip. Nothing quite like ripping your heart out of your chest and offering it to someone, but I didn't know what else to do. It didn't feel like I had anything to lose.

"I love you, too."

"Are you crying?" I ached to be able to hold her and wipe her tears. "I didn't want to make you sad."

"I'm not sad." She sniffled and I could tell she was trying to compose herself. "It's just hard to know what to do."

"I'm sorry. Is there a way I can help?"

"Keep praying." I heard a crash and some shouting in the background. "Oh, man. I gotta go. I'll try to call later."

I glanced at my phone. She'd definitely ended the call. What had happened? There was no way to even guess. I blew out a breath as I pushed up off the couch and headed into the kitchen. I should get that cleaned and then go check the laundry. And then? If there was still time before Beckett got up from his nap, I could spend a little time thinking about the fact that she'd said she loved me.

I focused on the chores and was just heading upstairs to stretch out on my bed for a few minutes when Beckett came padding down the stairs rubbing his eyes. So much for that.

"Hey, bud." I picked him up and settled him on my hip. Beckett burrowed his head into my shoulder and popped his thumb back in his mouth. "You sure you want to wake up? We could go rest together for a little if you're still sleepy."

He shook his head and talked around his thumb. "Want milk. And toast."

Beckett always wanted a snack when he got up from his nap and I was under the impression it was part of his routine. So I went with it. "All right. Milk and toast it is. Do you want butter or honey on the toast?"

"Can have both?"

"Hmm." I pressed a quick kiss to his forehead as we crossed the living room to the kitchen. I set him down and he climbed into his chair. "I guess. This time."

He laughed.

I winked and went to the cabinet for one of the cups with a built-in straw. They were a little bit of a pain to clean, but they didn't spill if they got tipped and that was a good thing. Because they always got tipped. He *could* use a regular cup, but I definitely didn't risk it when he was sleepy. "Whitney called while you were sleeping. She said to tell you she loves you."

"She coming home?"

My heart broke a little at the hopeful lift in his question.

"She doesn't know yet." I set the filled cup at the table in front of him and started fixing the toast. Maybe I shouldn't have brought it up, but he missed her. Just like I did. "But I know she wants to."

That seemed to appease him. I just prayed it was true. When the toast popped, I spread butter and added a light drizzle of honey before slicing it in half and giving it to him. "I'm going to run down and see if the dryer is finished. You work on that. I'll be right back, okay?"

"K." Beckett took a huge bite of toast and started to chew.

I shook my head and hurried downstairs. An idea was beginning to take shape. I took out my phone, leaned against the silent washer as the dryer continued to tumble the final load of clothes, and called Austin.

"Hey, man." There was a lot of noise in the background of the call. Shoot. I hadn't checked what time it was before calling. He'd answered, so he obviously wasn't in class, but still.

"Hey. I'm not getting you at a bad time, am I?"

"Nope. School's out. I'm just watching the hall to make sure people don't get into too much mischief as they're heading to lockers and all that. What's up?"

I rubbed the back of my neck. "I have an idea and I need to know if it's stupid."

Austin laughed. "It's you, so probably, but let's hear it. Stupid isn't always wrong."

"Yeah, yeah." I shook my head. I could always count on my friends to keep me humble. "I'm thinking maybe Beckett and I won't go to the Caymans."

"Heading to Kansas?"

"Yeah." I waited. Austin didn't speak. "Am I an idiot?"

"Well, yeah, but not for this." He chuckled. "Kidding. No. You're not an idiot. You would be if you didn't go after her, though. Think you can convince her to come home?"

I swallowed. "She mentioned a job. In Kansas. Once. I

haven't asked what's going on there, but...I'm thinking maybe this trip could turn into a house-hunting adventure."

"Oh. That's big."

"Good big or bad big?" My stomach was unsettled. I honestly couldn't answer the question for myself. Austin wasn't wrong, it was big. And it felt right. But I'd been wrong about things before.

"I don't know, man. I don't want you to move." Austin sighed. "But I don't blame you. She's worth that kind of change. And hey, we have a plane now, it's not like we can't still get together to hang out."

"Probably not for poker every week." I frowned. Was I really going to give up everything to be with Whitney? Yeah. Yeah, I was. "Sorry about that."

"Nah, man. Don't be." Austin cleared his throat. "When do you want to go?"

"I guess Sunday. That way I'm not disrupting all of your plans. You guys go down on Saturday as planned. I'll get in touch with the pilot and see if he's up for another trip on Sunday. If not, I'll get someone else lined up." I didn't think Beckett would be disappointed. He'd probably rather spend time with Whitney than go to a beach he knew nothing about. While he'd enjoyed the sand in Florida, it wasn't as if this was the last time he'd get a chance to go. I squashed the tiny thought that the Caymans would make a good honeymoon spot. That was getting ahead of myself.

"Sounds good. Say hi to Whitney for us."

"Hey. Can you try and keep Megan from spilling the beans? I'd kind of like this to be a surprise."

"Will do. Shouldn't be too hard. She's been grumbling about Whitney being an idiot lately. I haven't pressed, but I suspect she'll be all about you going out there and getting this fixed."

"Hope so. Pray for us, would you? I don't know how this is

going to work out—I'm not a hundred percent sure where God's leading beyond this trip to Kansas. After that? I want to make sure we're doing what He wants. You know?"

"I do. You got it. Shoot a text and keep me in the loop if you can."

"I will. Thanks. See ya." I ended the call as the dryer turned off. With a laugh, I scooped the warm clothes out into the basket with the other load in it, hitched it onto my hip, and headed back upstairs to tell Beckett about our change of plans.

30

WHITNEY

I opened my eyes and looked around the bedroom I'd grown up in. Mom and Dad hadn't changed it much. There was a stack of boxes in the corner of the room. Mom had apologized for them—they were marked for donation but she hadn't managed to take them to the church thrift store yet. Otherwise? It was like I'd never left.

I couldn't decide if that was horrifying or comforting.

Maybe somewhere in between.

The bed was better than the hotel's bed had been. None of us had been upset to finally be able to check out yesterday when they'd agreed that there was no medical reason to keep Wendy at the hospital. She was struggling with brain fog and memory loss. Her arm was broken and they'd had to remove her spleen and an ovary during the initial surgery.

Mom and Dad had insisted she stay at their house for a while, too. There was no way she needed to be living alone in the home she'd shared with Mark and the girls while everything was so raw.

"Knock, knock." Mom poked her head through the door. "Did you want to try to go to church?"

I wriggled until I was sitting up. "You're going? Is Wendy going?"

Mom shook her head. "She's still sleeping. Dad and I figured we could get there and back without much trouble. You don't have to come."

I could hear the underlying censure in her words, but chose to take them at face value. "I don't think we should risk leaving Wendy alone. What if she's disoriented when she wakes up?"

Mom's lips thinned, but she nodded once. "All right. I guess that makes sense. And if you're here, Dad and I won't have to rush quite so much."

"Thanks, Mom." I rubbed my eyes and tossed back the covers. "Is there coffee?"

"Of course. I need to finish getting ready, but then I can fix you some breakfast before we go." She turned and left before I could tell her it wasn't necessary.

I stretched my arms over my head and yawned, then grabbed my phone and unhooked the charging cable. I headed downstairs to the kitchen.

Dad was at the table with the newspaper and a cup of coffee. He was already showered and dressed for church in a bright red sweater over a white collared shirt and some khakis.

"Hi, Dad."

"Morning, honey." He glanced at me over the top of the paper and smiled. "Mom says you're going to stay here in case Wendy wakes up."

"Yeah." I set my phone at the table before moving over to the coffee machine.

"Sounds good. Oh, be sure to check your email. I got a text from George, over at the college. He said they'd made an offer on that drama teacher position. I didn't ask who, but I doubt he'd give me a heads-up if it wasn't good news." Dad winked then returned to his perusal of the news.

My heart raced and my hand shook a little as I finished pouring coffee. I forced myself to add cream and sugar and wipe up the spill after my shaking hands proved incapable of the task. I sipped, closing my eyes briefly before heading back to the table.

This was it. I took another gulp of coffee and opened my email. A couple of messages down, I spotted the email I was looking for. I tapped it and read, my heart sinking with each word. They were super polite. Friendly, even. But the end result was the same: I hadn't gotten the job. I clicked off my phone and stared into my coffee.

Now what?

I'd been so sure. Mom had made it sound like I was a shoo-in. Honestly, even though I'd tried to demur, I'd been confident the job was mine for the asking. I'd asked. They'd said no.

Dad put his paper down. "No email?"

"Oh, no. I have an email. They hired someone else."

"Huh." Dad frowned. "I'm sorry to hear that."

"Yeah. Me, too." I blinked back tears and stood. "I think I'm going to drink my coffee in my room."

"Sure, sure. Just bring that mug back down. You know how your mom gets about her dishes." Dad smiled and reached for his coffee. "Want us to grab lunch after church and bring it home?"

I nodded, though I couldn't imagine having an appetite. "Sounds good. Would you let Mom know I don't need breakfast?"

"Are you all right?"

"I don't know, actually. I'm surprised. Maybe I shouldn't be." I shrugged and picked up my coffee. "I'll see you at lunch."

Dad started to say something, but I kept walking. I didn't want to hear his reassurance that God would work something out. I honestly believed He would—that wasn't a question—but it still hurt, and I didn't think it was wrong to feel that pain and be upset. Emotions always made Dad a little uncomfortable.

In my room, I crawled into bed and leaned against the headboard. *Okay, God. Now what?*

It wasn't an eloquent prayer by any stretch of the imagination, but it was what I had. I looked at my phone. I could call Scott—but there was a part of me that didn't want him to see how disappointed I was that I hadn't gotten the job. He'd say it was God's way of showing me that I should go back to Virginia.

Well, that wasn't true. He probably wouldn't. Because Scott wasn't the kind of guy who rubbed your face in problems. No. He'd be supportive and empathetic.

I was the one who was wondering if that was the takeaway.

I missed Scott. And Beckett. I wanted to be with them. But I felt an obligation to be here and try to help my family. I sighed. Why weren't there ever clear, easy answers?

I tapped Megan's entry and waited as it rang. I had no idea what the time zone for the Caymans was, but they were probably east of me. So it shouldn't be too early.

"Hey! Listen to this."

Before I could say anything, my room was filled with the sound of the ocean.

"It looks even better than it sounds."

"Ugh. Now I'm jealous and depressed."

"Jealous, I get. But you can still come. You know the guys would send the plane for you. Then you don't have to be jealous or depressed."

"I didn't get the job." I don't know why I blurted it out like that, but Megan was smart. I was sure she could keep up.

"You didn't...oh. Oh, Whit. I'm sorry. Well, I'm sort of sorry because I know you're disappointed, but I'm secretly pretty happy because that means you're going to come home, right?"

I groaned and banged the back of my head against my headboard. "I don't know. I still don't think Scott needs me. Although…"

"Although?" Megan's voice rose at the end, teasing. "I sense something juicy."

"He told me he loves me."

"I knew it!" She yelled it. Hopefully there weren't too many people on the beach wondering about the psycho on her cell phone.

"Yeah, yeah. You called it."

"And?"

"And I told him I loved him, too." I sighed, but I don't think Megan heard me. She was busy screaming like a crazy woman. I waited until she calmed down. "It doesn't solve anything."

"Yes. It. Does."

"How? My sister still has a long road ahead of her. My parents aren't exactly spring chickens. I feel like I could do more good here than I was doing in Virginia."

"Uh-huh. Where do you want to be?"

"With Scott and Beckett." The admission cost me. "Saying it makes me feel small. Shouldn't I want to be here?"

"Have your parents even asked you to stay? Or your sister?"

Trust Megan. I sorted through the conversations I'd been part of with my parents and those I'd only overheard pieces of. And…no. No one had said anything to me, directly, about staying to help out. "Well, no. But—"

"But nothing. Your parents understand that you have a life. I'm guessing they even actively support it. Come home."

I needed to talk to Scott. I didn't want to leave without knowing what was going on with us and Beckett and…everything.

"Do you know if Scott's up yet? I'm betting yes. Beckett isn't exactly a kid who sleeps in. But I also don't want to risk waking them on the off chance."

Megan's pause was long enough that I started to worry I'd lost her. Then she finally said, "I haven't seen him today."

"Hrm." I frowned. "I guess I'll wait a little. Or, if you see him? Have him call me."

"I can do that." Megan cleared her throat. "I have to go. I'll check in later."

"Wait—" The phone was dead. I grunted and tossed it on the bed. I didn't blame her. Or not much. Megan was on vacation in a tropical paradise. Who wanted to spend time listening to their friend whine about her existential crisis when the sand and surf beckoned?

I reached for my coffee and drained it before setting it back on my nightstand. I should get in the shower and get dressed so I was ready for the day whenever Wendy woke up. I flipped the covers off me, grabbed an outfit out of my suitcase, and headed to the bathroom in the hall that I'd been sharing with my sister for most of my life.

I hurried through my morning routine, not bothering to do anything with my hair or face. I didn't spend a ton of time as a general rule, but I did usually do more than I'd bothered with today.

I stopped in my room to get my mug—Dad wasn't wrong when he said Mom would be salty if I didn't bring it back down —and headed downstairs. I rinsed the mug before loading it into the top rack of the dishwasher.

Looking around, I spotted Dad's newspaper on the table. With a shrug, I sat at his spot and scanned the headlines. I was nearly finished with the first section of the paper when the stairs creaked.

I stood and rushed to the steps. "Wendy. You should have called me."

She shook her head. "The doctors said I could walk as long as I went slow and was careful."

"I know. It's just—"

"Stop. Please? It's bad enough Mom and Dad treat me like I'm going to fall apart. Don't you start."

I licked my lips and watched her make her way down the stairs. "Okay. Coffee?"

"Please. And maybe some aspirin?"

"Do you want something stronger? You have painkillers."

"I don't want that. They make me sleepy. I don't hurt badly. It's more of an ache."

"Okay." I frowned, but went back into the kitchen. I filled a mug with coffee and rummaged through the medicine drawer to find the aspirin bottle. I shook out two and carried them with the coffee to the table.

"Thanks." Wendy lowered herself carefully into a chair. She reached for the pills first and swallowed, then chased them with a drink of coffee.

"I will never understand how you drink it black." I shuddered.

"Practice."

We exchanged a smile.

Wendy sighed. "I want to go home."

"But."

She shook her head. "It's my home, Whit. And I understand —I do—that it'll be hard. But it's not like living there was always easy."

"What do you mean?"

Wendy just lifted her coffee mug.

I wanted to push, but I recognized the stubborn set to her jaw. She wasn't going to explain. "I can talk to Mom, I guess. You scared us. I don't know how happy she'll be to let you go again."

"I guess I can see that. But you need to get back to your life. Mom and Dad can check in on me—even every day, if that's what they want. For a little while at least."

"Don't you think you should give it a little time? A week? Two?"

"If I have to. But I'd rather be home. You understand, don't you?"

I nodded. I did. Even though I was disappointed about the job, Kansas didn't feel like home anymore.

"Good. So you'll drive me?"

My eyes widened. "No way. Mom and Dad are bringing lunch after church and then you can talk to them. But I am not helping you sneak off."

"Worth a shot, I guess." Wendy smiled and pushed her mug toward me. "Will you at least get me another cup of coffee?"

"That I can do. I can even make some eggs if you want."

"I wouldn't mind that. Thanks."

I smiled and took her mug over to the coffee pot. Before I could pour, the doorbell rang. "I'll be right back."

I hurried to the front door and tugged it open. Then froze. "Scott?"

31

SCOTT

"Surprise." I grinned and tried to decipher the expression on her face.

"Whitney!" Beckett launched at her legs the moment the door was clear.

"Hey, bud." Whitney tore her gaze away from mine and squatted so she was at Beckett's level. She drew him into her arms and squeezed until he grunted. "It's good to see you."

"Missed you." He didn't let go of her as she tried to stand, so she hitched him onto her hip.

I tucked my hands in my pockets because they were itching to grab her and hold her tight. "That goes for me, too."

She met and held my gaze. Her eyes filled. "Me, three."

I chuckled and closed the distance between us. I pulled her into my arms, including Beckett in the hug, and my lips found hers. I closed my eyes and sank into the sensation. This was right. This was home.

She was home.

I eased back. "I didn't want to go to the beach when I could come see you. Beckett agreed."

"I'm so glad." Whitney blinked back the tears that still

threatened to spill over. "Come on in. I was just about to make my sister some eggs. Are you hungry?"

"I eat!" Beckett bounced a little on her hip.

She laughed and drilled a finger into his belly causing him to giggle madly. "Then I'll scramble you some eggs. Scott?"

"If it's no trouble."

"None. At all."

I followed her through the house to the kitchen. It was a homey place. There was a tree up, but not decorated, in one of the rooms we passed. It made sense, given the timing of the accident. It added to the lived in, welcoming feel.

"Wendy? Um. This is Scott. And Beckett."

I held out my hand to the woman at the table. It was obvious they were sisters. "It's nice to meet you. I'm glad you were able to come home. I've been praying for you."

"Thanks." Wendy offered a weak smile, her gaze drifting back to Beckett. "Hi there."

Beckett buried his face in Whitney's shoulder.

"Sorry. He gets shy." Whitney kissed the top of Beckett's head.

"It's okay. I know how it is." Wendy's eyes filled and she turned her face away.

I couldn't imagine what she was going through. I stuffed my hands in my pockets and glanced in the other direction. "What if I made the eggs and the three of you hung out and chatted?"

Whitney shifted, trying to hand Beckett off, but he threw his arms around her neck and clung.

She rubbed his back. "Hey, bud. It's okay."

He shook his head.

I smiled. "I can scramble eggs. Just point me in the direction of the skillets."

Whitney pointed to the oven. "Mom stores them in there."

"Baking must be fun." I reached for the oven door and

pulled it open, shaking my head a little at the stacks of pans inside.

Wendy and Whitney both snickered.

I found a skillet that would work and set it on the stovetop, then busied myself looking through cabinets for the other things I'd need. I didn't focus on the words, but the quiet hum of conversation between Whitney, Beckett, and Wendy was soothing.

Before long, I'd dished scrambled eggs onto four plates and carried them over to the table.

"These look delicious, thank you." Wendy's smile showed strain at the edges.

"You're welcome." I hesitated a moment before holding out my hand for Whitney. "I can pray, if you want?"

"Sounds good." She put her hand in mine and reached across for Wendy's hand.

I closed my eyes and blessed the food, adding on thankfulness for Wendy coming out of the coma. There was so much more to say, but the eggs were cooling, so I said amen.

"Thank you. Again." Wendy took a bite of the eggs, then steadily shoveled them into her mouth.

I didn't imagine she was tasting them. I glanced over at Beckett. He was pushing them around the plate more than eating, though some did occasionally make it to his mouth.

My gaze met Whitney's. She shrugged and offered an apologetic smile. I shook my head slightly. I wasn't bothered. As glad as I was to see her, as much as coming here felt like what God was prompting me to do, it was awkward to sit here with her sister in her obvious grief and pain.

"I'm going to go upstairs and rest." Wendy pushed back from the table and stood. She wobbled on her feet a moment. She lifted a hand as both Whitney and I started to stand. "I'm okay. Wake me when Mom and Dad are home from church, okay?"

"Okay. Call if you need something. Anything." Whitney chewed her lip as she watched her sister leave. When Wendy's footsteps on the stairs faded, Whitney sighed, her body slumping. "She wants to go home. She wants me to help convince Mom and Dad."

"She seems to be getting around okay?" I understood the desire to be at home. To have privacy. "Would it be so bad?"

"I'm just worried about her. She took some hard knocks. It's a miracle that she's as uninjured as she is. But losing Mark and the girls...should she really be alone?"

"I imagine she's the one who knows best on that score."

Whitney frowned at me.

Beckett put his fork down with a clatter. "All done."

"You sure are. Nice job." I scooped up the last bite of my eggs and then collected the empty plates. I gestured to Whitney's. "You should eat them before they get gross. Then, do you maybe want to go for a walk?"

Whitney looked down at her clothes then sighed. "Yeah. If I'd known you were coming, I would have taken the time to put on makeup."

I set the dishes down and moved around the table to where Whitney sat so I could cup her face in my hands. "You're beautiful."

Her lips curved and her cheeks pinked.

"I love you." I leaned down and pressed my lips to hers. I'd intended the kiss to be quick. Friendly, even. But she grabbed a handful of my shirt and held me in place, deepening the kiss.

Something rammed into my legs, and I stumbled forward a step.

Whitney broke the kiss, laughing. "Beckett."

"Me, too!" He crawled onto her lap and kissed her cheek.

Chuckling, I rested my forehead on hers for a moment

before straightening and collecting the dishes. I carried them to the sink and opened the dishwasher.

"You can leave them. I'll get them later."

I looked over at her and shook my head. "It just takes a minute. I've been getting into the habit."

"Maybe that's not a bad thing."

I laughed. I was never a slob, but having to do everything without Whitney to help had definitely tightened up some of my chore doing schedules. I never would have guessed that one extra person—even a toddler—could make it so much more necessary.

I ran hot water into the pan I'd used for the eggs and added a squirt of dish soap before starting to scrub. I could feel Whitney's eyes on me as she finished her food. What was she thinking?

I was rinsing the pan and setting it in the drying rack when she brought her plate and fork over and added them to the dishwasher.

"Just let me go get shoes and we can take that walk." She cocked her head to the side. "Did you and Beckett bring a coat? It's probably chilly."

"They're in the rental car."

She headed out of the room. I shifted my gaze to Beckett. "You ready to walk, kiddo?"

He grinned. "I can run."

"Sure you can." I closed the dishwasher and held out my hand. Beckett slipped his little fingers into mine. Would I ever get tired of that feeling? Used to it, even? Somewhere along the way, he'd wrapped himself around my heart. I squatted down so we were at eye level. "I love you, buddy."

"Love you." He grinned and threw his arms around me.

A noise drew my attention and I looked over to see Whitney

standing in the doorway, one hand on her heart. I smiled and slowly stood, lifting Beckett onto my hip. "Ready?"

"I am."

We went out the front door and I stopped at the rental car to grab coats for Beckett and me. It was cool, but I wouldn't say cold. Still, no one wanted to get sick right before Christmas.

True to his word, Beckett started to run as soon as he was zipped.

"Stay on the sidewalk." Whitney called after him.

I threaded my fingers through hers and we walked along the neighborhood sidewalk behind Beckett. "I missed you. A lot."

"I've missed you. Both of you."

"I'm glad to hear that. I know you're worried about your sister. And then there's the job situation."

She glanced over at me; her brow furrowed.

I hurried on. "Now that I'm not working at Robinson Enterprises, I have a lot more flexibility. Even if I do some consulting —and Stephanie's been emailing me about some projects every week, so there's work if I want it—I can do that from anywhere. I want to be where you are. So I was thinking maybe this afternoon you could show us around Gilead. Point out the good neighborhoods, that kind of thing, so I know where to start looking for a place."

Whitney stopped. "A place? Here?"

"Well, yeah. If you need to be here, then so do we. Beckett agrees, by the way." I glanced away to check on Beckett. He'd stopped and was squatting beside a mailbox that was surrounded by rocks. I tugged her hand. "We should catch up to him."

Whitney didn't say anything as she followed.

"Let's leave the rocks, okay? The people who live here want them for their mailbox." I gently pried open Beckett's little fists and shook the rocks out.

"No! My rocks!"

Becket made a grab for them, but I scooped him up. He kicked out and I twisted to avoid having his feet make contact with parts of me that were more sensitive to assault.

"Rooocccckkkkkssss."

His wail tore at me, but we weren't going to steal rocks from around someone's mailbox. There were rocks everywhere.

"There's a playground if we turn left here." Whitney pointed.

I started in that direction. I didn't bother trying to talk over Beckett's wailing. I just held him close and patted his back. It had been working at home when he tried to have a tantrum.

It was another block before I spotted the little playground. "Look, Beckett. What's that?"

Beckett scowled at me before turning to see. His expression morphed into joy and he began to wiggle in my arms. "Down. I can play?"

"You can play." I set him on the ground and chuckled as he took off.

"There's a bench over here." Whitney angled toward it.

I followed and sat beside her. "So. Do you think you'd like to go for a drive?"

She shook her head.

My stomach dropped. "Oh. Okay." I frowned. "Actually, it's not okay. I'm confused. I love you. You said you love me. Why wouldn't you want us to be together?"

"I didn't get the job." Her words came out in a rush as she stared straight ahead. Then she turned and met my gaze. "They emailed me this morning to let me know they were going in another direction. Which kind of sounds like a nice way of saying I never had a shot."

"I'm sorry." I wasn't really. I was sorry she was upset—I could see she was—but it made things simpler. "So can you come back? To Virginia?"

She nodded. "Yeah. I'm pretty sure I can. My sister's made up her mind that she's going home. I could see that this morning. Mom and Dad don't stand a chance of convincing her otherwise. I just…"

"What?" I wasn't sure how to feel. She wasn't exactly leaping at the opportunity for us to be together. Had I completely misunderstood the situation? Did being in love mean something different to her?

"I don't want things to go back to the way they were. I don't want you to find me another place to live. I want to stay in the house with you and Beckett."

My heart sped up and a tiny glimmer of hope blossomed. "I thought we agreed that wasn't the best idea. That we didn't want to give the wrong impression."

She cocked her head to the side, one corner of her mouth poking up. "What if it wasn't the wrong impression?"

"Are you asking me to marry you?" I couldn't stop the teasing grin that formed on my face.

Whitney shook her head, her eyes dancing with laughter. "No. I'm suggesting that if you asked me to marry you, the answer might be something you wanted to hear."

Laughter bubbled up and out as I leaned close. I slid my arms around her and, lips touching hers, murmured, "Will you marry me?"

"I will." Her kiss was full of promise and I never wanted her to stop. She drew back and tapped my nose. "More later. Have I ever mentioned that my father's an ordained minister?"

My heart soared. "I don't believe you ever mentioned that, no."

Whitney winked. "Come on, let's head back. I know my folks will want to meet you. And Beckett."

"Speaking of Beckett." I glanced over and watched him climbing up the slide. He got to the top, flipped over, and went careening back down. "I've had Tristan working on paperwork to legally adopt him."

She nodded.

"I guess I'll give him a call and see how hard it is to add you to that. If you want."

Joy shone from her face. "I'd like that. Very much."

32

WHITNEY

"I'm glad you and Scott and Beckett were able to spend the last two weeks with us." Mom fussed with the edge of my sleeve and wouldn't meet my gaze.

"Me, too." I turned away from the floor-length mirror, the picture of me in my wedding dress seared into my memory, and caught her hand. "I love you, Mom."

"I love you, too. You're sure about this?" Her eyes searched my face, then she nodded once. "You are. So I will be, too. He seems like a good man. And it's clear he adores you. So does Beckett."

"My little instafamily." I grinned and pulled Mom into a hug. I understood why she worried. I would have worried, too. Neither she nor Dad had greeted the news of our engagement with excessive joy, but the last two weeks as we waited for our marriage license to process had eased their minds enough that they were on board with having the small ceremony here at home.

"I wish your sister would come." Mom sighed. "I think, in time, she'll regret it."

"I understand. Sort of." It still hurt. Of course, she'd told me that I was cruel, getting married to a man with a child weeks after she'd lost hers. I wasn't trying to be cruel.

Scott and I had talked about waiting until spring, but the logistics were a problem. Plus, this way Tristan could adjust the paperwork and I'd be part of Beckett's adoption right off the bat instead of having to do it separately later.

"Don't stop praying for her, okay? She has a long road ahead of her."

"I know. I won't." Wendy wasn't who I wanted to dwell on right before my wedding.

"Well. Enough. Today is a day for happy things. Are you ready?"

"Yeah. I am." More than ready. I thought back to the conversation I'd had with Megan not all that long ago when I'd tried to convince her—and myself—that I wasn't in love with Scott and it was too soon for anything like this to happen. But she'd known. How she'd laughed when I called to tell her.

There was a brisk knock on my bedroom door and Megan poked her head in. "Are you ready?"

I held out my arms. "How do I look?"

"Amazing." Megan struck a pose. "Just like me. This dress is gorgeous. Completely not something I can ever wear again, but still gorgeous. And I'm glad you let me choose it."

"Like I had a choice." I grinned. She did look good. "Is everyone ready downstairs?"

"Yep. You have more groomsmen than guests. Or bridesmaids for that matter. I guess that's what happens when you plan a wedding in two weeks."

I chuckled. That definitely factored in. As did the fact that Scott had a larger friend circle than me. "Is Kayla ready?"

Megan rolled her eyes. "Of course she is. She's waiting at the top of the stairs."

I looked at Mom. "I guess it's time."

Mom leaned forward and kissed my cheek. "I guess it is."

We made our way out into the hallway.

Kayla gave me two thumbs up and a big grin. "You look awesome. Let's do this."

"Get going. They're supposed to start the music as soon as you get to the landing." I leaned forward, trying to peek over the stairs. Sometimes, if I angled myself just right, I was able to see into the living room from up here—it was how I'd spied on Wendy when she was dating Mark.

Megan pulled me back. "Stop it."

Kayla started down the stairs with a giggle. The music did, indeed, start when she reached the landing and turned.

Megan reached back and squeezed my hand before she started her trip down the stairs. As she neared the landing, I linked my arm through my mom's and we started down together.

Since Dad was doing the ceremony, it seemed only fair that Mom walk me down. There was already so much that wasn't traditional happening, I didn't see the harm in adding one more. Mom had balked for a moment, but when Dad said he thought it was great, she gave in.

We reached the bottom of the stairs and my gaze swept over Scott's parents standing with Beckett, to Scott. I locked in on him like a homing beacon as my heart began to race. I knew I was walking too fast, but I was helpless to do anything about it.

When we reached him, everyone in the room was laughing.

"I guess I can skip the part about anyone having questions." Dad grinned at me as Mom placed my hand in Scott's and gave it a squeeze. "Marriage is a holy and beautiful thing that should never be entered into recklessly. It's a lifetime commitment and a daily choice. There will be days when you want to give up. Those days are the ones I pray you remember that you didn't make this union. Nor did I. God did. And He is the author and the finisher here."

I nodded, blinking back tears.

Scott squeezed my hands and mouthed the words, *I love you.*

I mouthed them back.

Dad led us through our vows and the exchange of rings. My eyes might have bugged a little as Scott slipped a thick, glittery band of multicolored gems on my hand. I'd told him I wanted him to choose. All I cared about was being his wife. But apparently, I got some bling anyway. His band was less ornate. A fat band of etched platinum I'd had engraved with our initials and the year.

"I now pronounce you man and wife. You may kiss the bride." Dad stepped back, his eyes shining with unshed tears.

Scott pulled me close and dipped me, kissing me with tenderness and enthusiasm before righting me and stepping away.

Beckett broke free of Kayla's hand and raced to me. He wrapped his arms around my legs. I leaned down and hoisted him up.

"Hey, buddy. You look handsome in your suit."

"Don't like it." He frowned. "You're pretty."

I grinned and kissed his nose. "Thanks, baby."

He wriggled down and headed for the little stash of toys my parents had gotten down for him.

Scott's arm came around my waist and he leaned close to whisper in my ear, "I love you."

I turned to look at him, my heart full and content as our eyes met. "Thank you."

He cocked his head to the side. "For what?"

"For being Mister Wright."

He laughed and lowered his mouth to mine.

It was the perfect way to start forever.

EPILOGUE

Austin

I looked away as Scott and Whitney started kissing. Again. If you couldn't kiss at your wedding, when could you? But still.

"Get a room." I'd meant it to stay inside my head, but Kayla started to laugh.

She jabbed me in the ribs. "Jealous much?"

I shrugged. "Maybe. A little. You're not?"

She shook her head. "Nah. Scott's not my type."

I grunted. "You know that's not what I meant. He's not mine, either."

Kayla poked me again.

I held up my hands. "Okay, okay. Neither is Whitney. I just think it must be nice to finally find the one who your soul loves, you know?"

Kayla frowned at me. "What are you quoting?"

My face heated. My Bible reading plan had reset in September, so I was in Song of Solomon while the majority of the world was in Genesis. And of course that's the line that stuck in my head.

She narrowed her eyes. "Song of Solomon."

"Shh." I glanced around, but no one was paying us any attention, thankfully. Everyone was chatting and trying to ignore Scott and Whitney. Megan and Cody were playing cars with Beckett in the corner of the living room. Kayla touched my arm, drawing my attention back to her.

"I do know. But maybe instead of getting jealous, take this as a confirmation that it happens. God still brings people together in His time. We just have to wait and trust and pray."

"You're right." I slung my arm over her shoulders. "This is why you're my best friend. You talk me down off the ledge."

Kayla's smile was more teeth than anything. "Yep. You and me, BFFs."

"Forever and always." I patted her shoulder and stepped away. I'd keep praying for God to bring me a wife. In the meantime, I'd remember to be grateful for my friends.

READ MORE in The Billionaire's Best Friend, coming soon.

ACKNOWLEDGMENTS

It feels like these should get easier to write with every book that comes out, but in fact, for me? It's a lot harder.

I owe so many people thanks. Author friends. My author squad girls. My husband and kids. My sister. My editor (shout out to Lesley McDaniel for knowing what participles are and why I'm using them wrong!)

This book was written while I was wrestling with some pretty significant depression and self-doubt. It seems like for every person who's excited when you tell them you're narrowing in on a specific sub-genre of CCR, there are six others who are happy to tell you why that sub-genre is awful and shouldn't exist. And I tend to internalize stuff like that and chew on it rather than letting it go. I'm working on it.

For all of that? I love this story and I'm excited about the next five books in the Billionaire Next Door series. I hope you'll come along for the ride. Because in addition to the friends and family I appreciate, I also owe you, my reader, an incredible amount of thanks. Without readers, books are just little piles of electrons or scribbles of ink on paper. They only come alive when you lend your imagination to them.

So thank you, from the bottom of my heart, for being a part of my author journey.

Solo deo gloria.

WANT A FREE BOOK?

If you enjoyed this book and would like to read another of my books for free, you can get a free e-book simply by signing up for my newsletter on my website.

OTHER BOOKS BY ELIZABETH MADDREY

Billionaire Next Door

The Billionaire's Nanny

The Billionaire's Best Friend

The Billionaire's Secret Crush

The Billionaire's Backup

The Billionaire's Teacher

The Billionaire's Wife

Postcards, A Novel

So You Want to Be a Billionaire

So You Want a Second Chance

So You Love to Hate Your Boss

So You Love Your Best Friend's Sister

So You Have My Secret Baby

So You Need a Fake Relationship

So You Forgot You Love Me

Hope Ranch Series

Hope for Christmas

Hope for Tomorrow

Hope for Love

Hope for Freedom

Hope for Family

Hope at Last

Peacock Hill Romance Series

A Heart Restored

A Heart Reclaimed

A Heart Realigned

A Heart Redirected

A Heart Rearranged

A Heart Reconsidered

Arcadia Valley Romance – Baxter Family Bakery Series

Loaves & Wishes

Muffins & Moonbeams

Cookies & Candlelight

Donuts & Daydreams

The 'Operation Romance' Series

Operation Mistletoe

Operation Valentine

Operation Fireworks

Operation Back-to-School

Prefer to read a box set? Find the whole series here.

The 'Taste of Romance' Series

A Splash of Substance

A Pinch of Promise

A Dash of Daring

A Handful of Hope

A Tidbit of Trust

Prefer to read a box set? Get the series in two parts! Box 1 and Box 2.

The 'Grant Us Grace' Series

Wisdom to Know

Courage to Change

Serenity to Accept

Pathway to Peace

Joint Venture

Prefer to read a box set? Grab the whole series here.

The 'Remnants' Series:

Faith Departed

Hope Deferred

Love Defined

Stand alone novellas

Kinsale Kisses: An Irish Romance

Luna Rosa (part of A Tuscan Legacy)

For the most recent listing of all my books, please visit my website.

ABOUT THE AUTHOR

USA Today bestselling author Elizabeth Maddrey is a semi-reformed computer geek and homeschooling mother of two who lives in the suburbs of Washington D.C. When she isn't writing, Elizabeth is a voracious consumer of books. She loves to write about Christians who struggle through their lives, dealing with sin and receiving God's grace on their way to their own romantic happily ever after.

facebook.com/ElizabethMaddrey

instagram.com/ElizabethMaddrey

amazon.com/Elizabeth-Maddrey/e/B00A11QGME

bookbub.com/authors/elizabeth-maddrey

Made in the USA
Monee, IL
05 October 2024

67269406R00184